kiss her goodbye

kiss her goodbye

ROBERT GREGORY BROWNE

ST. MARTIN'S PRESS ✠ NEW YORK

Browne

This is a work of fiction. All of the characters, organizations, and events portrayed in this novel are either products of the author's imagination or are used fictitiously.

www.stmartins.com

ISBN-13: 978-0-312-35839-6
ISBN-10: 0-312-35839-3

First Edition: February 2007

10 9 8 7 6 5 4 3 2 1

For my father, mother, and sister,
who always supported the dream

And for Leila, Lani, and Matthew,
who long ago fulfilled it

author's note

In service of this story, I've taken a few liberties with setting, geography, law-enforcement agencies, and folklore. As Faulkner once said, a writer is congenitally unable to tell the truth and that's why we call what he writes fiction.

part one

CAUSE

1

It all started when the pregnant girl went crazy.

Walt spotted her right away, standing amid the knot of customers who waited out front as he unlocked the doors: nineteen, twenty years old. Belly about to burst. Sweet smile.

When Walt saw that smile, the first thing that came to mind was Emily. He remembered the fresh-scrubbed look she'd had when she was pregnant with their first child; an effervescence she had carried through to old age; the ability to smile even as Death reached up and put a hammerlock on her heart.

Walt looked at the girl and felt a choke of emotion bubble up as he swung the doors open. He had loved his wife, but he didn't really like thinking about her. He'd never been one to dwell on the past, and as sweet as this little lady seemed to be, he felt uncomfortable looking her in the eye.

She, on the other hand, didn't seem to have a problem with it. As customers filed past him into the bank, she waited her turn, then let her smile widen as she approached, looking directly at him.

"Beautiful morning, isn't it?"

Her voice had a carefree, I've-conquered-the-world lilt to it. The kind only kids her age are able to muster. Walt himself had never been much of a conqueror—as thirty-seven years working security for the same bank easily demonstrated—but he envied those who seemed to feel they were invincible.

Avoiding the girl's gaze, he stared out at the sky, which was as blue as Emily's eyes.

"Yes, ma'am," he said. "A morning like this makes me wish I had wings."

It didn't really, but he believed in being polite and the words sounded good. Almost poetic.

Walt didn't think it possible, but the girl's smile grew even wider as she slipped past him, her shoulder brushing against the gray of his uniform.

He watched her waddle to the counter at the center of the room, where she grabbed a withdrawal slip and began filling it out with deliberate strokes, as if the final result would somehow be worthy of framing.

Walt realized it wasn't just her smile that reminded him of Emily. It was everything about her. Her build, the little yellow sundress, the short-cropped hair, the way she kept her purse cocked on her hip as she stood there, all of her concentration centered on the task at hand.

For just a moment he wished he were young again. Wished he could wipe away all these years without his woman and go back to a time when the only thing that mattered was how much they loved each other. When laughter was a way of life, and a leaky pipe or a pet on the loose or a wrong turn was an adventure rather than a chore. An adventure they shared as comrades-in-arms.

Try as he might, Walt couldn't stop thinking about these things. This girl had somehow opened the floodgates and he knew now that her beautiful morning was just the beginning of his bad day.

Then, it happened.

As Walt watched, the girl turned slightly. He could see she was still smiling. Then something flickered in her eyes and the smile abruptly disappeared. Clutching her swollen belly, she stumbled back and released a small cry of pain, her withdrawal slip fluttering to the floor.

Walt went to her and caught her by the shoulders as she started to fall. "You alright, ma'am?"

"Peachy," she said.

This wasn't even close to the response Walt had expected, but before he could give it too much thought, the girl twisted away from him and brought her hand out of her purse.

She was holding a Smith & Wesson nine-millimeter.

Pointed at his sixty-three-year-old paunch.

All at once the sweetness evaporated, the lilt in her voice replaced by a cold, hard edge.

"On the floor. Now."

At first Walt couldn't believe it. A pregnant girl was pointing a weapon at him. A *crazy* pregnant girl who no longer reminded him of Emily at all.

He hesitated, thinking about his own weapon that hung heavy at his side.

"Now," the girl said. "Or you *will* have wings."

Walt started to move, feeling his old bones creak as he did what he was told. Halfway down, he heard a shout from across the room and immediately recognized Sam's voice.

Sam was his partner. A ten-year man with a wife and two cute kids who giggled a lot and called him Uncle Wally.

"Drop your weapon!" Sam shouted.

Without even the slightest hesitation, the pregnant girl spun around and leveled the Smith, letting loose two quick shots.

Walt jerked his head up just in time to see Sam—hand resting on a weapon that hadn't even cleared its holster—take two bullets to the face and fly backward, landing in a heap on the linoleum.

It was then that Walt decided to act.

No thinking, no planning, just action.

His hand dropped to the butt of his pistol and with a quick jerk he pulled it free.

But the pregnant girl was too fast.

As if sensing what he was up to, she spun back around, and this time Walt looked her right in the eye. What he saw there sent a chill through him:

The gaze of a predator.

A fierceness that froze him to the spot.

His weapon was only halfway out of its holster when she pointed the muzzle of the Smith & Wesson at him and squeezed the trigger.

And the last thing Walter O'Brien thought before the lights went out was *I'm coming, sweetheart.*

See you soon.

2

Everyone was screaming. Tellers. Customers. The haughty little banker bitches who sat behind their desks with their oh-so-superior smiles.

They weren't smiling now.

Sara raised the Smith over her head and fired a round into the ceiling, just like Alex had taught her. Gotta let them know right away who's boss.

"Everybody down!" she shouted. "Noses to the floor!"

What a rush.

She almost let out a giggle, but held back. No time for levity now. This was serious business.

All around her, people dropped to the floor, keeping their heads down, afraid to look at her for fear she'd put a bullet in somebody's brain.

And she would, too.

No mercy, Alex always said. Show them no mercy. Mercy is a sign of weakness. And weakness will never be respected.

He was a genius, Alex was. Poet. Philosopher. Mystic. Activist. All the clichés rolled into one.

Only Alex wasn't a cliché.

Alex was the real deal.

Sara had known that the moment she'd met him back at Knox College. Her roommate, a giggly bitch named Tiffany, had picked him up at The Passion Pit and brought him to their dorm room for a quick tuck and tumble—a guy with a ponytail, no less. But once he laid eyes on Sara, Tiffany ceased to exist. He gave Tiff the quick brush-off, then caught up to Sara in the hallway and invited her outside to smoke a joint.

Tiffany was miffed, to say the least, standing in their doorway with her famous fuck-you scowl, but Sara didn't care. This guy had magnetic green eyes that bored into you as he spoke. Like he knew you were really there. Like you weren't just some hole he was sniffing around, hoping to get lucky.

They sneaked into the bell tower atop Old Main, got high, and spent the night laughing and talking. And in those hours, she discovered that he could read her feelings like no one she'd ever met. By the time the sun came up, they'd made love twice and Sara knew this was it.

He was the one.

A month later they married and Sara dropped out of school. Her old man nearly had a brain aneurysm when he found out, but there wasn't much he could do about it. She knew he had tried to buy Alex off, but Alex had told him to go take a flying fuck. For once Daddy's money was useless.

Besides, Alex had his own financial strategy.

"Please, don't hurt anyone else." This from some sweaty little ass-bag in a bow tie. "Take whatever you want."

Sara figured him for the bank manager. Probably treated his employees like shit. You could see in his face what a creep he was.

He reminded her of her father.

She leveled the pistol at him and he ducked, covering his head with his hands. She had half a mind to pull the trigger just because the sight of him made her sick, but that wouldn't be right.

Another of Alex's tenets: no unnecessary killing.

The two guards had been shot in self-defense. If they hadn't been crazy enough to try to draw on her, they'd still be alive instead of lying in pools of their own blood and waste.

Sara felt kind of bad about the older one. When she gave him the look and pointed her gun at him, his watery gray eyes got all big and scared. She'd practically had to force herself to pull the trigger.

But it was his own fault. He should have gotten down and stayed down like she told him to.

Stupid old fool.

There was movement toward the back of the room and Sara fired another round into the ceiling. A woman screamed as plaster showered down around her.

"I'm not gonna tell you again," Sara shouted. "You move, you die. Got that?"

She gave *everyone* the look now—that flat, deadly, animal stare she'd practiced for hours. Alex said she had a natural propensity (his word) for sweetness, and he'd spent days working with her, teaching her to turn it on and off. He said her ability to do that was better than any weapon he owned, and Alex owned a lot of weapons.

Speaking of which, where the hell was he?

The guards had been immobilized; the room was under her control . . .

He should've been here by now.

Before she completed the thought, the bank doors burst open and the love of her life strolled in.

Gunderson hated bank jobs. They were messy and unwieldy and full of unknown variables. You never knew when some nutcase might decide it was more important to die a hero than tuck his kids into bed that night.

On top of that, the labor-to-profit ratio was a bit too thin to make it all worthwhile. He could make more money copping credit card numbers off the Internet.

But bank jobs generated heat. And if you've got a message to get across, as Gunderson did, then heat is what you need.

He pushed the bank doors wide and gestured for Luther and Nemo to go in first. Like Gunderson, they sported black battle gear, ski masks, and Colt Commando 733s. A bit showy, but that was the point.

Their armbands featured hand-sewn Chinese characters against a black background, the symbol for *warrior*, a favorite of Gunderson's. Sara had designed them one night after a particularly athletic bout of lovemaking. He was *her* warrior, she'd said. His energy inspired her.

And she, in turn, inspired him.

Gunderson hefted the 733 and pushed in after Luther and Nemo. Sara was near a counter at the center of the room, her game face on, the nine-millimeter he'd given her for her birthday clutched in her left hand.

Her wedding ring glinted under the fluorescent lights—a $40,000 work of perfection he'd stolen off some fake-n-bake bitch in Boulder City after he'd boned her silly.

Nothing but the best for his Sara.

Gunderson crossed to where Sara was standing and handed her a Kevlar vest. She waved the nine, indicating the crowd of civilians face-down on the floor. "Proud of me?"

Gunderson smiled and rubbed the swell of her abdomen. The kid was kicking like crazy. "Always, baby. Always."

As he helped her into the vest, he marveled at how good she looked pregnant. He couldn't imagine anyone more beautiful than she was right now. Or any other time, for that matter.

She was the kind of woman men write sonnets about. Fight duels over.

And she was his. All his.

Gunderson pulled off his ski mask, kissed Sara's forehead, then turned and pointed his 733 at the nearest surveillance camera, blasting it right off its swivel mount.

There was an audible reaction from the crowd as camera guts blew everywhere.

Gunderson smiled. "Alright, folks, settle down. This, as they say, is a stickup."

3

D-E-A-T-H.

A five-letter word for *crossing over.*

Donovan was trying to pencil it in when A.J. spun the wheel and took a turn at high speed. The Chrysler's tires groaned beneath them, the shift of force pinning Donovan against the passenger-side door.

"Easy, Hopalong, you're messing up my perfect penmanship."

A.J. grunted and took another turn, this one only slightly less severe. A.J. never said much when he drove. Especially if he was in a hurry.

The call from Sidney Waxman had come in at 9:15 a.m. The Madison Street branch of Northland First & Trust was normally a ten-minute drive, depending on traffic, but with the siren on and the bubble flashing, A.J. swore he could make it in under five. That meant two to go, give or take, allowing Donovan just enough time to polish off this bitch of a crossword he'd been struggling with all morning.

Donovan was seriously addicted to crosswords. Every workday started with a glass of grapefruit juice, a sharp No. 2 pencil, and the Tempo section of the *Trib*, where the checker-box monstrosity was nestled among the art reviews and horoscopes.

Working the puzzle prepared him for the day ahead. Sharpened his mind. Unfortunately, he was notoriously bad at solving the damn things. So bad, in fact, he couldn't remember the last time he'd actually finished one.

But he was close this time. Very close.

"Four blocks and counting," A.J. said, breaking his silence. "If I push it, I can beat my own record."

Donovan glanced up from his newspaper. "Why settle for silver when you can grab the gold?"

A.J. grinned and punched the accelerator, a man with a mission, living life on a perpetual caffeine high. Donovan was only a dozen years his senior, but working next to a live wire like A.J., he sometimes felt like a very old man.

Of course, that might have something to do with all the pain and aggravation he'd managed to pack into his thirty-nine years. Both parents were dead. His sister had committed suicide when he was seventeen. And his wife and kid—make that ex-wife and kid—barely knew he was alive. Donovan wasn't quite sure how or when he'd let it all slip away, but he had and felt guilty because of it.

Actually, guilty was too mild of a word. What he really felt like was an A Number One shitheel and held no illusion that either wife or daughter would disagree.

The only part of his life Donovan really had a handle on was the job. He'd been a special agent with the Bureau of Alcohol, Tobacco, Firearms and Explosives long enough to consider it a lifetime commitment and had spent ten years prior to that with the Chicago PD. He was a rising star in a vast federal bureaucracy and, so far, hadn't managed to disappoint.

There was always tomorrow, of course. Or the rest of today, for that matter. But Donovan had enough confidence in his abilities on the job to ignore the failures of his personal life and approach the future with optimism.

Cautious optimism.

A.J. turned a corner. "You think we're looking at another snipe hunt?"

"Sidney says it's the real thing."

"Doesn't make any sense. Why would Gunderson take down a bank?"

Donovan shrugged. "I stopped trying to figure out that asshole a long time ago."

Alexander Gunderson was another puzzle Donovan had yet to solve. The task force he headed had been formed specifically to investigate a local arms-trafficking ring with suspected ties to a nationwide network. The deeper they dug, the more Gunderson's name had come up. So Donovan kept digging and was introduced to the organized anarchy of a small but potentially destructive new militia organization: the Socialist Amerikan Reconstruction Army.

S.A.R.A.

Gunderson was its founding father.

The group's recent stockpiling activities had put them squarely on Donovan's radar screen. Yet despite his insistence that they be taken seriously, both the FBI and the Department of Homeland Security considered a ragtag band of malcontents hardly worth their time. They were too busy scooping up olive-skinned bogeymen and carting them off to Guantánamo for a round of zap my privates.

Donovan knew different. With all the weaponry Gunderson had accumulated, the guy was capable of doing just about anything.

But a bank job?

A.J. was right. It didn't make much sense. Unless, of course, Gunderson was vying for more attention. Something he seemed to crave.

"Home stretch," A.J. said. "Twenty seconds to spare."

Shooting through an intersection, they made yet another quick turn that had Donovan gripping the armrest. Why A.J. never took the straightforward route was beyond him. With a sigh of resignation, he dropped the crossword to the seat next to him. No way he'd finish it now.

Up ahead loomed the forty-story building that housed Northland First & Trust, the carnival already in motion. Patrol cars formed a barrier near the bank's front doors. The street had been blocked off; a throng of rubberneckers had lined up behind long wooden sawhorses, anxiously awaiting the big showdown. News vans struggled to find a place to perch that was within camera range. A SWAT van sat at an angle several yards behind the patrol cars. Standard procedure meant a platoon of sharpshooters already occupied various sweet spots in neighboring buildings.

Gunderson or not, Donovan didn't envy whoever was inside that bank.

Waxman and the local SWAT commander were waiting for them as they pulled up next to the van. Donovan swung his door open, climbed out. "Sing to me, Sidney."

Waxman and Donovan had come up together through the ranks of the ATF, and Donovan had long considered him his best friend.

He was also a damn fine agent.

"It's him, Jack. Gunderson, the missus, and two shooters in ski masks. Video feed was cut right after they made entry, so we're flying blind."

A.J. joined them as they crossed toward the barrier of patrol cars. "He make contact?"

Waxman shook his head. "Not a word."

Donovan shifted his attention to the SWAT commander—a barrel-chested guy with a neatly trimmed mustache. "What about hostages?"

"We're estimating as many as thirty. What's this asshole's story, anyway?"

"Just another pretty boy looking for attention," A.J. said.

Donovan gestured toward the bank. "Any way out besides the front doors?"

"Not without a sledgehammer and a whole lot of elbow grease. We've shut down the elevators and sealed off the lobby. There's a fire door in back, but it doesn't connect directly to the bank. He's boxed himself in."

"Trust me," Donovan said. "He went in, he's figured a way out." Gunderson always had an angle. The trick, of course, was figuring out what it was before he had a chance to use it.

They crouched low as they reached the patrol cars, taking position behind them. A.J. aimed a pair of field glasses at the front doors.

Like those in the windows, the blinds were drawn shut.

"Visibility stinks," he said. "Shooters don't have a prayer."

Donovan pulled his cell phone from a pocket of his flak jacket. "Let's see if he's in a talkative mood."

He punched in the number for dispatch and had the operator patch him through to the bank. He had never considered himself much of a negotiator. Found it difficult to buddy up to these scumballs. But if it meant getting the hostages out of there alive, it was worth a shot. Maybe he'd get lucky and Gunderson would tip his hand.

He thought about that a moment and almost laughed out loud.

What's an eight-letter word for *fat chance*?

4

Kinlaw was pissed. Three years wearing the uniform, busting his ass on the streets, taking shit from civilians who considered him barely a step above Hitler's Schutzstaffel, and here he was pulling duty at the *rear* of the crime scene. You'd think the dues he'd paid, he'd at least get a front-row seat.

But no. The supervising officer had decided Kinlaw and a handful of his fellow uniforms were best put to use at the backside of the bank building, just in case the suspects got clever.

The way Kinlaw saw it, they'd have to be friggin' geniuses, considering there was only a single fire door and no ground-floor windows back here, and the building was made of solid concrete and steel. But who knows, maybe they'd launch hang gliders off the fortieth floor and make their getaway at three hundred feet above street level.

Uh-huh. Sure.

Just once in his life, Kinlaw wanted to be out where the action was. Maybe even get in a shot or two when the fireworks started. Assuming there'd be any fireworks.

Instead he'd have to stand here like an idiot for God knows how long, feeling like the designated driver while everyone else partied hardy. Sometimes he wanted to take this badge of his and . . .

Shit.

Some bozo in a van was trying to edge past the barrier at the top of the block. Big Channel Four news wagon that wasn't even supposed to be back here. Kinlaw sighed and trudged up the street toward it. All his time on the force and he was nothing but a glorified—

Wait a minute—what's this?

He nearly stopped short when he saw the driver, a hot-looking babe in a tight-fitting wife-beater tank top. Hard to tell through the windshield, but it looked like she wasn't wearing a bra.

And what a set of rockets she had.

Kinlaw threw his hands up to stop her. "Excuse me, ma'am. You can't be back here."

The news van squeaked to a halt and Kinlaw approached the babe's window, waiting for her to roll it down.

Damn, she was hot. Steaming, in fact. Short-cropped, blond hair, body of a goddess, cute little radio-com headset that made her look sexy as hell.

And those tits. Ouch.

She eyed him quizzically. "I'm sorry. What was that?"

"This is a restricted area," Kinlaw said. "Pull to the side and cut your engine."

"But I've got a story to—"

"Trust me, you're not gonna find it back here."

"But I'm late and everything's blocked out front and my producer'll kill me if I don't get something on tape before the noon broadcast." Her face flushed as she said it, a twinge of desperation in her voice.

Ahh, Kinlaw thought. A woman in distress.

He smiled. It was a smile he normally reserved for off-duty hours, the smile he took with him to the dance clubs and used as often as he could to charm his way into the sack.

He took a casual glance at her tits again, noting that her nipples were diamond hard. Then he said, "Tell you what. Pull to the side and cut your engine."

"But—"

Kinlaw silenced her with a firm but patient wave of the hand, making sure to infuse his words with just the proper amount of charm. "I'll make a call," he continued, "and see if we can get you some kind of exclusive."

Kinlaw knew there wasn't a snowball's chance in hell of *that* ever happening, but he could make the promise now and apologize later over dinner and drinks. And dessert, of course.

She looked at him. "Really?"

Kinlaw nodded and relief shone in her eyes.

"Thank you. Thank you so much."

"My pleasure, ma'am. Protect and serve. That's what I'm here for." He extended a hand. "Name's Randy, by the way."

She shook the hand, holding it a split second longer than necessary. "Tina," she said, her eyes telling him she was definitely interested.

Oh, yeah, Kinlaw thought. I'm in.

Maybe getting stuck back here in the boonies wasn't so bad after all. If he played this right, by midnight tonight those hefty ta-tas of hers would be warming the palms of his hands.

He was busy picturing every exquisite detail of the evening ahead when a muffled explosion came from inside the bank building.

Kinlaw turned. What the hell?

The blast knocked the vault door right off its solid-steel hinges. Gunderson saw it at half speed, like a scene from an old Peckinpah flick—the door teetering, then falling to the linoleum with a booming crash.

Somewhere behind him a phone was ringing, but Gunderson ignored it, enjoying the spectacle. He relished his ability to slow the world around him to a crawl whenever the mood suited him.

He grinned at the exaggerated looks of surprise on the faces of bank tellers and customers. Marveled at the fluidity of motion with which Luther and Nemo wielded fire extinguishers as they put out stray flames and climbed into the vault to fill their duffel bags.

He watched as, backpack full of Semtex in tow, Sara glided past the Plexiglas teller windows toward the rear of the bank, moving with an easy grace that only his slow-motion point of view could provide.

Gunderson felt high. As if he'd taken a dozen hits of ecstasy. But he never took drugs of any kind when he was working, didn't need them to see the world this way. This was his gift. His power. One he used sparingly and never took for granted.

And it wasn't his only gift.

Better yet was what the bitch who'd raised him—his nasty old bat of an aunt—called his Inner Eye, an acute intuition he had inherited from her, a sensitivity to the vagaries of human emotion that sometimes offered him a peek into the darkest corridors of the soul.

It was a gift that had made the old woman an outcast, the neighborhood crackpot. He himself had been smart enough not to flaunt this gift, learning to use it with stealthy precision to gain trust and manipulate. Because, after all, Trust was his true weapon of choice.

Despite his hatred for the old woman, who had been as cruel as they come, Gunderson shared her fascination for the workings of the mind and soul, and the belief that there was a world beyond this one, where both could thrive and flourish.

And where anything was possible.

The phone continued to ring. Gunderson snapped out of his reverie, turned toward the nearest desk where an extension light blinked.

It was the cops, of course. Most likely the Feds.

He checked his watch. Still on schedule. The police response had been quicker than he'd expected—someone had probably triggered the silent alarm the moment Sara started shooting—but everything was going smoothly, all according to plan.

Not that this surprised him. *The Book of Changes* was rarely wrong. His interpretations might be off sometimes, but you could never blame the *Ching*.

Patting his breast pocket, he heard the faint chink of the I Ching coins he always carried with him and wondered if he should bring them out for one last consult. Instead, he fished for his pack of Marlboros, shook one out, then tore off the filter and lit up, listening to the phone ring.

He picked it up at ring number forty-seven.

"Let me guess," he said into the receiver. "ATF? FBI? Mom?"

"Jack Donovan, Alex. I'm guessing the explosion we heard was the vault?"

Well, well. Mr. ATF himself.

Special Agent Jack had been trying for quite some time now to put a damper on Gunderson's plan to reeducate the country. So long, in fact,

that he'd become a regular source of irritation. Despite their mutual inter-
ests and a couple of semiclose encounters, however, this was the first time
they'd actually spoken.

Donovan's vaguely condescending tone was annoying as hell, but Gunderson kept his cool. "How you been, Jack?"

"Better than you'll be if you don't release those hostages. You've blown
it big-time, my friend. There's no turning back now."

Gunderson laughed. "Turning back? I'm moving forward. Just like a
shark."

"You let those hostages go, we'll talk about getting you out of there in
one piece."

Gunderson sucked on the Marlboro. Exhaled. "You sound awfully sure
of yourself, Jack. You know something I don't?"

"Only that you're fighting a lost cause. Why don't you give it up like a
good boy and let those people go. They aren't involved, anyway."

"We're all involved, whether we like it or not. You call 'em hostages,
you're right. They're hostage to a country you, and people like you, created." He took another hit off the cigarette, then flicked it aside. "But I
don't mean these folks any harm, so I'll tell you what—you want 'em, you
got 'em. Just remember one thing: the water's cool and clear right now, so
don't for a minute think you can slow me down."

He hung up. In the movie of his life, Gunderson was Che Guevara and
this idiot was Barney fucking Fife. Donovan had been haunting him on
the evening news for months now, spreading the Gospel According to the
ATF. Didn't he realize that sooner or later the tide would turn as more and
more citizens began to see the U.S. government for the inbred den of
hypocrisy it was? The country had wasted valuable resources blasting
sand rats in the Middle East, when it should have been looking inward.
The real threat didn't come from outside. It came from right here, within
our own borders. From our own selected officials.

It was only a matter of time before the people of America came around,
and Gunderson would be there, leading the charge.

Luther and Nemo climbed out of the vault carrying duffel bags full
of cash.

Gunderson looked over at them. "How we doing, boys?"

"We're clear," Luther said.

"Excellent. Baby?"

At the back of the room, Sara looked up from a patchwork of Semtex—or plastic boom-boom, as she liked to call it—part of a shipment Gunderson had had smuggled in from Prague. "All set, sweetie."

He clapped his hands together. "Alright then, let's put some wheels on this wagon and ride." He gestured to Luther, who immediately dropped his duffel bag, flipped open a vest pocket, and brought out a mini-DV cam about the size of a cigarette pack. The wonders of technology.

The only thing the traditional media offered Gunderson was exposure—which, of course, was his real reason for being here. But the traditional media was controlled by gutless corporate stooges. Expecting them to broadcast his true message was like expecting the late, lamented Mother Teresa to take a dump on the steps of the Vatican.

Gunderson knew full well that Fox and the nightly news would reduce him to a six-second sound bite courtesy of ATF lackeys like Jack Donovan. So he took matters into his own hands by pirating various high-traffic Internet sites to spread the word.

That's where the video cam came in.

Gunderson smoothed his hair back, adjusted his ponytail, then waited for Luther to take a good pan shot of the damage they'd done. As the camera turned on him, he addressed the hostages.

"All right, listen up," he said. "This little garden party has been brought to you courtesy of the Socialist Amerikan Reconstruction Army. We're ordinary folk, just like yourselves, striking a blow against a New World Order that uses mind control and propaganda to beat its citizens into submission and turn us into slaves. It's all about freedom, folks, and we're taking it back. If any of you want to join us, check out our Web site at S-A-R-A dot com."

He looked directly into the camera. "Get ready, America. The revolution is now."

He scraped a finger across his neck, gesturing for Luther to stop rolling. Unhooking a two-way radio from his belt, he flicked it on. "Big Daddy to Tina. You out there?"

A voice crackled in response. "Roger, Big Daddy. Already in position."

"Thirty seconds and counting," Gunderson said, then returned his attention to the hostages. "Everybody on your feet."

The hostages, still facedown on the floor, glanced at each other as if the command had been too much for their minuscule brains to comprehend. Fucking morons.

"Come on, come on," Gunderson snapped. "Hop to it."

One by one they started to rise, still looking at each other, fear in their eyes. Some of the women broke into tears.

When they were all on their feet, he said, "Okay. I'm gonna start counting. When I get to three, I want you to run your asses straight into the street. The last one out those doors gets a bullet to the back of the brain. Understand?"

Wide stares. More tears.

"I'll take that as a yes. Here we go: one . . . two . . ."

Before he could finish, a beefy boy in a three-piece suit cut loose and beelined it for the doors. The room filled with shouts and screams as the rest of the hostages scrambled after him.

Gunderson watched the stampede in slow motion and smiled. "Three."

The bank doors flew open without warning. A fat man in a three-piece suit stumbled out, fell to his hands and knees, and was nearly trampled by a dozen or more hostages as they clawed their way past the bottleneck and spilled into the street. It was as if someone had fired a starter pistol in the middle of a herd of buffalo. Not exactly the orderly hostage release Donovan had envisioned.

As he watched them pile out, their faces tight with panic, all at once he realized what this was.

Gunderson's angle.

"Sonofabitch," he muttered, turning to his men. Sledgehammer or no sledgehammer, Gunderson was going out the back. "He's using them for cover. Get in there—now!"

Donovan vaulted the hood of a patrol car and bolted. Yanking his government-issue Glock from its holster, he plowed through the exiting crowd and fought his way toward the entrance.

Something hissed past his head—something from inside the bank—and hit the ground nearby, smoke billowing. A smoke bomb, courtesy of Gunderson's well-stocked arsenal. Judging by the explosion they'd heard earlier, that arsenal included a significant amount of C-4 or possibly Semtex. Donovan had to get inside that bank before Gunderson could put it to further use.

But just as he reached the doors, another explosion rocked the building, its message rumbling in the pit of his stomach.

He was too late.

The deed was already done.

5

The cop named Randy was staring at her tits, asking her, "Who the hell is Big Daddy?" when the second explosion blew a hole the size of a freight wagon through the rear wall of the bank building. Chunks of cement flew everywhere, taking a couple of blue boys with them.

"Holy shit," the cop said, and as he spun toward the building, Tina put a bullet in his ear.

How's that for an exclusive?

She had the van in gear before his body hit the pavement. Behind her, in the well of the van, her partner, Gabriel, popped a grenade into the breech of an M203 launcher, then rolled open the side door and fired.

The charge pounded the gas tank of the nearest patrol car, sending up a mushroom cloud of fire and smoke and debris.

"Hold on!" Tina shouted.

Punching the accelerator, she slammed through a wooden barrier and blew past the flaming patrol car.

Cops were running everywhere, dazed, weapons drawn, looking to each other for direction and getting none. Tina heard Gabe pop another charge into the breech and fire.

A second patrol car exploded, noxious smoke and fumes billowing, giving them cover from any potential sharpshooters stationed above. Tina held her breath, feeling the heat of the flames as she roared past the patrols cars and angled the van toward the ragged hole in the building.

The chatter of Colt Commando fire came from inside the bank. Out on the street, one cop went down in a burst of blood, followed by another and another, as Alex and crew stepped out into the open, bulging duffel bags in hand.

Woo-hoo, Tina thought. We are gold.

"Come on! Come on!" Alex shouted, gesturing with his weapon. He kept looking over his shoulder into the bank. Someone or something was coming and they didn't have a moment to spare.

Tina swung around next to them, screeched to a halt. As Luther and Nemo tossed in their duffel bags, Alex helped Sara climb inside. "Easy, baby. Get up front and strap yourself in."

Luther and Nemo jumped in after her. Alex was about to follow when Tina heard a shout from inside the building.

"Freeze, Gunderson!"

Tina swiveled her head. A guy in a navy blue flak jacket stood in a haze of smoke inside the bank, his weapon pointed directly at Alex's back.

The Fed. Jackass Donovan.

Tina had been telling Alex for weeks to get rid of the motherfucker, but Alex had repeatedly blown her off. "In due time," he'd said, in typical Alex fashion, as if the world could wait until he was good and ready to give it his attention.

Tina figured that nasty piece of hardware in the Fed's hands was enough to make him reconsider. She looked at Alex, remembering the only motivational phrase her dear departed prick of a father had ever uttered in her presence. The old bastard had been sucking crack for two days straight when he offered her a hit off his pipe. "What's it gonna be, hot stuff? Shit or get off the pot."

Those words never seemed more appropriate than they did right now.

Donovan kept his Glock leveled at Gunderson, finger resting against the trigger. "I mean it, Alex! Don't you move!"

Smoke stung his eyes. Gunderson wasn't much more than a silhouette in the haze, but Donovan's aim was good. If he pulled the trigger, the man would go down and go down hard. This was the closest Donovan had ever been to collaring the prick and he wasn't about to let him slip away.

Gunderson froze for a split second as he stood outside the van door. For a moment it looked as if he might actually turn and give himself up.

Then Donovan spotted the remote detonator clutched in Gunderson's right hand.

Sweet Jesus.

He hadn't counted on a third explosion.

Before Donovan had time to react, A.J., Sidney, and a handful of SWAT sharpshooters burst into the room behind him and fanned out.

Donovan immediately threw his hands in the air. "Down! Everybody down!"

But it was too late.

With a deafening roar, the teller windows erupted. Plaster, Plexiglas, and chunks of cement and linoleum rocketed past Donovan's head as he tackled A.J. and Sidney and knocked them to the floor.

More smoke filled the room, along with the pungent odor of cyclonite and burning flesh. Beneath the agonized wails of the injured SWAT team, Donovan heard gunfire and the faint squeal of tires.

Gunderson's van, digging out.

Move, Jack, move.

Donovan looked into the dazed faces of Sidney and A.J., checked to make sure they were still in one piece, then jumped to his feet and raced to the hole in the wall.

The carnage out back mirrored the scene behind him. It was a war zone. Patrol cars in flames. Smoke everywhere. Uniformed cops dead on the blacktop, others wearing the same dazed expression as A.J. and Sidney.

Down the street, tires squealed as the Channel Four news van smashed through a row of police barriers and shot toward an intersection, a few shell-shocked cops firing after it.

Donovan scanned the area, sprinted toward an undamaged patrol car. Halfway there, pain stabbed his leg. A dark red stain spread across his right thigh, blood bubbling up through a tear in his slacks.

Shit. He hadn't realized he was hurt.

Reaching the cruiser, he threw the door open and jumped in. His thigh throbbed mercilessly now, but there was no time to think about it. No time to think, period. The news van was still in sight, but it wouldn't be for long.

He found the key in the ignition, twisted it, and the engine coughed, roaring to life. Jamming his foot against the accelerator, he spun the wheel and shot toward the intersection.

The news van was two blocks ahead now, weaving crazily through midmorning traffic. Donovan searched the dash, flipped a switch, and the patrol car's siren kicked in.

Traffic parted grudgingly and he punched the pedal, picking up speed—two blocks, a block, half a block—steadily gaining on his prey.

The van turned, a hard right into an alley. Donovan raced after it, honking his horn as he went. He whipped the wheel and turned into the alley just as the news van cleared the opposite end. It made an arcing left, nearly sideswiped a parked car, and continued on without slowing.

Donovan sped up, made a quick left.

Up ahead, the van blasted through another intersection. As Donovan struggled to catch up, some idiot in a Volvo crossed his path. Donovan swerved to avoid him, but clipped the Volvo's rear bumper and sent it into a spin.

Stupid bastard.

Donovan straightened the wheel and continued on without slowing, glancing in his rearview mirror as the Volvo slammed into a lamppost with a metallic crunch. He could only hope the driver was okay.

The wound in his thigh felt like a lump of molten lava. He probed it with two fingers and discovered something hard and jagged embedded in the flesh. He couldn't be sure, but it felt like a sliver of Plexiglas.

Biting back a wave of nausea, he tried to concentrate on the van. It was within striking distance now, its rear bumper only feet away.

Donovan nudged the accelerator and pulled up along the right rear side. Jerking the wheel hard, he smashed the side of the van.

It swerved, losing speed.

That's right, you son of a bitch, I'm right on your ass.

Without hesitating, Donovan jerked the wheel again. Metal crunched.

The van fishtailed, its driver nearly losing control.

He had them now. One more hit and this race was over. He was about to jerk the wheel a third time when the van's side door flew open and Alexander Gunderson pointed the business end of an M203 grenade launcher directly at him.

6

So Barney wanted to play.

Moments earlier, Gunderson was watching him through the van's rear windows, watching him work the wheel with a ferocity he didn't know the man possessed. Fucker blew right past that Volvo with barely a backward glance.

Driving like that took balls.

Until today, Special Agent Jack had been more of an annoyance than a threat. Gunderson had never considered him much more than a minor itch he'd eventually have to scratch. That opinion had changed, however, with every jerk of Barney boy's wheel.

So maybe he wasn't Barney after all. Maybe he was Chuck Heston, NRA poster child, crashing his chariot into theirs, jostling Gunderson's crew and forcing Tina, Queen of the Gladiators, to fight the wheel.

If Jack wanted to play, Gunderson was more than happy to oblige.

He'd even brought along his toys.

After that second jolt, he tore himself away from the window and gestured to Gabriel, who immediately tossed him an M4 carbine with an underbarrel launcher. Squeezing past Luther and Nemo, he moved to the side door.

Sara, strapped in up front, looked at him over her shoulder. "Careful, sweetie."

She was trying to mask her fear, but he could see it in the way she kept her shoulder muscles tensed, as if bracing for an impact.

Poor kid. He'd tried to convince her to sit this one out, but she'd insisted on coming along. Refused to be left behind. She was a True Believer, Sara was—her passion and his skill the perfect marriage. And despite her condition, she was the best soldier on his team.

She was his muse. His inspiration.

His only true cause.

He smiled at her, reached over, and rubbed her belly. Alex Jr. was kicking around like crazy. Probably scared, too. "Hang on, baby. It'll all be over in a minute."

He popped a charge into the breech. With a grunt, he rolled the side door open, then pointed the launcher at Donovan's windshield.

"Send up a prayer, motherfucker. You're about to kiss God."

The grenade launcher barked and Donovan swerved. The charge hissed overhead and a parked car behind him exploded, erupting in flames.

Score one for the good guys.

But Gunderson wasn't a quitter. He popped another charge into the breech, let it fly.

Donovan braked and swerved a second time, hearing another ominous hiss as the grenade streaked past his windshield and blew a chunk out of the blacktop.

Two–nothing, home team.

But he'd been lucky. If Gunderson fired that weapon a third time, there was a pretty good chance they'd be peeling Donovan's hide off these car seats with a pair of forensic tweezers.

He floored the accelerator, regaining his momentum, and just as Gunderson finished loading up charge number three, Donovan jerked the wheel, hard.

The van shuddered and fishtailed, the impact knocking Gunderson off his feet. He fumbled the carbine, which tumbled past the doorway, slammed onto the hood of the cruiser, then bounced into the street. Gunderson was about to follow when big hands grabbed him and yanked him back inside.

But Gunderson's troubles were far from over. The news van swerved wildly now as its driver fought for control of the wheel.

Up ahead, a road crew had set up shop in the middle of the street, signs warning drivers to PROCEED WITH CAUTION—and the van was doing anything but.

The next happened so fast it barely had time to register in Donovan's brain:

Swerving to avoid the road crew, the news van tilted sideways onto two wheels, then tipped over with a rusty groan and began to roll. Gunderson and a big guy in a ski mask were launched through the open side door by the force of the impact. As they tumbled onto the street, the van rolled and rolled, metal pounding blacktop, windows splintering, until it finally barreled through a row of parked cars and came to rest against the fresh carcass of a BMW.

Donovan, meanwhile, jammed his foot against the cruiser's brake pedal, feeling the tires melt beneath him. But it was too little, too late. The patrol car skidded into the mangled leftovers and stopped cold.

That's when Donovan's forehead met the steering wheel and everything went black.

7

A baby was crying. Somewhere far away.

Gunderson lifted his head off the blacktop, felt the burn of road rash against his left cheek, the tickle of blood on his forehead. He pushed himself up on his elbows and looked around, trying to figure out what the hell had just happened.

Someone was lying near him on the road. Dressed in black. Groaning.

Luther?

Sounded like him. Looked about his size. Still wearing his goddamn ski mask, the paranoid fuck.

Luther always said he'd back Gunderson's play with everything he had—everything except his face. "I'm no superstar," he'd once told Gunderson. "You tell me what to do, I'll do it, but my ma ain't gonna see my face all over the TV news."

Luther wasn't the sharpest tool in the shed, but Gunderson had to respect his point of view.

But then Luther wasn't the concern right now, was he? Something else sat unformed at the periphery of Gunderson's mind, something he needed to take care of. Unfortunately, his head felt like a can of soda that had been shaken up and left in the freezer too long.

In the distance, the baby was still crying. Getting closer now. Couldn't somebody shut that fucking kid up so he could concentrate?

No, wait. Not a baby.

A siren. A police siren.

Then all at once it hit him: Special Agent Jack. The van. Tina losing control of the wheel.

Oh, shit.

Sara.

Body screaming in protest, Gunderson jumped to his feet and spun, scanning the area until he found the van, which lay on its side like a dead elephant amidst a litter of old bones. There was a spray of blood across the cracked front windshield.

Oh, my fucking Christ.

"Sara!"

Gunderson stumbled toward the van, scrambled up and over it, and climbed in through the side door. He nearly stopped short at the sight of the carnage inside.

Gabe was gone for sure, lying at an impossible angle in back, head canted, eyes open and glazed. Nemo lay faceup across the middle seats, half-conscious and blinking. "What the fuck just happened?"

Then there was Tina. Jesus. Poor Tina had half a steering wheel embedded in her face, her once blond hair now wet and stained crimson, Queen of the Gladiators no more.

And Sara.

She was strapped in front next to Tina, eyes closed, arms dangling, a pregnant Raggedy Ann.

Gunderson felt gut-punched. He climbed over to her, touched her face, her neck, searched for a pulse.

Nothing there.

"No," he groaned, and unbuckled her seat belt. She fell into his arms, all bony angles and beach-ball belly, as lifeless as a sack of potatoes.

This can't be happening. Not this.

Blood dripped from the car seat. A dark stain spread at the crotch of her dress.

Gunderson groaned again. He slapped her face, trying to rouse her. "Wake up, baby, wake up!"

He slapped her again and then again, her head flopping listlessly beneath his blows. "Goddamn you, you little bitch, don't you fucking do this to me!"

The sirens were even closer now. He heard movement behind him, Nemo sitting up, probably still blinking.

"We're dead, man. We gotta get out of here."

Gunderson cradled Sara in his arms. He'd never been much for tears, but he felt them coming on now and struggled to choke them back.

She was alive. He knew she was alive. Her pulse was too weak to register, that's all. There's no way she was gone. Not Sara.

He turned to Nemo. "Help me get her onto the sidewalk."

"Are you kidding me? We don't have *time* for this shit."

Gunderson wrapped his fingers around Nemo's neck and jerked him forward. "Help me get her onto the sidewalk, needle dick, or I swear to Christ you'll wish you were Tina."

Nemo shot a nervous glance at Tina's bloody corpse.

"You're the boss," he said.

When Donovan came awake, he saw the big guy in the ski mask getting to his feet. Donovan's brain kicked into autopilot, sizing him up: six-three, 240 pounds, most of it muscle. He ran the catalog of possibilities through his mind, thinking he knew the names and faces of everyone on Gunderson's crew, but this guy was a mystery to him.

Of course, the ski mask didn't help much.

The guy staggered a bit, cradling a nasty gash that ran the length of his left inner forearm. The gash didn't seem to slow him down. Still wobbling slightly, he glanced back at Donovan, then stumbled toward the overturned van, which lay on its side several yards up the street.

Police sirens screamed in the distance, as if connected to an alternate universe, and Donovan wondered what the hell was taking them so long. He felt as if he were caught in some weird kind of limbo, where time and distance weren't measured the way they were in the real world.

He tried to move, but couldn't. The front end of the patrol car looked as if it had been crushed in the jaws of a trash compactor, the crumpled dash pinching his wounded leg. Blood pumped steadily from his thigh, seeping down to the seat beneath him. The entire limb was prickly numb, as if he'd slept on it for two days straight.

Donovan had been wounded twice before in the line of duty. Once as a patrolman in Lakeview. He was chasing a suspect in a liquor-store robbery, a kid no more than sixteen years old, when the kid wheeled around, opened fire, and struck gold with his first shot.

The bullet entered Donovan's right pectoral and exited just below the armpit. It ripped the hell out of muscle and tissue—he still had the puckered pink scars to prove it—but it had somehow managed to miss any vital organs. The attending physician told Donovan he was lucky his right lung was still sucking air, but Donovan hadn't felt all that lucky at the time.

The second incident was more serious. Donovan had a detective's shield by then, working Special Crimes, chasing down a serial rapist who had slit the throats of three of his latest victims, all thirteen-year-old girls.

On a tip from victim number four, who had miraculously escaped un-harmed, Donovan and his partner tracked the rapist to a run-down apart-ment building on the South Side. They cornered him in a dingy basement laundry room, where the suspect, a wild-eyed Neanderthal named Willy Sanchez, had dragged yet another thirteen-year-old.

He was holding her at knife point.

Donovan tried to reason with Sanchez. One hostage is the same as an-other, right? He set his .45 on a washer top and offered an exchange. "Come on, Willy, let her go. Take me instead."

Scared out of his wits, Sanchez at first balked, but finally agreed. Keep-ing his blade pressed against the terrified girl's throat, he told Donovan to turn around and back slowly toward him. Donovan did as he was told, sharing a quick glance with his partner, who had his own .45 trained on Sanchez.

The message was clear: as soon as the girl is free, take the shot.

But as he drew closer to Sanchez, Donovan caught the wild man's reflection in the window of a nearby dryer. Just a flicker of movement in those eyes told him that Sanchez wasn't about to let the girl go. He'd sooner slice her throat and let her bleed all over the laundry room floor.

Instinctively, Donovan quickened his step, brought his elbow up fast, and rammed it into the center of Sanchez's startled face, shattering his nose. Sanchez screamed, reaching for the damage as Donovan grabbed the girl's arm and spun her halfway across the room.

But Sanchez wasn't down. With a surge of pure rage, he lunged at Donovan, knocking him sideways against a jumbo dryer. The knife arced upward, sank deep into Donovan's side, and punctured his left kidney.

As Donovan slid to the musty cement floor, his partner pumped six bullets into Sanchez's back and head, sending him to the great boneyard beyond in five seconds flat.

The last thing Donovan remembered was the smell of stale dryer sheets and the hysterical sobs of a frightened little girl.

A team of surgeons managed to save both Donovan and his kidney, but the memory of that night still sent a shiver through him. Any pain he suffered was always compared to the heat of that blade piercing flesh.

Thanks to the numbness, the fire in Donovan's thigh was almost nonexistent now, but he'd gladly suffer a little pain in exchange for mobility. He watched helplessly as the big guy in the ski mask reached the overturned news van. Gunderson and another guy—Bobby Nemo from the looks of him—climbed out carrying a pregnant woman in a Kevlar vest and blood-stained sundress.

Sara Reed Gunderson. The girl next door with a heart of stone.

They laid her on the sidewalk and Gunderson knelt over her, almost reverently it seemed, and felt for a pulse. He obviously wasn't getting one. Head drooping, he closed his eyes a moment, then abruptly stood up and turned in Donovan's direction.

Even from this distance, Donovan could see the rage in those eyes. A greater rage than even Willy Sanchez had been able to muster, broken nose and all. Donovan didn't need a course in advanced logic to know what was coming. He tugged at his leg, trying desperately to pull it free, but the damn thing was wedged in tight.

Gunderson's hand dropped to a holster strapped at his thigh and pulled out a Beretta nine-millimeter.

As Donovan fumbled for his own weapon, he heard a sound—a sound that came from deep within Gunderson's gut and erupted into a roar of pain and rage that only a truly wounded soul could articulate. There were no words, just that sound, as Gunderson pointed the Beretta at him and squeezed the trigger.

Donovan dove sideways, flattening against the seat as the shot rang out. His windshield shattered, glass showering down on him.

Two more shots followed, punching leather directly above his head. Donovan raised his Glock over the dash and returned fire, but it was a fruitless gesture. The bullets ricocheted harmlessly.

The sirens were closer now, finally part of the real world and close enough to be a threat. The distant *thup-thup* of a helicopter accompanied them.

Bobby Nemo shouted, "We gotta get outta here, man!" but another shot rang out and metal clanged nearby.

A weightier voice said, "He's right, Alex. We'll deal with this motherfucker later."

Apparently Gunderson was incapable of speech. He made a strangled sound that seemed to indicate a reluctance to leave, but after a moment he was silent.

And a moment later, hurried footsteps carried them away.

Donovan raised his head and peered over the dash, his gaze immediately drawn to Sara, sprawled on the sidewalk. He knew what she was capable of, but that didn't equate with what he saw before him.

She was somebody's daughter. Someone's sister, wife, grandchild, and, until now, a mother-to-be. Donovan found himself thinking of his own little girl, wondering what his life would be like if he ever lost her. Maybe he *was* an A Number One shitheel, maybe he hadn't paid as much attention to her as he should, but he still loved her and couldn't imagine a world without her.

He stared at Sara and almost couldn't blame Gunderson for his rage, for wanting him dead. And in his heart and mind, he knew this wasn't over.

Not by a long shot.

Alexander Gunderson had a new cause.

part two

EFFECT

8

Jessie Donovan could count on one hand the things she hated in this world, and among them was the alarm clock in her father's bedroom.

At 7 a.m. on a chilly Thursday, that clock started buzzing, just loud enough to pierce the armor of her bedroom wall and pull her out of what had, until then, been a sound, dreamless sleep.

The alarm wasn't meant for her father. No, chances were pretty good he'd been up since dawn. He'd showered, shaved, and hit the street by 6:45, true as always to his workaholic lifestyle.

But because Jessie refused to set her own alarm and had consistently demonstrated a failure to rise on time, Daddy dear had taken it upon himself to make sure she didn't sleep in. She had school to think about. And grades. And a tardy student does not bring home the kind of grades that make the future bright.

What made matters worse was that Jessie couldn't simply roll over and smack the alarm silent. Instead, she had to force herself out of bed and stagger into her father's room.

By then, she was awake. Groaning, but awake. Irritated, but awake. And she knew that somewhere out there in the working world, her sadistic jerk of an old man was smiling.

A shower put her in a better mood. She liked the water needle-hard and hot enough to redden the skin. She shampooed, shaved her legs, and by 7:35 was wrapped in a towel and ready for breakfast.

As always, her father had left a bowl, a spoon, and a box of Cocoa Puffs on his breakfast nook counter. She had been staying with him for nearly two weeks now and the routine had never varied. This time, however, she was surprised to find a small, neatly wrapped box sitting next to her cereal bowl.

Not a birthday gift, that's for sure. Number fifteen had come and gone months ago. So what the heck was this all about?

A note card was taped to the box. She ripped it free and unfolded it, the neat, economical strokes of her father's pen staring up at her:

TRY NOT TO LOSE THIS ONE

She could hear him saying it in that no-nonsense tone of his. A tone of authoritative disapproval he'd cultivated after too many years on the job. She knew immediately what was in the box and felt like throwing it across the room.

But what would that accomplish?

Truth was, Jessie was too impatient for her own good. At least when it came to her father. It was obvious he loved her, and okay, okay, maybe she loved him back. But cut her a little slack. This was all new to her. She'd barely seen the guy in years. After half a lifetime of awkward, two-minute phone calls on birthdays and holidays, they had only recently reestablished contact.

She supposed part of that could be blamed on distance. Before moving back to the city, she and Mom and Roger had been trapped in gooberville for what seemed like an eternity. But her father hadn't exactly strained himself to keep in touch.

Until now, that is.

Something had happened, he'd told her. Something that had made him realize what a fool he'd been for allowing their relationship to become so fragmented. What that something was remained a mystery, but at the time he said it, his words had been like a melody to Jessie, a sad but reassuring song about love and loss and hope.

Unfortunately, the second verse didn't quite live up to the hype.

Shortly after he contacted her, Jessie had agreed to meet with him for lunch. Hot dogs and malts at Superdawg, one of the family's favorite haunts when she was a kid. But the meeting turned out to be just as awkward as those two-minute phone calls. And what talking they *did* do felt like an interrogation—Daddy dear obsessed with her love life, wanting to know who she was dating and how he treated her.

Jessie didn't hide her irritation.

"Who I hang out with," she finally told him, "is none of your fucking business."

She'd thrown in the F-bomb for shock effect, showing him that she was no longer his darling little girl. And it worked. That moment, in fact, was the sour note that knocked the entire melody off-key.

By the time he dropped her off at home, their conversation had been reduced to monosyllabic, caveman grunts. And after he left, she went directly upstairs and cried into her pillow for three straight hours.

But Jessie wasn't a quitter.

Despite the disaster, she couldn't escape the feeling of longing she had whenever she thought of her father. She wanted to hate him, but couldn't. Something about the smell of him reminded her of her childhood, of a time when all was good and clean and safe in the world.

He smelled like home. And Jessie wanted more than anything to be back beneath his protective cover.

So she called him, and they met again.

And a third time.

Better, but not perfect.

But maybe perfect was a pipe dream. Because no matter how hard she tried, Jessie just couldn't rid herself of the resentment she felt. A resentment that seemed to underscore their entire relationship.

Yet here she was now. Standing in his apartment on a chilly Thursday morning.

Mom and Roger had gone away for the month, and despite her

mother's skepticism, and her own serious misgivings, Jessie had accepted her father's invitation to spend the time with him.

It was almost as if he wanted to prove himself. To prove to her that this newfound desire for contact was more than just a passing fad, or half a decade's worth of guilt piling up on him.

The least she could do was give him that chance.

So instead of throwing the box across the room, she ran her thumb up under the spot where the edges of the wrapping paper met and tore it open. Just as she suspected, inside was a single key, attached to a tiny, ceramic figurine of Lisa Simpson.

The key chain was a nice touch. Jessie had been a *Simpsons* fan for as long as she could remember. When she was small, she and her dad had watched the show together every Sunday night, and she still made an effort to catch the nightly reruns.

The key fit the front door to his apartment. He'd given her a copy her first day there, but she had lost it at school a few days ago and had been forced to wait in the lobby until he came home that evening.

He was really pissed at first, lashing out at her with a sarcastic remark about teenagers and their lack of responsibility, but one thing she had learned in these two weeks was that he was the kind of guy who couldn't stay mad for long.

Not at her, at least.

And while that small fact didn't exactly have her jumping for joy, it was, she supposed, a step in the right direction.

She missed her bus and had to catch a cab to school. Not something she liked to do, but she was a big girl. It was either that or be late again, and late was not an option.

"Bellanova Prep," she told the driver, and gave him the directions.

The driver was a bald-headed perv who acted as if the only time he'd ever seen a girl in a school uniform was in some cheesy porn flick. All the way there he kept glancing at her in his rearview mirror.

Jessie shifted uncomfortably on the backseat and folded her arms across her chest, watching the morning whip by.

Vendors washed down sidewalks in front of flower shops and bakeries and delicatessens that promised mile-high pastrami sandwiches; harried moms dropped their squealing kids off at concrete nursery schools; men in gray suits with gray faces marched dutifully toward gray office buildings. It seemed to Jessie that people were always in such a hurry to get somewhere, but did any of them really know where they were going?

She sure didn't. Not yet, anyway.

After a while, some guy in a funky old Jeep pulled up alongside the cab and blocked her view. Not that she minded. He was pretty cute. *Way* too old for her, close to thirty probably, but he looked familiar and she was sure she'd seen him on TV. Maybe on SOAPnet. Or one of the entertainment channels. She couldn't be sure.

The ponytail was a bit much—who the heck wears ponytails these days?—but the body wasn't bad. Taut, muscular, looking like he'd spent a lot of time outdoors chopping wood or something. He had nice gray eyes and an easy smile, which he flashed in her direction as he sped up and turned a corner.

Bellanova Prep was less than a mile away. Jessie had half a mind to tell the driver to turn around and "follow that Jeep," but that would be a little reckless, now, wouldn't it?

Jessie was not a reckless girl.

Moments later, as she paid the driver and got out of the cab, she could swear she saw the Jeep again, out of the corner of her eye. She glanced up the street, but saw no sign of it—if it had even been there in the first place.

As she hurried up the steps and fell in with the crowd of kids piling in through the school's cathedral-like entrance, she found herself thinking about that Jeep, and about sixth-period math and a guy named Matt who sat across the aisle from her.

She wondered how *he* would look with a ponytail.

9

The hot item on drive-time talk radio was the transfer of Sara Reed Gunderson to yet another critical-care facility. This was the third such transfer in little over a month. The first came ten days after she was brought to Franklin Memorial, her baby lost, her pulse nearly nonexistent, and her brain showing little, if any, activity.

In other words, Sara was about as dead as you can get without actually crossing over to the other side. The doctors should have pulled the plug that first day, but Sara's parents wouldn't hear of it. They still held out hope for their little girl.

Sara's father, the CEO of a topflight investment brokerage, used his considerable influence and deep pockets to call in medical experts from around the world. They'd take his money and study her charts and quietly shake their heads.

Sara's mother appealed to God, but her prayers had apparently fallen on deaf ears. Sara had been in a coma for a month and a half now, and the prognosis wasn't even remotely hopeful.

Despite Sara's crimes, and despite her leftist leanings, she was something of a cause célèbre to the right-wing fanatics who dominated the talk-radio waves. Whenever a new transfer was announced, discussions about government agencies out of control were renewed with venomous vigor. Most of that venom was reserved for the ATF.

Remember Waco, they'd cry.

The children of Walter O'Brien, and the wife of fellow bank guard Samuel R. Kingman, pointed fingers at no one. They believed Sara Reed Gunderson was an icy-hearted bitch who got exactly the punishment God intended: an eternity in hell.

Their only hope was that her husband would soon join her.

Unfortunately, no one expected that hope to come to fruition anytime soon. Despite the best efforts of the Chicago Police Department, the FBI, and the ATF, neither Alexander Gunderson nor his two surviving comrades could be found.

The FBI, plagued by the more pressing concerns of Middle East terrorist cells, speculated that Gunderson and crew had fled the country, possibly to Cuba. The police commissioner, countering criticism that the CPD was asleep at the wheel, insisted they had headed for the mountains of Wyoming or Iowa, seeking refuge among the local militias.

Neither scenario made sense to Jack Donovan. And as the publicity surrounding the Northland First & Trust robbery sank deeper and deeper into the back pages of the daily newspapers, he refused to give up. He maintained that Alexander Gunderson hadn't left at all, but was holed up somewhere within the city limits.

Waiting. Watching. Planning.

Gunderson would never, Donovan insisted, leave his beloved Sara behind.

10

"Will you hurry up, for crissakes? He's waiting."

"I'm coming, I'm coming."

The bitch in the Chevy Suburban dabbed at her nose, snapped her compact shut, then climbed out and slammed the door. The sound reverberated through the underground parking lot like cannon fire.

Her husband, a balding butterball in a three-piece suit, was already standing at the parking-lot elevator, watching with a scowl as she straightened her skirt and checked her reflection in the passenger-side window.

"Oh, for Christ's sake," he said. "You're not gonna screw the guy. Come on!"

Gunderson had half a mind to cap the butterball right then and there.

Count your blessings, asshole.

At least she can walk.

Gunderson sat behind the wheel of his Jeep Commando, which was parked across the aisle from the Suburban. He'd been watching these two pathetic retards ever since they'd pulled into the stall five minutes ago. Neither looked particularly happy, and he had no clue where they were headed, but when they returned, they'd be considerably less jovial than they were now.

He was about to steal their wheels.

Gunderson had spent six months of his sophomore year of high school at the Illinois Youth Center downstate. His offense had been unsophisticated and impulsive: a smash and grab of his shop teacher's prized Datsun 240-Z.

If six months at the IYC taught him anything beyond what the juvenile-court schools called an education, it was the wonders of the slim-jim and the screwdriver. No more smashing and grabbing for Gunderson, he now had the tools he needed to forge a career, and forge it he did.

The next few years were spent organizing and operating a car-theft ring that quickly became a top priority for the Chicago Major Crimes Division. Cars were stolen, stripped, and dismantled in less than two hours, their parts often sold for three times the value of the car itself.

Those days were long behind him now, but Gunderson still knew how to use the tools of the trade. In fact, he'd copped this crappy old Commando with nothing but a slotted two-inch Craftsman. The Jeep had served its purpose well, but now he needed something roomier. Something that said *soccer mom*.

The Suburban was the perfect choice.

The elevator bell rang and Mr. and Mrs. Waste-of-Space stepped inside, the Husband of the Year still complaining about how late they were as wifey-poo adjusted and readjusted her ample, if sagging, bosom.

Gunderson waited for the doors to close, checked to make sure the aisle was clear, then swung his legs out of the Jeep and crossed to the SUV.

Approaching the driver's-side window, he fed the length of a slim-jim down past the rubber, gave it a little shake and a tug. The lock popped open. Once inside, he pulled a stubby screwdriver from his pocket, jammed it into the ignition, and started the engine.

The whole operation took less than forty seconds.

On his way out of the parking lot, Gunderson paid the attendant five bucks (and they called *him* a criminal), rolled the Suburban up the ramp into traffic, and headed back the way he'd come.

As ripe little Jessie exchanged shy glances with the pimply-faced geeks in her biology class, Gunderson thought about his sweet Sara lying silently in her hospital bed and allowed himself the slightest of smiles.

Retribution is a wonderful thing.

11

When the buzzer buzzed, Bobby Nemo's muscles tensed. An instinctive reaction. He'd been on edge for weeks.

"Oww," Carla groaned, "you're hurting me."

"Shut up," Nemo said. He got off her, told her to get dressed, then pulled his pants back on and eased onto the sofa, letting his gaze drift to the television set across the room. ESPN extreme sports.

He was trying to look relaxed, but he didn't feel so relaxed.

"That's it?" Carla said. "We're not gonna finish?"

The buzzer buzzed again.

"Get your clothes on and answer the goddamned door."

Carla pouted. Pushed her lips together and got all teary-eyed. Nemo hated when she did that. Made her look like some needy skank, especially when she sat there on the floor with her tits and ass hanging out. He knew what was coming next.

"You don't love me anymore."

"Jesus, Carla, don't start, okay?" He picked her T-shirt up off the carpet and threw it at her. "Just shut up and get your ass in gear."

She got quiet then and pulled the T-shirt on, the words MAN BAIT plastered across her surgically enhanced chest. She reached under the sofa for her panties, started to slip into them, then had a sudden change of heart and flung them at Nemo instead. "Asshole."

She got to her feet and sashayed toward the door, the T-shirt barely covering the crack of her ass. She was planning to give their caller a beaver show, doing it to spite Nemo, because she knew how much he hated it when she did that.

Of course, Carla made her living giving beaver shows. Let guys stick dollar bills up her snatch even though a sign at the back of the club where she was headlining clearly said TOUCHING OF DANCERS STRICTLY PROHIBITED. God knows what she let them do during the private dances.

But that was work. This was different. Nemo had been staying with Carla for a few weeks now, and this was the second time she'd gotten pissed enough to go to the door bare-assed. Last time some poor geek of a Mormon kid got a glimpse of that little Brazilian wax job of hers and almost shot his wad right there in his Fruit Of The Looms.

Carla had laughed like a friggin' hyena, but Nemo didn't think it was funny. Not one bit.

The buzzer buzzed a third time. Nemo's hand slipped under the seat cushion next to him and touched the grip of his Desert Eagle.

Carla called out, "Who is it?"

"Chu's Chinese. I've got your order."

About goddamned time, Nemo thought, and withdrew his hand. His muscles relaxed. Everything was cool. Nothing to worry about.

For now, at least.

The first time Nemo saw his face on TV, he almost shit a brick. This was the day following the Northland First & Trust disaster, when he, Alex, and that dimwit Luther were nursing their wounds at a house on Lake Shore Drive, a big mother of a place owned by Sara's brother, Tony.

Reed was an unwilling participant in the proceedings, a petulant little prick who spent one minute crying about his kid sister and the next threatening to call the police. So Alex wasted no time setting him straight.

They were watching CNN on Tony's big screen, watching a report on the robbery, when Nemo's face filled all sixty-two inches of the thing, some candy-assed news anchor telling the world what a fuck ball he was.

Nemo didn't feel like a fuck ball, and he sure didn't feel like spending the rest of his life in a federally franchised HoJo, so he split from Alex and Luther that day, telling them they'd all be better off if they didn't travel in a pack.

They kept in touch, using stolen and hacked cell phones, Luther the lucky one because he'd never been identified, living back home with Mommy. Alex carved his own shithole out in the boondocks while Nemo grew a beard and played nomad, bouncing from place to place. He thought about leaving the country altogether, but that would make him a stranger in some strange land and he didn't exactly relish that thought.

In the end, he stayed where he belonged, right here in the city, where he felt comfortable. The Feds probably figured he was holed up somewhere in South America, but he never got overconfident, always stayed alert. Keeping to himself during the day, he cruised the bars at night, constantly looking for a safe place to perch. He spent a few nights out at Fredrickville, holed up in some cracker-box motel that a friend of Luther's managed, but a restless spirit sent him back to the city, prowling for a better grade of poon.

Then he met Carla, a dancer at the Pussy Palace, a G-string-optional strip dive on South Clinton.

Carla always opted to go without.

That night, she took him to a private booth and gave him head like you wouldn't believe. Nemo didn't know if it was the size of his unit or the fact that he thanked her afterward that made her fall for him, but she invited him home and he'd been here ever since. It had worked out real good, because Carla didn't watch the news or read the papers and had absolutely no idea who he was. Carla was a cute little piece of ass, but she'd never be a contestant on *Jeopardy*.

Nemo watched her get up on tippy-toes and look out the peephole. She was short, but it was all muscle and soft curves.

"Puny little oriental guy," she said, then turned and gave Nemo a defiant grin. "Let's give him the full show."

She peeled off her T-shirt and tossed it aside. Her tits probably would've bounced if they weren't so pumped full of silicone.

"Jesus, Carla. You're gonna get your ass popped for indecent exposure."

"You call this indecent?"

She turned back to the door, reached for the dead bolt, twisted it.

The moment the latch clicked, the door burst open, knocking Carla on her ass. She yelped in surprise as a horde of federal flak jackets barreled past her and piled into the living room. "Federal agents! On the floor! Now!"

Every one of them carried heavy firepower.

Nemo's hand ducked under the cushion again, but before he could reach his Eagle, three agents were on him. Big hands grabbed his shoulders, spun him around, and pushed him to the floor. He felt the pressure of a knee digging into his back as his arms were jerked behind him and nylon cuffs looped his wrists.

The room got quiet then, except for Carla, who squealed like a terrified puppy as they dragged her naked hide outside. After she was gone, Nemo heard footsteps thump toward him across the carpet—someone with a slight limp to his gait. A moment later, an agent knelt down next to him and got right in his face.

Jackass Donovan. Wearing a grin that Nemo felt like putting a fist in.

"Hiya, Bobby." Despite the grin, there was no hint of humor in Donovan's eyes. "We need to talk."

12

He is *so* cute," Jessie whispered.

She and her best friend, Laura, stood near the foot of the steps outside Bellanova Prep, trying to look nonchalant as Matt Weber strolled by. It wasn't easy, but Jessie managed by pretending to have a sudden intense interest in the zipper of her backpack.

Matt tossed her a quick glance as he passed.

Jessie caught it, giving him an equally quick smile in return. He was way out of her league, but that glance meant something. She was sure of it.

Laura thought so, too. "Did you see that?" she said, keeping her voice low. "Did you see the way he looked at you?"

Jessie just nodded, momentarily unable to speak. She had been admiring Matt for weeks now and this was the first time he'd shown any real interest. Could she be misreading the look?

"You've *got* to ask him," Laura said.

"No way."

"Come on, Jess, he'll go. You know he'll go."

She was referring to Bellanova's upcoming Ladies First dance. Girls were expected to do the asking, a thought that terrified Jessie, especially when Matt Weber was factored into the equation. Jessie felt confident about many things, but the thought of asking him to the dance scared the heck out of her.

She watched Matt cross the parking lot, step around a maroon Suburban parked at the curb, then dash across the busy street. Horns honked in his wake, but he ignored them and headed down an alley.

Normally Jessie would keep her eyes on him until he was completely out of sight—staring at that tight little butt of his could easily become a full-time occupation—but something else caught her attention, and it had nothing to do with Matt.

Her gaze shot back to the Suburban parked at the curb.

The guy behind the wheel looked familiar.

It was hard to tell from this distance, but she could swear he had a ponytail.

Was it the guy from this morning? The cute one driving the Jeep?

"Hey, Jess! Laura!"

Jessie turned. Karen and Kathy Northam approached from the top of the steps, both out of breath.

"Better hurry or we'll miss our ride," Karen said. She pointed toward the street, and true enough, their bus had already pulled up to the curb.

Tossing all thoughts of Mr. Ponytail from her mind, Jessie ran with her friends to catch it.

How much longer you stuck with your dad?" Laura asked.

They sat near the back of the bus, close to the engine. Jessie had always liked the sound it made, a low rumble she found soothing and somehow reassuring.

"I'm not stuck," she said.

"Doesn't sound like it, the way you've been talking."

Jessie shrugged. "We're a work in progress."

"Uh-huh, sure. Just be prepared for the big letdown." Laura's own father had been gone for years. "When do your folks get back from the Caymans?"

"Couple of weeks."

"I don't see why they didn't just take you along."

Jessie made a face. "It's some kind of second honeymoon thing."

"Yuck."

"Tell me about it."

The mental image of her mom and Roger doing it in their beachside hotel room was not a pretty one. Jessie couldn't count the number of times she'd heard them moaning and groaning through her bedroom wall at home.

Double yuck.

Not that she had anything against Roger. He was an okay guy. He gave her space and didn't hassle her too much about homework and grades and junk like that. He and Mom had been together since she was eleven, so she was used to having him around. He was by far the least offensive of the jerks her mother dated during the year following the divorce.

Jessie had spent that year wondering why Mom preferred these idiots to her father. To her it wasn't even a close call. Then Roger Nolan came along and he always had a smile and something nice to say. The next thing Jessie knew, he and Mom got married and four years passed, most of it stuck in Nebraska, where Roger worked.

As the bus rumbled beneath her, Jessie thought of those four years, of the isolation she'd felt—a city girl trapped in a place so flat and wide and open that it had the opposite effect on her than you might expect.

She'd felt trapped. Trapped in a town she hated, a school she despised, surrounded by kids who treated her like a freak of nature. She'd wanted so much for her father to come and rescue her, but he was missing in action at the time. A voice on the telephone. A signature on some cookie-cutter birthday card.

But who knows, maybe it was all *her* fault. Right after the divorce she had grown cold and distant toward him, blaming him for her mother's tears, for his inability to make her happy. When he tried to contact her, Jessie had closed him out, refusing to see or even speak to him.

After a while, he stopped trying—which, of course, angered Jessie even more, because he'd given up too easily. The bastard.

Why did life have to be so freaking complicated all the time? Why couldn't it be like TV, where everything was wrapped up nice and neat in a single half hour?

It just wasn't fair.

"One good thing came from moving in with your dad," Laura said.

"Yeah?"

"We finally get to ride the bus together."

Jessie grinned and squeezed her hand. She and Laura had been close before the move to Nebraska and picked up right where they had left off the moment Jessie came back.

They grew silent now, Laura opening her journal as Jessie watched the afternoon traffic buzz by. The bus chugged toward its next stop, the low roar of the engine vibrating against her seat.

Bus rides always lulled her to sleep, and today was no exception. She closed her eyes, feeling the vibration play against her back and thighs, letting herself be carried into the world of the half-awake, where dreamlike images flitted through her mind.

Matt Weber was there, walking with her hand in hand toward Bellanova. They talked and laughed and the next thing Jessie knew she was pressed against a wall as Matt kissed her, his hot tongue scraping against her teeth. She kissed him back, feeling a tingle between her legs, wanting him to put his hand there. Then he pulled away and smiled at her.

Only it wasn't Matt.

It was the guy from the Jeep. Mr. Ponytail.

Jessie jolted awake in her seat. Where the heck had *that* come from?

Then, a sudden, odd chill ran through her and all at once she felt as if she was being watched.

No, it was more than that.

Something more . . . invasive.

She turned, glancing out her window toward the left rear of the bus, surprised to find the maroon Suburban rolling alongside it.

Mr. Ponytail was behind the wheel.

Looking straight at her.

Smiling.

Jessie snapped her head back around and faced front, her whole body rigid with fear. Her stomach lurched.

What the hell? What was he doing here?

Karen and Kathy sat behind her, completely oblivious to her sudden alarm. Karen leaned forward in her seat. "You guys hear about Steve Hugard?"

Laura, who had been writing in her journal, swiveled her head in their direction. "No, what?"

"He grabbed Mrs. Lehman's boobs in Health today."

Laura's eyes widened. "He *what*?"

"Right in front of the whole class."

"Oh, my God, what a perv."

"Yeah. They're trying to keep it a big secret, but Skinner kicked his butt right outta school. Told him he has to get therapy before they'll let him back."

"I never could stand that jerk," Laura said. "Guys like him give me the creeps."

I know the feeling, Jessie thought.

Through her window she heard the muffled whine of an engine accelerating. Glancing sideways, she saw the Suburban pull up parallel to her. She didn't dare chance a longer look, but she was sure Mr. Ponytail was still smiling at her.

Go away, she wanted to scream.

Leave me alone.

She thought back to this morning, to that funky old Jeep he was driving. Had he been following her to school? Was today the first time, or was he stalking her?

"Jess? You okay?" It was Laura. "Your face is all white."

Jessie didn't answer. She'd barely heard the question. This morning she'd thought this guy looked familiar, that she'd seen him on TV, and now she remembered where it was.

The afternoon news.

A few weeks ago she'd come home from school, flipped on the set. Channel Two had a story about a woman in a coma being transferred to a new hospital. The woman was young and pretty, but she'd done some really horrible stuff, most of which they blamed on the Svengali-like influence of her husband—whatever that meant—a big, badass bank robber that practically every cop in the country was looking for.

A big, badass bank robber with a ponytail.

Knowing he was now only feet away made Jessie sick to her stomach. A dozen different scenarios ran through her mind, none of which made any sense.

Why was he following *her*?

And what the hell did he want?

Sitting here wondering about it didn't help. She had to do something and do it now.

One thing her dad had always drilled into her head, even when she was just a kid, was this: if you find yourself in a situation beyond your control, don't be shy, do everything you can to regain that control—immediately.

And that's what she intended to do.

Without even thinking about it, Jessie tossed her backpack off her lap and shot up from her seat.

Laura looked up in surprise. "Jess? What's wrong?"

Jessie didn't look at her. Her eyes were on the bus driver.

"Stop!" she shouted. "Stop the bus!"

13

Interrogation Room 3 wasn't much more than a table, two chairs, and four blank walls that always felt as if they were closing in on you. Whether they had an effect on Bobby Nemo was anybody's guess.

Jack Donovan dropped a tagged and bagged submachine gun to the tabletop. An H&K MP5. Unlicensed. Fully automatic. They'd found it under Carla Devito's bed—part of a shipment they'd been tracing for months. They'd also found something in Carla's bathroom, something distinctly incriminating, but Donovan was keeping it under wraps for the time being. Saving it for leverage.

"Here's how it plays, Bobby. Just on the HK alone, you're looking at five in the bucket. Throw in Northland First and Trust and a handful of dead cops and we're talking some very serious sphincter time."

Nemo sat in one of the aluminum and vinyl chairs, his shackled hands in his lap. He eyeballed Donovan, but said nothing.

Donovan grabbed his own chair, straddled it. "You hearing me, Bobby? Multiple counts means consecutive sentences, my friend, so you can kiss off any hopes of an early release."

Nemo remained silent.

"I'd be happy to show you the guidelines."

"Fuck the guidelines. What are you selling?"

"I think you know." Donovan pulled a manila file folder from under his arm, flipped it open, and slid it across the table. Inside was a Most Wanted flyer featuring a grainy black-and-white photo of Alexander Gunderson.

Nemo snorted. "This is a joke, right? You think I'm some kinda half-wit?"

"I figure you've got enough rattling around in there to know when someone's offering you the only prayer you have of ever seeing daylight. Gunderson's underground and I'll bet dollars to donuts you know where to find him. Help me out and I'll talk to the AG's office. Who knows, they might even go for immunity."

"Bullshit."

"Is that yes or no?"

"It's you're outta your fuckin' mind, is what it is. Where's my lawyer?"

So that's how it's going to be, Donovan thought. A month and a half searching for this piece of shit and the wall immediately goes up.

"Don't make a mistake here, Bobby."

Nemo shook his head. "You're the one making the mistake. Gunderson's had a hard-on for your ass ever since you turned his bitch into creamed cabbage. You think I'm gonna get in the middle of that?"

"Beats the middle of a federal cellblock for the rest of your natural life."

Nemo eyed him dully. "You're so anxious to find him, why don't you give Sara a jingle, see what she has to say?"

"Very funny, Bobby."

Nemo shrugged. "Doesn't seem to be a problem for Alex."

Donovan just looked at him.

"You think I'm kidding? Guy thinks he can commune with the dead, for crissakes—and I guess creamed cabbage is close enough to qualify."

"Uh-huh," Donovan said. He'd heard rumblings about Gunderson dabbling in mysticism, but had never taken them seriously. Was Nemo pulling his chain?

"He doesn't make a big deal about it," Nemo continued, "but you get him high enough, he'll start spouting all this ancient Book of the Dead bullshit he picked up from his whack job of an aunt. Reincarnation, mind control, swapping souls and shit . . . Guy's convinced he's got a suite re-served in the afterlife. Tells me, 'Don't be afraid to die, Bobby, that's when all the fun starts.' " Nemo snorted again. "Thanks but no thanks, baby. I'll take my chances right here and now."

Donovan remembered reading a report in Gunderson's juvenile file about his wayward aunt, a two-bit fortune-teller. When Gunderson was twelve, she was dragged off to the nut farm after she strangled one of her clients. Proclaiming innocence, she told the arresting officer that the client had committed suicide. That he'd been taunted by "the voices." When the officer asked her what voices, she told him matter-of-factly, "Why, the voices of the dead, of course."

If Nemo was on the level, maybe the apple hadn't fallen too far from the tree.

"So if Gunderson's such a head case," Donovan said, "why join his crew in the first place?"

"Shit, man, I *was* his crew until Sara and the rest of those idiots showed up. And for all his bullshit, there's one thing you can say about Alex: he knows how to generate cash."

"Doesn't do you a whole lotta good right now."

"Excuse me while I break down and cry. What's your point?"

"I think you know," Donovan said. "Why not use the only leverage you have and tell me where to find him?"

Nemo's eyes glazed over. "Tell you what. You wanna deal?" He made fists with his shackled hands, then raised the middle finger of each and pointed them at Donovan. "Deal with this."

Six weeks. Six weeks nursing a wounded leg that still hadn't healed right, calling in favors from informants, staking out the homes of known associates, looking for something, *anything* that would lead him to Gunderson . . . and Donovan had popped a foul.

Finding Bobby Nemo had been pure luck. Nemo's new girlfriend had flashed a Mormon missionary kid, who, despite the distraction (and Nemo's freshly grown beard), had recognized a wanted fugitive parked on the naked woman's sofa. The kid sat on the information for close to two weeks, afraid the incident would either get him in trouble with the church or with Nemo himself. But he'd finally let good sense get the better of him and picked up the phone.

That was this morning. Donovan and his team had spent half the day staking out Carla Devito's apartment, then decided to make their move when a take-out man showed up with a couple boxes of Chinese noodles. Donovan had high hopes that nabbing Nemo would get him that much closer to Gunderson, but now Nemo was playing hard-ass.

And there wasn't much Donovan could do about it.

He slammed out of Interrogation Room 3 and found A.J. waiting for him in the hallway. A.J. had observed Nemo's display of affection through a two-way glass.

"That was a regular laugh fest," A.J. said. He looked restless. Ready to get busy. "Think you'll ever wear him down?"

Donovan shook his head. "Not without a serious breach of his civil rights."

"I'll bring the beer if you bring the peanuts."

Donovan put a hand on A.J.'s shoulder. His muscles were twitching. "Easy, Rambo. That kind of thinking makes the boys from D.C. nervous."

A.J. smiled. "Yeah," he said. "But it feels so goddamn good."

The task force command center was in motion as usual, a well-oiled machine that pushed forward relentlessly but never seemed to get a lock on a specific path to follow. The harried agents and support staff who populated the place had a purpose but no real sense of direction.

Donovan shared their frustration. Probably felt it stronger than all of them combined. But his only solution to the problem was to keep going, keep working, keep waiting for something to break.

Gunderson was still in town, he was sure of it. Sooner or later the bastard would have to show himself, and Donovan would be there, the full force of the attorney general and United States Treasury behind him.

He and A.J. exited the elevator and crossed the command center toward Donovan's office. A.J. made an abrupt turn, heading for the break room. He still looked jittery. "You want coffee? I brewed up something special."

"Maybe you should lay off a little."

"Lay off? I'm two cups shy of my quota. You want one or not?"

"No thanks," Donovan told him. "I'm trying to cut down."

"Jesus, Jack. No booze, no cigarettes, now you're turning your back on the almighty java bean? What exactly do you do for fun?"

Donovan tossed him the tagged and bagged MP5, wondering himself what the answer to the question was. After twenty years in law enforcement, he supposed it hadn't changed.

"Chase bad guys," he said.

14

"Stop! Stop the bus!"

When he heard the shout, Lavare Singleton's attention snapped to his rearview mirror. Near the back of the bus, a girl stood at her seat, a look of pure panic in her big blue eyes. One of the little cuties from Bellanova Prep.

Come on, kid. Maneuvering a ten-ton hunk of steel through afternoon traffic is tough enough without you giving me grief.

Chances were pretty good her dilemma wasn't much more urgent than a forgotten history book. These kids got rattled over the dumbest stuff.

"What's the problem?" Lavare sighed, not bothering to hide his irritation.

"You have to stop, call the police," blue eyes said. "I think . . ." She paused and looked around. Everybody on the bus was staring at her. "I think I'm being followed."

Oh, for criminy sake, Lavare thought. You're on a bus, you little twit. Who the hell could be following you? The two blond chipmunks on the seat behind you?

Lavare kept his foot steady on the accelerator, not about to surrender to her demand. "I'm sorry, miss, you'll have to sit down. I'll let you off at the next stop."

But blue eyes didn't sit down. "Listen, you jerk. You think I'm making this up?"

Lavare scowled. Jerk, huh? Little bitch.

"There's a guy driving next to the bus," she said. "He keeps looking at me. I've seen him before. I think he may be stalking me."

"Look," Lavare said, "just sit your butt down and we'll take care of it at the next stop."

Blue eyes continued to protest. She was babbling on about this imaginary stalker being some kind of fugitive, when a maroon Suburban cut in front of Lavare and screeched to a halt.

Son of a bitch.

Lavare stiffened and shifted his foot to the brake pedal. The bus yanked to a stop, air brakes hissing. His passengers reacted audibly, and blue eyes nearly toppled over into the next seat.

A few of her classmates giggled.

The Suburban sat in the middle of traffic, blocking Lavare's path. What the hell was this all about?

He angrily slid the side window open and leaned out. "Hey, fool, you wanna move that piece of tin before I mow it down?"

More giggles rose behind him. At least somebody was having a good time.

The Suburban didn't budge. Instead, the driver's door flew open and a guy with a ponytail climbed out.

Uh-oh, Lavare thought. Road rage alert.

Only he had no idea what this guy's beef was. Traffic was bad, sure, but he hadn't cut anybody off for at least half an hour.

Not that it mattered. It was Lavare's experience that these nut bags didn't need much provocation. Their whole day was centered on confrontation, the more the better.

If Lavare had it his way, he'd be happy to oblige.

Unfortunately, CTA policy made it clear that in tense traffic situations an operator must always use wisdom and diplomacy and keep an even temperament. Calling the guy a fool probably hadn't been too wise or particularly diplomatic, but Lavare was more than willing to do a little backpedaling to avoid any job-threatening situations.

The guy with the ponytail walked past the windshield and came around to the door. Lavare studied him through the glass, but didn't see any sign of rage on his face. In fact, he was smiling. As friendly as a neighbor looking to borrow your lawn mower.

Then it hit Lavare.

Had blue eyes really been serious? Could this be the somebody she claimed was stalking her?

The guy kept smiling and gestured for Lavare to open the door, but Lavare didn't budge. He had to think this thing over, figure out exactly what was going on here.

Behind him, a voice said, "Jessie, what're you doing?" and Lavare checked his mirror again.

Blue eyes was in the aisle now, working her way toward the gap in the middle of the bus where the side door was.

Lavare was about to tell her to get back to her seat when he heard a rap on the glass and returned his attention to the guy with the ponytail. Smile still intact, ponytail gestured again to open the door.

Something wonky was going on here and Lavare wasn't about to start speculating what it might be. Instead, he picked up his two-way and clicked it on.

"Base, this is Unit 219. Looks like I got me a situation." No judgment calls for Lavare. Leave them to the brass. "Unit 219 to base, do you read me?"

He was waiting for a response when the guy with the ponytail pulled a handgun from behind his back and pointed it at the glass.

Jessie heard a firecracker pop, then glass broke, and the bus driver jerked backward, his chest bursting blood.

She screamed. The bus erupted in panic, passengers looking around in confusion as others immediately ducked in their seats and covered their heads with their hands.

The forward door slammed open with a loud crash. Mr. Ponytail came up the steps carrying an ugly black gun, then turned and looked directly at Jessie, his smile gone, his eyes flat, reptilian.

Stranded in the middle of the aisle, Jessie dove for the side door. She tried desperately to pry it open, but Mr. Ponytail was on her in seconds flat. Grabbing her by the hair, he yanked her out of the door well. Needles of pain shot through her skull.

Jessie cried out and stumbled backward, losing her footing. Mr. Ponytail readjusted his grip, pulled her to her feet again.

Jessie winced, the pain nearly unbearable. "Please . . . ," she cried.

Mr. Ponytail leaned in close, his breath hot against her cheek. "Make a fuss, sweet pea, and this is only the beginning."

He released her hair, then grabbed her collar and jerked her backward. Jessie struggled to remain standing as he dragged her toward the front door.

Off to her side, a big guy in a Megadeth T-shirt started to rise, a threatening look on his face. "Let her go, asshole!"

Jessie heard another firecracker—this one loud and close to her head—and a hole the size of a dime opened up in the guy's neck. He flew backward, slamming against his window.

Jessie screamed again. A half dozen passengers echoed her, including Laura, Karen, and Kathy, who sat riveted to their seats, their faces twisted in terrified disbelief.

Mr. Ponytail spun Jessie around now and shoved her toward the steps. She stumbled down them, glass crunching beneath her shoes. Feeling his hand on her back, she stepped through the doorway and onto the blacktop.

Horns were honking, angry drivers oblivious to anything but the snarl of traffic backing up behind the bus and the Suburban. All along the sidewalk, startled pedestrians stood frozen in place, gaping at Jessie.

"Somebody help me!" she cried. "Get the police!"

A hand smacked the back of her head—"Shut up, bitch"—and a burst of hot, white heat shot through her brain. She stumbled again and Mr. Ponytail grabbed her arm and dragged her toward the Suburban.

Take control, Jessie, take *control*. Don't let him get you into that truck.

She tried to wriggle away, battering his shoulder with her free hand, screaming again for help. A couple of men in business suits started toward her, but froze in place when Mr. Ponytail waved his gun in their direction. "Think about your loved ones."

An arm slipped around Jessie's waist and jerked her off her feet, nearly knocking the wind out of her. Then the Suburban's rear passenger door was yanked open and Jessie was thrown inside as if she were nothing more than a sack of cement.

"Ladies first," he said.

She fell hard across the seat and the door slammed shut, nearly clipping her left foot. The engine idled beneath her, but there was nothing soothing about it.

Mr. Ponytail climbed behind the wheel, popped the gearshift into Drive. "Get your clothes off."

Jessie tried to catch her breath. "W-what?"

"Get your fucking clothes off, *now*," he said, then hit the gas pedal.

Jessie stared at the ugly black gun in his hand, knowing he wouldn't hesitate to use it. Too stunned to cry, she reached a trembling hand to her regulation Bellanova Prep sweater and fingered the top button.

All control was lost now, relinquished to the stranger behind the wheel.

Help me, Daddy.

Please help me.

15

"Any luck with Nemo?"

"Don't ask."

"Uh-oh, somebody's grumpy."

Donovan had learned a long time ago that there wasn't much point in trying to hide his moods from Rachel. She'd been the team's investigative analyst for over two years now and could read him like a polygraph.

"Grumpy's an understatement," he said as he trudged into his office and shrugged out of his coat. "I've got half a mind to gather up my toys and go home."

Rachel Wu stood in front of an open file cabinet near his desk, trying to jam a bulky manila folder into its proper slot in the drawer. She was young, Chinese-American, and had a fresh-scrubbed beauty that Donovan never got tired of admiring. More than once he'd thought about asking her out to dinner. Unfortunately, a pesky little thing called office protocol kept him in check.

He draped his coat over the back of his chair and sat. The wall next to his desk was a shrine to the evil that was Alexander Gunderson, a compilation of newspaper clippings, police reports, and mug shots that chronicled a life of crime and social anarchy. An eight-by-ten of Gunderson's face was riddled with tiny holes. A tight circle of darts adorned the spot between his eyes.

Anyone entering Donovan's office would immediately realize he had a serious obsession. He sometimes joked that he was a stalker with a badge, Gunderson's Number One Fan. Now if only he could tie the bastard to a bed, grab a sledgehammer, and hobble his ankles . . .

Donovan glanced at the mess atop his desk and sighed. More police reports, a stack of aging newspapers neatly folded to the crossword puzzle, a couple of federal procedure manuals. Amidst the chaos, a smiling, freckle-faced six-year-old stared up at him from a framed photograph. It was an old one, but one of his favorites.

His daughter, Jessie. In better times.

Despite their problems, Donovan thought of her as his salvation. His only lifeline to a normal world. A line that, unfortunately, was a little frayed at the moment.

Which reminded him. He checked his watch, looked up at Rachel. "Any word from the wayward one?"

"Not so far."

"She's running late."

Rachel shoved the file drawer shut. "They always run late at this age."

"Oh? You read that in the manual?"

"I'm studying up, just in case." Rachel was divorced and childless. Donovan had no idea what kept her from taking another dive into the deep end of the pool, but it certainly had nothing to do with looks or personality. Maybe she was simply as puzzled by relationships as he was. Whatever the case, she was a good sounding board for his parental insecurities.

He glanced at Jessie's photo again. "You think I'll ever see the day she actually *wants* to spend time with me?"

Rachel raised an eyebrow. "You're lucky *any* of us do."

Donovan shook his head and smiled as she gathered up an armload of files and headed for the door. Shifting his attention to the collage on the wall, he stood up, grabbed the cluster of darts adorning Gunderson's forehead, and pulled them free. "Tell me something, Rache."

She turned, waited. She looked good framed in the doorway like that, her straight, dark hair parted at the side and cut just below the shoulder. Her brown eyes were always bright and clear and attentive. And her body . . .

Donovan moved around to the far side of his desk, putting some distance between himself and Gunderson's photo. "What do you see when you look at that face?"

Rachel frowned. "Besides the bad complexion? Killer. Sociopath. Someone who enjoys inflicting pain. He's what my grandmother would call a *si futt lou.*"

"*Si futt lou?*"

"An asshole," she said flatly. "Reminds me of my ex."

Donovan knew he was supposed to laugh, but instead returned his attention to the dark malevolence of Gunderson's stare. "Sometimes I look into those eyes and it's like he's crawled inside my brain: 'Better come at me with everything you've got, hotshot,'cause I'll take you down the very first chance I get.'" He looked back at Rachel. "Live with that long enough and you're bound to be grumpy, too."

Rachel gave him one of her patented smirks. As always, it looked great on her. "Jack, I mean this in the nicest possible way: have you ever considered therapy?"

With that, she spun on her heels and walked to her desk outside. Donovan watched her go, thinking thoughts he knew he shouldn't be thinking, then turned and fired a dart toward that well-worn spot between Gunderson's eyebrows.

Bull's-eye.

A.J. Mosley had never met a cup of coffee he didn't like, and today's blend was particularly satisfying. A buddy from the Federal Public Defender's Office in Honolulu had shipped him an entire case of Kona dry-processed beans that produced a full-bodied cup of perfection that went down oh-so-smooth, without even a hint of bitterness.

A.J. had sampled just about any bean you could think of, from the mild sweetness of the Sul de Minas crop, to the heavy acidity found only in Zimbabwe's Chipinge region. He didn't consider himself a connoisseur by any means—even a stale cup would do in a pinch—but he certainly knew what he liked. If it started with a *C* and ended with double *E*, chances were pretty good it would bring a smile to his face.

He was savoring a much needed second cup when the telephone on his desk bleeped.

He snatched up the receiver. "A.J."

It was one of the division operators. "Got a call from a Ron Stallard at Chicago PD. Want me to transfer it?"

"Send it on over."

After a couple of clicks, Stallard was on the line. A.J. had sent him a bag of the Kona and figured this was a thank-you call. "Hey, big guy, am I a god or what?"

"I'll leave that to you and your flock to figure out. Got a situation you'll definitely be interested in."

"Yeah?" A.J. said. "What's going on?"

"You sitting down?" Stallard's voice was tight with excitement and A.J. knew this was something big.

"Come on, Ron, spit it out."

"Strap your balls on, buddy boy. Guess which weasel just popped his head out of the hole?"

16

Half a city block was cordoned off. Chicago PD had been generous with the yellow tape, steering the press and any curious bystanders clear of the immediate area. A couple of police choppers hovered high overhead, keeping the sky clear of pesky newscopters and their telephoto lenses.

The only pedestrians who remained were the handful off the street who had directly witnessed the incident, and the busload of passengers who now waited on the sidewalk as police technicians scurried about both in and outside the bus.

Donovan and A.J. pulled in next to one of the half dozen patrol cars parked just outside the tape. Al Cleveland, a member of Donovan's team, was there to greet them as they climbed out.

Donovan eyed the bus. "What are we looking at?"

Cleveland waved a hand toward the flurry of activity around them. "All I've been able to get so far is Gunderson snatched a schoolgirl."

A.J. frowned. "Schoolgirl? What the hell's he want with a schoolgirl?"

What indeed? Donovan thought. This wasn't something you'd expect from a guy like Gunderson. His first public appearance in over a month and he snatches a kid? It didn't make sense.

Then again, his wife, Sara, had been a schoolgirl when Gunderson had first come into her life. Maybe the sick son of a bitch was shopping for a replacement.

"Are we sure it's our guy?"

"Witnesses recognized him from all the media coverage," Cleveland said. "But don't expect much cooperation from the CPD. They're looking for the gold star on this one."

"Who're we talking to?"

"Fashion plate with the comb-over." Cleveland gestured toward the sidewalk where a rumpled, balding plainclothes detective was interviewing a witness. It must've been fifty-six degrees out, with a windchill of God knew what, and the guy was sweating. "Name's Fogerty."

Donovan turned to A.J. "I thought Ron Stallard was in on this."

A.J. shook his head. "Just a courtesy call. He warned me that we might run into a little resistance."

Donovan sighed. "This should be a treat. You know the drill."

He took his badge from his coat pocket, ducked under the yellow tape, and crossed the blacktop toward the sidewalk.

Lack of cooperation between branches of law enforcement seemed like a cliché reserved only for pulp novels and bad television, but nine times out of ten Donovan found it to be true. In his experience, cops both city and federal were a territorial bunch. What they hated most was some dildo trying to encroach on their jurisdiction.

Even within departments the competition for case control was stiff. Donovan had seen it time and again during his years on the local force. In the end, everyone followed the proper chain of command, but they rarely did it willingly or quietly. Add the invasion of outsiders like the ATF to the mix and the potential for verbal fireworks increased tenfold.

Like it or not, it was a reality that had to be dealt with. Donovan's solution was to take command immediately. He approached the sweating cop, held up his badge. "Jack Donovan. You in charge here?"

The cop, Fogerty, was busy talking to an elderly witness in a Cubs cap. He looked up at the sound of Donovan's voice, the sight of the badge provoking a weary sigh.

"Look," he said, "I already told Agent Numbnuts your invitation's rescinded. This is a city bus on city property. It ain't your party."

"It is when Gunderson's the guest of honor."

Fogerty turned toward him fully now. "Aren't you the chuckleheads who lost him in the first place? Look me up when you get your head outta your ass."

He was about to return to his witness when Donovan grabbed his meaty arm and pulled him off to the side.

"Hey, hey—what the fuck?" he squealed, wrenching the arm free.

Donovan nodded toward A.J. "You see my partner over there?" A.J. had his cell phone out and was busy punching a number. "Right now he's dialing Chief Dearborn's private line. In about two minutes your division commander'll be getting a call wanting to know why one of his detectives is waving his dick at the senior member of a federal task force."

Fogerty eyed him defiantly. "It's a big dick. Maybe I like showing it off."

"Good," Donovan told him. "Because what we have here is a circle jerk whether you like it or . . ." He paused, his attention drawn away from Fogerty to a cluster of shell-shocked girls standing on the sidewalk just outside the bus. Each wore a white blouse, blue skirt, and matching cardigan.

A school uniform.

Bellanova Prep's uniform.

He swiveled, stared at the bus, the destination placard like a swift, hard kick to the groin: Lincoln Park.

Oh, Jesus.

He turned back to Fogerty. "The girl Gunderson snatched—what was her name?"

"Look, you wanna observe, fine. But stay the hell out of my—"

A surge of adrenaline overtook Donovan. He grabbed Fogerty, swung him toward the nearest lamppost, and shoved him against it, hard. "What's her fucking name?"

Fogerty's eyes got big. He fumbled in his pocket and brought out his watch pad. "Uh, Jessica something . . ." He quickly leafed through it until he found what he was looking for. "Jessica Lynne—"

"Donovan," Donovan said, knowing the answer before it had even passed Fogerty's lips. He released Fogerty and stepped back, his knees weak. It was an effort to remain standing.

No. God, no.

Not Jessie.

"Hey, you okay? You don't look so hot."

A lump of bile formed in Donovan's throat, choking him as he tried to respond. Before he could get a word out, his cell phone rang. Fumbling it from his coat pocket, he clicked it on and raised it to his ear.

It took him a moment to find his voice. "Jack Donovan."

"Daddy?"

"Jesus Christ—Jessie?"

Please tell me she's alright. Please tell me she's—

Her words came out in a jumbled rush, her voice high and thin and filled with terror. "Daddy, he says he'll hurt me. He says he'll hurt me if you don't—" Donovan heard a noise and Jessie yelped. After a quick flash of static, a familiar voice filled his ear.

"Hiya, hotshot. Guess who's got himself a new girl? Not as sweet as my Sara, but she'll do in a pinch."

The words barely registered in Donovan's brain. His world was spinning. "You motherfucker . . ."

"Now, now, Jack, that's two demerits for bad manners. You're only allowed one more, so be careful what you say."

This isn't happening. Tell me this isn't happening. "If you touch her," Donovan said, his voice shaking, "I swear to Christ I'll—"

"You'll what? Hunt me down like the dirty dog I am? Oops, too late. Special Agent Jack and the United States of Fuck You have already put that plan in motion. You see, hotshot, short of blowing my brains out there's not a whole lot you can do to me that's worse than what you've already done. So the name of the game here is clarity. That's what I want. I hang on to the pea pod long enough for you to understand, with clarity, what you did to my Sara."

Donovan tried to breathe. Stay calm, he told himself. Figure a way out of this. "Listen to me, Alex. Let her go. We can make a deal. Anything you want."

Gunderson laughed. "You gonna forgive me all my sins, Jack? Huh? You gonna work up some miracle cure to solidify the mush that used to be Sara's brain? You gonna bring back my kid? I don't think we'll be making any deals. But I *will* make you a promise. If and when your schoolgirl comes home—and I'm stressing the *if* here—you can be absolutely certain of one thing: she won't be the same sweet Jessie we all know and love."

The line clicked in Donovan's ear.

He lowered the phone, trembling.

Donovan searched the street, not even sure what he was looking for, an overwhelming feeling of dread doing a kamikaze barrel-roll through his body. His head felt hollow, as if he'd just been smacked with a two-by-four.

How could he have been so careless? He knew what Gunderson was capable of. He should've seen this coming, should've stopped it before it had a chance to start.

All along he'd assumed that Gunderson would come after *him*. But he'd been wrong, and his mistake was inexcusable.

His mistake could mean Jessie's life.

Just this morning he had looked in on her as she slept, amazed by how quiet she was. No moans, no soft snores, no movement. She was so silent that for a moment he had wondered if she was alive; had put his hand under her nose just to make sure she was breathing.

As he looked down at that composed, expressionless face, he'd thought of Sara Gunderson lying motionless on the sidewalk so many weeks ago. He hadn't known whether *she* was alive or dead at the time, but he did know one thing: wherever she'd gone, she wasn't likely to come back. And she would never again feel her father's embrace.

Donovan had vowed then and there never to let his own daughter get away from him again. He would woo Jessie back into his life, and if nothing else, she would always know that he loved her.

Now, as he stood trembling in the street, her terrified cries reverberating through his head, he thought about their volatile reunion and wondered if that message had gotten across. Because now more than ever, she needed to know it.

Hang on, kiddo.

I'm coming to get you.

17

I want everything you've got. Notes, witness statements, forensics—anything that might tell us where that son of a bitch is headed."

"Now wait just a minute," Fogerty said, struggling to keep up as Donovan and A.J. strode toward the bus. "I know she's your kid and all, but I'm gonna have to get authorization for—"

Donovan spun on him. He couldn't believe this clown was still giving him static. Normally in these situations he'd try to work out some kind of peace agreement, but there simply wasn't time. Every second was critical.

He looked Fogerty square in the eyes. "Let me be clear about something. You do not want to piss me off."

Fogerty swallowed and said nothing for a moment, no doubt weighing the pros and cons of continuing this challenge. Then he raised his hands, a gesture of conciliation. "All I can offer you at this point is the tag on the Suburban."

"You put out a bulletin?"

"APB, roadblocks, the whole nine yards."

"You hear anything, even a rumor, you bring it to me before it goes anywhere else, or by this time tomorrow you'll be jockeying shopping carts at the local Wal-Mart."

"Lighten up, tough guy. I know my job."

"That remains to be seen." Donovan turned and climbed the steps into the bus. A.J. followed, Fogerty pulling up the rear.

Inside, two forensic technicians worked quietly. One was hunkered over the driver's seat, taking samples from the splatter of blood that marked where the driver had been slain. Another was crouched near the center of the bus, next to the side exit, studying something of interest on the plastic-gloved fingertip of his right hand.

Donovan approached him, carefully navigating the narrow strip of protective plastic that covered the aisle. "What've you got?"

The technician looked up with a frown, as if to say, who the fuck are you? then shifted his gaze to a spot over Donovan's left shoulder. He was looking to Fogerty for approval. It would be a while before word trickled down that the Feds were in charge.

Donovan heard a wheezy grunt behind him. "He's okay."

The technician nodded, then refocused his attention on the matter at hand. He gestured to a spot on the floor next to him. A grouping of muddy stains.

"Boot prints," he said. "Doc Martens from the looks of them."

Donovan glanced at the prints and noted the distinctive sole pattern.

Fogerty wheezed again. "They Gunderson's?"

The technician shrugged. "Everybody and his brother rides this bus, but they fit his general shoe size."

Donovan crouched, scraped a chunk of dirt free and rubbed it between his fingers. Relatively fresh. Damp to the touch. He held it to his nose, a sharp, acrid smell burning his nostrils. "Fertilizer."

"About half-half would be my guess."

A.J. crouched next to them. "You think he's cooking up a combustible?"

Donovan shook his head. "Our guy's a hair too sophisticated for home-made goods."

Fogerty jostled his bulk into view and tried to work it into a crouch. That idea was a bust, so he settled onto one of the passenger seats instead. "So what the hell's he up to? Digging himself a flower patch?"

A new wave of dread washed over Donovan. He glanced at A.J., whose eyes clearly mirrored the feeling.

Fogerty caught the exchange and raised his eyebrows. "What'd I say?"

"Few months ago," A.J. told him, "we found one of our informants in an empty lot in Calumet City. He'd been buried alive."

"Christ on a cracker," Fogerty said. "You don't think the asshole's planning to . . ." He stopped short, but everyone present had a pretty good idea where he was headed.

Especially Donovan.

He tried to drive the thought from his mind. Not even Gunderson could be that sadistic. Not with a fifteen-year-old girl. But he knew the evidence didn't lie. Whatever these boot prints signified, it wasn't good.

Not for him. And certainly not for Jessie.

He found her backpack on the floor between two seats near the back of the bus. Her name was scrawled across it in flowery print, the Lisa Simpson key chain safety-pinned to the strap, a shiny new apartment key dangling from it.

The sight of the key brought on a sudden rush of helplessness.

You go through your life putting locks on your windows, your doors, your car, hoping to protect your most valuable possessions. But how do you put a lock on a kid? How do you keep the Gundersons of the world from snatching them away and stealing their souls?

Donovan was a unit commander for one of the most powerful law enforcement agencies in the United States and even he couldn't prevent it from happening. No matter how much he tried to control his world, no matter how much knowledge and experience he brought to the task, he knew that life was nothing more than a cruel game of Russian roulette. You spin the chamber, close your eyes, and squeeze the trigger, hoping for that reassuring *click*.

He sank onto the seat and pulled the backpack into his lap, carefully unpinning the key chain. He ran his thumb over the ceramic replica of Lisa Simpson, recalling younger days with Jessie perched next to him on the sofa as they watched TV—the days before his betrayal of her trust.

He had failed her once. Would he do it again?

"Hey, Jack—A.J."

Donovan looked up. Al Cleveland was standing in the forward door well. "Sidney says he'll be here in five. He's got Bobby Nemo with him."

Donovan nodded, felt his jaw tighten. If anybody knew Gunderson, it was Nemo. They had a history that stretched all the way back to Gunderson's days at the Juvenile Offender Facility. So far, Nemo had refused to cooperate, but that would change. Donovan was sure of it.

He looked at A.J. "Time to break out the beer and peanuts."

18

"Alex, Alex, Alex. You are one crazy mofo."

The words were barely audible, little more than a mumble, really, but for all of Sidney Waxman's faults, he had one great virtue: a keen sense of hearing. When the radar was cooking, he could catch a whisper in a thunderstorm.

He glanced in his rearview mirror at Nemo's bloodshot eyes as they took in the furious activity around the crime scene. "You say something, Bobby?"

"Eat shit and die, asshole."

An original thinker, Nemo was. Waxman admired the man's ability to express himself with crude brevity, unimaginative though it might be. "Come on, Bobby, be nice. Maybe you'll come out of this with your balls still attached."

Nemo's eyes flitted toward him. Filled with contempt. "What the hell you bring me here for, anyway?"

"Boss is in the mood for a little conversation."

"We had our conversation. Where's my lawyer?"

Waxman shook his head. "You keep bringing up this lawyer bullshit. We don't work that way. Lawyers have a knack for getting in the way of the truth."

"Did I just wake up in Pakistan? You're violating my civil rights."

"Didn't you hear?" Waxman said, smiling. "You're a terrorist, Bobby. Guys like you don't have any rights."

Thank God for Congress, letting the White House bully them into circumventing the Constitution at a time of national turmoil. The War on Terror had been a boon to law enforcement. New laws relaxing the restrictions on evidence-gathering created lots of potential for abuse, sure, but this situation warranted a little abuse, didn't it? And, technically speaking, Nemo *was* a terrorist, even if the Department of Homeland Security didn't quite see it that way.

Waxman knew that sooner or later they'd have to break down and get him a federal public defender. Wouldn't want the poor SOB to incriminate himself. God no. In the meantime, they'd keep waving the Stars and Stripes and stall as long as they possibly could.

Nemo just stared at the back of his head. "You're full of shit," he said.

"Maybe so," Waxman told him. "But I'm the one behind the wheel. So you go ahead, keep asking for a lawyer. One of these days I might hear you."

"Asshole."

Ah, brevity, Waxman thought. A lovely thing.

Nemo stared at the back of the turd's head, halfway tempted to let a logy fly. But that would only get him in deeper shit. He figured he'd better just sit here quietly and let this thing play out.

Outside, a toothpick of a cop unfastened the yellow DO NOT CROSS ribbon and waved the turd through. As they pulled past him, Nemo looked out again at the bus parked in the middle of the street, big portable floodlights surrounding it, waiting for nightfall.. If it weren't for all the cops running around, you'd think this was a movie set.

Like his buddy Alex, Nemo had always been a big fan of movies and television. He'd even thought about going into acting once, back when he was in junior high. Buncha Hollywood assholes had come to town to shoot some Chuck Norris chopsocky piece of shit and this sweet-assed casting bitch showed up at the Center Street Arcade, looking for local color.

Nemo and a couple of other kids were chosen as possibilities, but in the end, the only one who made the cut was an emaciated little fuck named Joey Bustos.

Nemo didn't really care about the acting gig. His eyes were on that casting bitch, thinking how he'd like to bend her over the nearest foosball table and hammer Henry home. But he was a little peeved when Joey got the part instead of him.

The following night, just past dinnertime, he waited outside Joey's apartment until the little fruit came down to dump the trash. Nemo Chuck Norrised his ass right there in the alley. Left him inside the Dempsey Dumpster.

Needless to say, Joey never made it to the movie set. Didn't come to the arcade for a coupla months either. Turned out Nemo had fractured the fruit's skull, cracked a couple of ribs, and punctured a lung. Unfortunately, all of his hard work went to waste. The Hollywood assholes brought in somebody from L.A. instead, and Nemo never saw that sweet-assed casting bitch again.

The turd made a turn, pulling into an alley. A couple of Feds and a fat-ass cop were waiting for them, looking all serious.

Donovan stood in front, his cold, dead eyes on Nemo, and Nemo felt a tickle of fear. He knew Donovan was a hard case, but he'd never seen him like this before. The guy had a definite no-mercy vibe coming off him.

The turd pulled to a stop, killed the engine, then threw his door open and got out. Turning in his seat, Nemo glanced out the rear window. One of the Feds had moved to the mouth of the alley and was standing there with his back to the rest of them, keeping watch.

This was not gonna be a friendly conversation.

The turd opened Nemo's door, grabbed a couple handfuls of collar, and dragged him out of the car.

If Nemo hadn't been cuffed, he would've clocked the guy right there, but the turd wasn't his main concern right now. Donovan stood only feet away, never taking his eyes off him.

Once Nemo was clear of the car doorway and standing upright, Donovan moved in close.

"What d'ya say, Bobby? Something you want to share with me? And I'm not talking about Gunderson's twilight-zone bullshit."

Face-to-face it was a different story. Donovan was trying to look tough, but you could see the desperation in his eyes. Fucker was scared shitless.

Not that you could blame him.

Nemo relaxed a little. Felt a renewed sense of confidence coming on. He offered Donovan a slow smile. "Looks like somebody else got caught in the middle this time, huh, Daddy?"

The words were out of his mouth before he realized his mistake. Not only were they likely to piss Donovan off, they made it clear that Nemo had known about Alex's plan all along.

Bobby, you dumb-ass motherfucker.

In the tiniest fraction of a second, the desperation in Donovan's eyes morphed into hot, white anger. A hand shot up to the side of Nemo's face and sent his head straight into the rear fender of the turd's sedan. He hit it hard, pain exploding in his skull.

Hands grabbed him, spun him around, then someone hit him in the shins, knocking his feet out from under him. He landed on the alley floor like a bag of fresh crap, and one of the cops kicked him in the ribs.

Jesus, Mary, and Joseph.

Feeling something give, Nemo bit down on his lip, stifling a cry, thinking if he made any noise it might piss them off. At this moment in time, that was the last thing he wanted to do.

Then Donovan's fingers grabbed his chin, forcing his head upward, and the next thing he knew he had the business end of a Glock nine-millimeter in his face.

He could smell the gun oil.

"Listen carefully, asshole. You listening to me?"

Nemo nodded, which wasn't easy with the barrel of the nine stuck halfway up his left nostril.

"Your fearless leader just bit off a big old chunka shit, and unless you tell me where he's holed up—right now—I swear to Christ they'll be hosing little bits of your brain into the gutter tonight. You understand?"

The tickle of fear was back, only this time it felt like a thousand fingers attacking him simultaneously. He could call this motherfucker's bluff, sure, but he kept going back to those eyes, the way they shifted erratically between anger and desperation. He'd seen that look before, on the faces of lifers and junkies and the handful of crack whores he'd had the misfortune of hooking up with. And what it meant was this:

Donovan would not hesitate to pull the trigger.

Glancing at the others, he realized they had no intention of coming to his rescue. Not now. Not ever. The fat-ass cop was practically licking his chops, for crissakes.

Do or die time, Bobby. Do or die.

Donovan pushed in closer. *"Do you understand?"*

Nemo nodded again. Vigorously this time. He understood alright.

He just hoped and prayed Alex would, too.

19

It had taken him longer than expected to dig the hole. Despite being isolated these past few weeks, Gunderson had kept himself in shape—a hundred knuckle push-ups twice a day, double that in crunches—and he'd figured an hour tops for the digging.

Two and a half later, stinking of processed chickenshit, he had emerged from a hole six feet deep, three feet wide, and seven feet long. Just big enough to fit the box and all of its tanks.

Just big enough to fit a fifteen-year-old piece of sweet peach pie.

That was this afternoon, and he had finished right under the wire. He'd had maybe twenty minutes to fire up the Suburban and scoot on over to Bellanova Prep where his lovely one waited.

Sweet Jessie.

He had been watching her for weeks. Been witness to the pitiful display she and Special Agent Jack called a reunion. Had followed her to school every day since Monday, allowing her only a short glimpse of him this morning.

She was, he discovered, a perfect candidate for his plan. What his aunt would call a mark, a vulnerable. A girl who suffered from deep, conflicting emotions tempered by an intelligence that was beyond her years. And he was certain that a few days underground would condition her properly. Open the channel, so to speak.

After he snatched her off the bus, he watched her strip down in the back of the Suburban, her lower lip trembling, eyes refusing to meet his in the rearview mirror. He had been tempted to compare her to Sara—which was only natural, considering what he was about to do—but there was little similarity between the two. Sara eclipsed her in every way.

Even so, the sight of her flawless young flesh reminded him of that first night he'd spent with Sara, undressing her in the moonlit darkness of the bell tower atop Old Main. How she had looked directly into his eyes as he unhooked her bra and cupped those small but perfect breasts. The faint gasp as he ran his thumbs over her hardening nipples.

He'd known then and there that Sara was his forever. As his hands explored other parts of her body, he'd felt like a divine sculptor, turning raw, unblemished flesh into woman.

His woman.

With enough time and patience, Jessie could be his woman, too. But he had little time *or* patience right now. He had to work fast and he had to work crudely. No room for the subtleties of seduction.

Instead, he caught the interstate, drove the twenty miles back to the hole he'd dug, then quickly duct-taped Jessie's wrists and ankles and dropped her into her home away from home.

And if all went well, if everything the old bat had taught him proved to be true, he'd be one of the few people in this sad, sick world who could claim to have his cake and eat it, too.

Once Donovan was finally vapor, he'd come back here and dig this little one up. And as she sucked in her first breaths of fresh air, staring up at him with those big blue eyes, he'd pull her into his arms and murmur softly in her ear:

Welcome home, my darling. Welcome home.

It took him less than half an hour to put the dirt back. Once the deed was done, he took care of the rest of his business, ditched the Suburban, then called Luther to pick him up.

Luther was the only one of the surviving trio who hadn't been forced to go into hiding. His paranoia had paid off. Thanks to the ski mask he was so fond of wearing, the Feds hadn't been able to identify him. As a result, he was at Gunderson's beck and call, the perfect point man, gathering tools and weapons for the renewed crusade.

Gunderson waited for him in a nearby bar, one of those transient dives where every customer is treated with equal indifference. Pay your money, drink your drink. Nobody gives a damn who you are.

That's the thing about being a wanted man, your name and face plastered all over the news. You figure everybody you run into will take one look at you and start screaming for the cops.

But to Gunderson's surprise, as long as he was careful, he was virtually invisible. He quickly discovered that if you stick to yourself and don't attract attention, most people will walk on by without so much as a glance. They're too busy thinking about their mortgages or their sick kids or their cheating wives to bother with you. And a guy in a booth of some dumpy bar is about as anonymous as a stone in the ocean.

Nevertheless, he kept his head low, careful not to make direct eye contact with anyone.

Pulling his I Ching coins from a pocket, he gave them a quick shake, tossed them into the palm of his left hand, and carefully recorded the results on the napkin beneath his beer. After a few more tosses, his hexagram was complete and he felt more confident than ever.

Invincible, in fact.

Twenty minutes and two beers later, Luther pulled up outside.

"Saw you on TV," he said, as Gunderson climbed into the truck. "Everything go okay?"

"The bait's dangling from the hook as we speak."

Luther nodded, his expression grim. "You hear about Bobby?"

"Tell me."

"Feds picked him up."

Gunderson wasn't surprised. Bobby had always been careless. Right out of the box he'd hooked up with some strip-club skank, a mistake he was destined to regret—although Gunderson hadn't expected the inevitable to happen quite so soon.

No matter. It was, after all, what he'd been counting on.

"Good," he said, and smiled. "Things are about to get interesting."

Gunderson's own home away from home was an abandoned train yard near Cicero, an industrial suburb with smog thick enough to choke a rhino. The yard had once been a main stop on the metropolitan freight line, but the lines connecting to it had long ago been discontinued, and it quickly became a ghost town. Talks about clearing it out had dragged on for decades. Thirty-five years later it was still standing, but was so overrun with mangy cats and rodents that even the crackheads stayed away.

The perfect place to remain anonymous.

It was dark by the time Luther dropped him off, a mile and a half from the yard. Searching the streets of a run-down, blue-collar neighborhood, Gunderson found just the right car to take him home: a beat-up Corolla with missing hubcaps. No doubt its owner was already stationed in front of the tube, waiting for a beer and a blow job.

It was a chilly, moonless night. When he pulled up to the train yard gate, it seemed as if the Corolla's headlights were the only illumination for blocks. Killing the engine, he got out, unhooked the padlock, and rolled the gate open.

He stood there a moment, listening, studying the darkness. The maze of rusted-out train cars was barely visible beneath the blackened sky, but the yard seemed clear. No unaccounted-for sounds. No flicker of flashlight beams or glow of cigarettes.

He was alone out here, as always. Alone with the cats and the rodents and his thoughts of Sara.

She'd been lying in a hospital bed for weeks now, her body useless to her, her mind stuck in limbo.

He had visited her several times since her transfer to Saint Margaret's. The hospital was small, its security system a joke, and the graveyard shift was little more than a skeleton crew—a lone guard and a couple of nurses who spent most of their time yukking it up in the break room.

A temporary rerouting of the alarm wires and an accommodating fire exit had made it easy enough to slip into Sara's hospital room and watch her, the wheezy drone of the heart/lung machine and the steady beep of monitors telling the world that she was alive only because of them. One yank of the plug and she'd be on her way to the next life.

Gunderson had considered pulling it, but could never quite muster up the courage, always hanging on to the hope that he might somehow get her back.

Then, on his third visit, just as he was about to leave, he heard it.

Sara's voice.

. . . Release me. . . .

It was little more than a whisper in a corner of his mind, but he was certain it was her.

. . . Release me. . . .

Heart filling with joy, Gunderson leaned over her, looking for a sign of consciousness, but she was as still and as quiet as the dead.

"I'm here, baby," he said softly. "Talk to me. Tell me what to do."

The voice was so weak it almost brought tears to his eyes:

. . . Release me. Then she was silent.

Several minutes passed as Gunderson waited, hoping for more, but nothing came. He heard footsteps in the hall and knew that the night guard was making his hourly rounds.

Time to go.

He squeezed Sara's hand, promising to return, then took the fire exit out to the street, an idea forming at the periphery of his brain.

Sara's body might be useless, but she was in there somewhere, begging to get out. And while pulling the plug might free her, it wouldn't bring her back to him. Not in the flesh. Not to this world.

But what if he could find a way to make that possible? If he truly believed the things he said he did, how could he deny her that chance? How could he deny himself?

And then it hit him. The perfect solution. A marriage of vengeance and need, all wrapped up in a nice little fifteen-year-old package.

Sara would be his again. Not the same, perhaps, not as exquisitely beautiful, but the flesh was much less important to him than the mind and the heart and the soul.

And now that Bobby was in custody, the plan he'd waited to put into motion was about to kick into high gear.

And he was ready.

No, not just ready.

Eager.

20

When he heard the car pulling up, Donovan checked his watch: 8:35. He'd been waiting here twenty short minutes.

He stood in a corner of a dilapidated train car, near the rear door, his back pressed against the mottled fabric that lined the walls. The air was thick with the smell of stale cigarettes and half a century's worth of mold.

Earlier, a sweep of his Mini-Mag had told him that this had once been a passenger car. A luxury one at that, built at the turn of the century. How it wound up in the middle of a freight yard was anyone's guess.

A slower sweep had told him that amidst the litter of butt-filled ashtrays and Baby Ruth wrappers, Gunderson had stockpiled enough weapons and ammunition to launch a Cuban invasion. Donovan had them cleared out immediately, of course. No point in taking chances.

His earpiece crackled.

A.J.'s voice: "It's him."

Donovan raised his two-way. "Any sign of Jessie?"

"Negative."

"Alright. Stay put until I give the signal."

Outside, the car approached slowly, its engine rattling. It sounded small and foreign. Probably a beat-up Honda or Toyota, several years old, which undoubtedly matched its surroundings. Gunderson would be sure to steal a car that blended in.

The question was whether Jessie was inside. Could he have stashed her in the trunk? On the floor, between the front and back seats? Or was she with him at all?

The sight of those muddy boot prints had left a queasy feeling in Donovan's stomach. In his gut he knew Jessie wasn't in that car, and finding her would be problematic at best. All he'd managed to get from Bobby Nemo was this train yard and the location of Gunderson's makeshift digs. Nemo had claimed no knowledge of Jessie other than Gunderson's initial plan to snatch her.

Gunderson himself wasn't likely to be much more helpful, but Donovan would tie the bastard to a stake and strip the flesh off his body, piece by piece, if that was the only way to break him down. The moment Gunderson took Jessie off that bus, the boundaries had changed. All the rules Donovan had lived his life by went straight out the window.

The car rattled to a stop. A moment later, the door creaked open, then slammed shut. Just outside the train-car door, a cat cried.

Gunderson had a friend.

Donovan's earpiece crackled again. "Heads up, he's coming your way."

Donovan gave his call button two quick jabs, then clipped the radio to his belt and brought out his Glock. Keeping his eyes on the door, he listened intently as boots trudged onto the rear platform.

Welcome home, asshole.

The fireball was waiting for him. The little orange fuzz bucket had adopted him his first week here and wouldn't let go. Gunderson had always been partial to cats, liked their independence, but this one was a particularly needy beast, always there to greet him when he came home. It had been cute at first, but now he found it annoying as hell.

He had half a mind to snap its neck.

As he approached the train-car door, the cat meowed and rubbed against his leg, purring like a motorboat. He gave it a quick kick to the ribs, knocking it aside, then unfastened the padlock and rolled the door open.

Darkness greeted him. He had considered having Luther pick up a generator, but had decided against it. Unnecessary noise attracts attention. Not something he wanted to do.

Instead, he had lined the inside of the train car with portable fluorescents—the kind that look like Coleman lanterns—then boarded up all the windows to keep any clue to his presence hidden from the outside world.

He reached inside, just above the doorway, where he kept one such portable hanging from a hook.

It wasn't there.

Gunderson paused, his senses revving into overdrive. There was something different about the air inside. A hint of human beneath the mustiness.

He stood there, not moving for a moment.

Then he smiled. "Hiya, hotshot."

"Hello, Alex."

21

A portable fluorescent lamp flickered to life. Jack Donovan stood to the left, near a corner, the lamp in one hand, a Glock 19 in the other.

"Step inside," he said quietly. "Keep your hands in view."

Gunderson did as he was told. He took the threat of a weapon like the 19 very seriously. Once inside, he turned and faced the door.

Donovan set the lamp atop a seat back, then came out of the corner and stood just inside the doorway.

He didn't lower the Glock.

"Where is she?" he said.

Gunderson ignored the question. "You worked faster than I expected. I take it Bobby didn't offer you much resistance."

"I can be persuasive when I have to be."

"I'll bet you can. Maybe it's time I got myself some new friends."

Donovan stepped forward. "Cut the crap, Alex. Where is she?"

"Snug as a bug in a rug. Better pray nobody steps on her."

"Tell me or you're a dead man."

"I don't think so."

Donovan glared at him. Gunderson could sense the gears of desperation clacking away inside the man's head, trying to calculate the right move, searching for just the right thing to say. Seeing him in agony like this was like feasting on a fine meal. All the risks Gunderson had taken to get to this moment were more than worth it.

And the game had only begun.

"Look behind me, Jack. You see that oxygen tank leaning against the wall back there?" He'd had Luther steal a bunch of them, more than he was able to use. "There are six more just like it buried somewhere nice and cozy, all hooked up to switchover valves. Right now they're the only thing keeping your pumpkin alive."

Donovan's eyes flashed. "You sick fuck."

"Demerits, Jack, demerits. You don't want to get on my bad side. Look at it this way. I could've just popped that teenybopper cherry of hers and left her for dead. Instead I thought I'd give her a taste of what it's like to be my Sara." He looked directly at Donovan. "Have you seen Sara, Jack? Have you gone to visit her? I have, late at night, when nobody was watching. All those machines she's hooked up to? It's not a pretty sight."

"You're blaming the wrong guy," Donovan said. "If you love her so much, why was she even in that van? Why put her in harm's way?"

"You think that was my choice?"

"I think she did whatever you told her to."

"You're wrong. I couldn't have stopped her even if I wanted to. She wasn't exactly what you'd call a stay-at-home mom. She was committed. To me, and to the cause."

"Ahh," Donovan said. "The cause."

"You're a drone, Jack. You and the rest of America. You sit on your couches, mesmerized by the glitz of *Access Hollywood* and *Entertainment Tonight,* while a New World Order is put into place by a government you're supposed to trust. The Constitution doesn't matter anymore. There is no United States of America, only a global economy owned and operated by the Pentagon and big oil. You're a corporate lackey, Jack. And the corporation is set up to feed off its slaves."

"Nice speech," Donovan said. "I might even agree with you to some extent. But why do I get the feeling it's all hot air and bullshit?"

"Meaning?"

"I've read your sheet. I know your history. You're a thug, Alex. A sociopathic headline seeker who preys on the very people you claim you're trying to help."

"Thank you, Dr. Phil."

"You may have had Sara fooled, you may've even convinced *yourself* somewhere along the line that what you're doing makes you some kind of noble warrior, but we both know your only real cause is Alexander Gunderson."

Gunderson brought his hands together and clapped. "Looks like it's a night for speeches. But don't you think it's a little dangerous to be psychoanalyzing me when you've got so much at stake?"

"Then let's get down to it. What do you want from me?"

"Haven't we been over this? It doesn't have to be complicated." Gunderson nodded to the Glock. "At the moment I'd appreciate it if you'd point that fine piece of hardware in another direction."

Donovan's hand shifted, raising the barrel of the Glock, pointing it at Gunderson's forehead. "How's this?"

"At least you haven't lost your sense of humor."

Out of the corner of his eye, Gunderson saw a silhouette in the doorway and felt a sudden rush of excitement. God, in His wisdom, had sent him a four-legged savior. Not that he needed one. He was completely confident that he could reverse this situation with relative ease. But it never hurts to have an ally. Makes the game more interesting.

Tail snaking wildly, the fireball slinked silently into the room and approached Donovan's right leg. Good thing he hadn't snapped its neck.

Keeping his eyes on Donovan, he said, "Tell me something, Jack. Now that you and the pumpkin are back on speaking terms, how's it feel knowing you abandoned her for so long? You must feel pretty guilty every time you see that sweet little face of hers."

"That's between me and Jessie."

"No," Gunderson said. "*I'm* between you and Jessie—you keep forgetting that." He paused. "You ever think about death, Jack?"

"I've seen my share of it."

"Haven't we all. But I'm talking about your own mortality. Heaven and hell." The fireball was getting closer. "The ancient Egyptians believed the road to heaven was more dangerous than any place on earth.

That the newly dead had to go through a series of trials before they'd be allowed onto the Fields of Yaru. Kind of like a high-stakes cosmic reality show."

"Good for them," Donovan said. "And this affects me how?"

Gunderson smiled. "I know it's cheating, you being alive and all, but this is one of *your* trials, Jack. Right here, right now. And when you're done, you might just get that ticket to Yaru."

Donovan's finger brushed the trigger of the Glock. "Enough bullshit, Alex. *Where* is she?"

Gunderson said nothing. Remained perfectly still, every muscle in his body alert.

The fireball was only inches from Donovan's leg.

Donovan's eyes darkened. "I can hurt you without killing you, you know. It wouldn't bother me in the least to listen to you scream. You ever seen what a power drill can do to a man's scrotum? I really don't think you want to find—"

The fireball let out a cry and rubbed up against Donovan's leg. He flinched, the distraction lasting only a fraction of a second, but it was enough to give Gunderson the advantage he needed.

Gunderson lunged. Donovan's eyes registered faint surprise, but he didn't pull the trigger. They both knew that would be a mistake. Batting Donovan's weapon hand aside, Gunderson tackled him and drove him sideways into the wall.

Donovan hit with a thud and slid to the floor as Gunderson rolled away and reached for the Walther he kept strapped to his ankle. He dove for the doorway, paying no attention to the shout behind him. Reaching the platform, he sprang to his feet, then vaulted the rail, nearly losing his balance as he hit the ground.

From the yard, someone shouted, "Hold it, Gunderson!" and floodlights popped to life, lighting up the front of the train car. The lights had artfully been concealed by darkness and surrounding train-yard rubble, a platoon of uniformed cops lying in wait. More lights came to life at the back of the car, and the cops began to close in on Gunderson, their weapons drawn, a fat fuck with a comb-over pulling up the rear.

But Gunderson didn't slow down. Swinging his Walther upward, he let loose two quick shots. One of the floodlights shattered as the cops scrambled to take cover. Gunderson squeezed off another quick shot, then dove behind an adjacent train car just as the cops returned fire.

Bullets ricocheting around him, he scrambled to his feet and ran like hell, letting the darkness swallow him.

Donovan was already up and running when the gunfire started. Dashing to the train-car platform, he saw Gunderson dive to safety behind a broken-down cattle car as Fogerty and his men returned fire. Bullets ripped through the side of the car, splinters of wood flying everywhere.

Goddamned amateurs. He waved his arms. "Hold it! Hold your fire! We need him alive!"

A.J., Sidney, and the rest of Donovan's team filed in from their hiding places, A.J. echoing Donovan's command, signaling for Fogerty and his boys to stop shooting. As the gunfire died down, Sidney radioed the chopper: "The rabbit is loose! The rabbit is loose! Get your ass out here! Now!"

Donovan leapt over the platform rail and sprinted after Gunderson. Bringing out his Mini-Mag, he shone its narrow beam into the maze of train cars. It looked impenetrable from this vantage point, and Gunderson was bound to know every nook and cranny in the place. But Donovan could not let him get away. Would not. Not again. Not this time.

He pushed forward into the darkness, sweeping the light from side to side, his Glock gripped tightly in his hand.

Instinct. Pure blind instinct. That's what he'd have to rely on to find the bastard in this mess. Fortunately for Donovan, he and instinct had always been on close, personal terms.

22

Weapons and explosives had fascinated Gunderson for as long as he could remember. When he was thirteen years old, a year or so following the incarceration of his beloved aunt, he had been taken by his latest foster father into a special room in the family basement.

Its walls were lined with military weaponry. Amidst the AK-47s, Lugers, and shiny samurai swords was a shelf dedicated to a variety of Russian, German, and American land mines.

His foster father, an old prune named Vince, had picked up one of the mines—a German anti-personnel device complete with swastika on the side—and handed it to Alex.

"Careful," Vince said. "It's active."

Gunderson figured he should be scared, but he wasn't. He held the device with great care, captivated by the simplicity of its design.

Vince pointed to the detonator on top. "Step on that," he said, "and this sucker'll shred you into a thousand different pieces. You've never seen agony until you've seen what's left of your buddy after he's popped the cherry on one of these babies. If he's still got lungs, he's screaming like a six-year-old girl."

Two months later, while Gunderson was busy ditching school, old Vince accidentally blew himself, his wife, and half his basement to smithereens. Gunderson was forced to move on to a new foster home, but he'd never forgotten Vince's words, and the sense of power he'd felt with that precious baby resting on the palm of his hand.

All these years later, land mines continued to hold a special place in Gunderson's heart. He had long ago learned to rig his own and had recently turbocharged more than two dozen North Korean APDs, adding computerized detonator controls. With the aid of a remote, he could activate and deactivate them at will.

In anticipation of tonight's events, he had buried twenty-seven of these honeys around the train yard. Now, as he worked his way past an old caboose, he took the remote from his coat pocket and punched a combination of numbers on the backlit keypad—a global activation code.

Buried beneath a pile of rubble just twenty feet behind him, Shredder #1 (as he liked to call it) came to life with a faint beep. All around the yard, its brothers and sisters followed suit.

Come and get us, they said.

The fun's about to begin.

Crossing a set of rusted tracks half-buried in gravel, Donovan paused, trying to catch his breath. His leg throbbed, dredging up memories of his last encounter with Gunderson. The outcome was bound to be more positive this time.

He brought his Mini-Mag up to check his progress.

A collection of train cars in varying states of decay surrounded him. Weeds and tall grass grew out from beneath the cars and shot up between the tracks, showing no sign of disturbance. There was no way to know what path Gunderson had taken.

Police radios squawked in the distance. Fogerty and his trigger-happy bunch were all over the yard by now. If it had been up to Donovan, he would have left them all back at the bus, but phone calls had been made, and word from on high had reminded him that this was a joint effort that required both federal and municipal cooperation. Like it or not, that included Fogerty.

Donovan could only hope he'd keep his dick in his pants and not do anything stupid.

The squeal of another cat spun him to the right. The sound could mean a million different things, but he followed it anyway, heading toward an old caboose.

A moment later, a CPD chopper roared overhead and swept its searchlight across the yard. About goddamned time. A swarm of rats reacted in panic, surging up from beneath a pile of termite-eaten lumber, hundreds of them scrabbling over each other to avoid the light.

The sight sent a shiver of revulsion through Donovan. He'd never seen so many rats in one place. Cutting a wide path around them, he continued toward the caboose.

As the chopper roared overhead, Gunderson darted for the shadows, narrowly avoiding its beam. He watched it sweep by at half speed, saw a pack of rats scurry away in slow motion, felt the blood pumping through his veins.

Pumping sweet life.

The place was crawling with cops now, but they were well behind him and would soon have other problems to keep them occupied.

The yard was surrounded by a seven-foot-high aluminum fence, topped with barbed wire. Just beyond these cars, across a rubble-strewn clearing, was Gunderson's destination: a gap he'd made by prying back a section.

Even with the aid of the searchlight snaking across the yard, he could barely see in this darkness. But he'd have no trouble finding the gap. He knew this place like he knew the faint pattern of freckles across Sara's upturned nose.

Everything was working perfectly. If Donovan managed to avoid getting himself blown to bits by an APD, Gunderson would have the pleasure of destroying him emotionally. He'd enjoy playing Donovan. Seeing him scramble fruitlessly for clues to Jessie's location. And when the time was right, he'd reel ol' Barney in and gut him like a two-hundred-pound tuna.

But best of all, when everything was said and done, he'd have his Sara back.

Since the day he'd first knelt over her comatose body, searching for a pulse, he'd been dead inside. But now, for the first time in weeks, he felt alive again. Vibrant.

He hoped and prayed Donovan made it through the yard in one piece.

This feeling was just too good to let go.

102 ROBERT GREGORY BROWNE

———————

When Donovan reached the caboose, he heard another sound. Not a cat this time, but the faint creak of footsteps on wood, followed by the trampling of weeds.

Gunderson?

Flicking off his Mini-Mag, he backed against the side of the caboose and listened. Whoever it was, was trying like hell to be as quiet as possible. Definitely moving in this direction.

Donovan eased his way toward the back end of the caboose, Glock ready. The footsteps slowed, close now, no more than ten feet away.

Donovan waited, feeling his adrenaline rise.

The footsteps came closer. Slowly. Just around the corner, on the other side of the caboose.

Resting his finger against the trigger of his Glock, he raised his flashlight to shoulder level and waited until the footsteps were nearly on top of him.

Then, in one fluid motion, he pushed away from the caboose, turned, leveled the Glock, and flicked the flashlight on, a startled face caught in its beam. "Hold it!"

The face didn't move. Nor did the body beneath it.

"Hey, boss."

It was A.J.

"Jesus Christ," Donovan said.

When the light came alive in his eyes, A.J. was sure he was a goner, cursing himself for holstering his weapon. Then he heard Jack's voice, and sweet relief washed over him. Thank God the boss wasn't quick to pull the trigger.

Jack lowered his flashlight. After they both got their stomachs out of their throats, A.J. said, "This place is a labyrinth. Gunderson could be anywhere."

"Maybe," Jack said, keeping his voice low. "But I think he's close."

"Yeah? What makes you think so?"

Donovan tapped a temple with the tip of his finger, a gesture A.J. had seen a hundred times before. It was true that Jack had always had pretty good instincts, a kind of sixth sense when it came to bad guys, but with this particular bad guy it hadn't exactly paid off yet.

A.J. loved Jack, loved working with him, but the guy wasn't functioning on all cylinders right now. When he'd insisted on taking Gunderson alone in that train car, A.J. had known it was a mistake. Gunderson was not somebody you *took* alone.

As soon as word got out that Jessie had been snatched, somebody upstairs should've pulled the plug on Jack. Let the FBI take over. They were arrogant assholes, yeah, but they specialized in this kind of shit.

Of course, you'd never hear A.J. say a word of this out loud. Especially not to Jack.

He didn't even like *thinking* it, but there it was.

Donovan said, "We'd better split up. If Gunderson's around here, I don't want Fogerty's bozos getting to him before we do."

A.J. nodded, understanding the concern. "Watch your back."

"You, too."

As Donovan headed away, A.J. cut a diagonal path across the narrow strip of land that separated the caboose and another train car. Trampling over the weeds and piles of trash that had collected over the years, he realized how sluggish he felt. A taste of the bean would do him wonders right now. The smooth ecstasy of, say, a little Café Atarazu.

Moments like these made A.J. realize just how bad his addiction was. Considering the circumstances, coffee should've been the last thing on his mind. But he just couldn't help himself. No doubt about it, he was a bona fide caffeine junkie.

Oh, well. At least it wasn't booze.

Halfway to the adjacent train car, a faint beep brought A.J. to an abrupt stop. What would only be a nanosecond for anyone else stretched to several times that for A.J. as he analyzed the situation:

That beep—it wasn't good.

He was pretty sure it had come from beneath the flattened old hubcap he'd just stepped on, and it wasn't the kind of sound you expected to hear in the middle of a dump like this.

No, something was seriously amiss. And it didn't bode well for Arthur James Mosley.

In the latter half of that nanosecond, A.J. sensed what that something was, giving him just enough time to close his eyes.

The prayer, unfortunately, would have to wait.

23

The explosion knocked Donovan off his feet. He toppled backward, hitting the ground hard, dropping both Glock and Mini-Mag. Pain radiated through his back as something hard and splintery dug into it.

He rolled away, both ears ringing. Biting back the pain, he pulled himself upright.

His back throbbed. His vision was blurred.

The caboose and adjacent train car were completely shredded, flames shooting up from what was left of them. Between them was a small crater in the earth, and in that crater was a sight so horrible, it didn't even register in his brain as human.

Donovan had never been a military man, so the only action he'd seen was on the city's streets. He'd seen some pretty heavy things, but none of it had prepared him for this.

What was left of A.J. lay in pieces scattered between the two cars, glistening in the light of the flames. Part of a torso. A leg that looked as if it had been run through a meat grinder. A severed hand with only two of its fingers.

And A.J.'s head. Eyes closed. Half the skull missing.

Jesus God, Donovan thought, then leaned forward and vomited into the gravel.

He sat there, dazed, barely remembering what he was here for, knowing that shock had set in and was liable to overcome him. Then another explosion, followed by an ear-shattering shriek, reverberated through the train yard.

Donovan looked again at the remains of his friend and partner, a renewed sense of rage pounding through him. Patting the ground blindly, he found his Glock half-buried in a clump of dry weeds, then stood up, his feet starting to move involuntarily, carrying him into the darkness.

Soon he was running, knowing that he could easily suffer the same fate as A.J., yet he barreled forward with complete abandon, thinking only of Gunderson and what he'd do to the bastard when he got hold of him.

He was pretty sure Gunderson wouldn't be hiding. The train yard was surrounded by a high fence, and Gunderson was smart enough to have prepared an escape hatch. All Donovan had to do was keep him from reaching it.

As he ran, yet another explosion rocked the yard. A distant scream. Picking up speed, he zigged and zagged through the last of the cars and emerged at the edge of a clearing.

It was too dark to see, but Gunderson was out here. He *knew* it. Could feel him.

Then, as if in answer to a prayer, the CPD chopper buzzed overhead, throwing its beam down on the clearing. And there, caught in the light, was Gunderson, legs pumping, headed for a break in the fence.

Donovan ran faster than he'd ever run in his life, his back still throbbing, his breathing ragged, his bad leg about to give out on him as he steadily closed the gap that separated him from his prey. Raising his Glock, he fired a shot into the air, shouting over the roar of the helicopter.

"Hold it, Gunderson! Freeze!"

But Gunderson didn't slow, only a few short yards from his escape hatch.

Donovan fired another round. "Freeze, goddammit, or the next one goes in your back!"

Gunderson stopped, pinned in place by the chopper's search beam.

He turned around, clutching a Walther.

Donovan moved in closer, struggling to catch his breath. "Drop your weapon to the ground!"

Another explosion echoed in the distance.

Gunderson smiled. "And spoil all the fun?"

"Do it, asshole!"

"Don't forget Jessie, Jack. No food or water. Only enough air for what—a coupla days? Maybe three, if she breathes through her nose."

Donovan pulled the trigger. The bullet whizzed past Gunderson's ear. "Throw down! Now!"

Gunderson didn't even flinch. "You keep fucking with me, the worms'll be snacking on her intestines before Sunday school lets out this weekend. So cut the horseshit and call off the hounds."

Donovan had never wanted to take someone out as badly as he did right now. Every gesture, every word this bastard said, was an invitation to pull the trigger.

And Gunderson knew it. Reveled in it. "This ain't a drill, hotshot. Get on that radio of yours and tell your buddies to take five, or you can kiss Jessie's ass goodbye."

Donovan stood there, thinking of Jessie and A.J., feeling helpless and outmaneuvered. He knew that his only choice was to do what Gunderson told him.

He brought out his radio, flicked the call button. "This is Donovan. Everybody fall back. You read me? Fall back and hold your fire."

The radio crackled in response, the words unintelligible. A moment later the chopper backed off, but kept its beam on them.

"Attaboy," Gunderson said, moving closer. "You say you wanna deal? Looks like I've got no choice but to bring an offer to the table."

"I'm listening."

"Oh, I bet you are. So here it is, Jack, a simple proposition: your life for Jessie's. All you have to do is escort me out of here in one piece—no tails, no surveillance, nobody but you and me. When I'm done punishing you for your multitude of sins, I'll give your buddies a jingle and tell them where to find her."

Donovan searched Gunderson's eyes. "You expect me to trust you?"

"Your negotiating position is tenuous at best. Think of it as the ultimate test of daddyhood. Are you willing to die for your little girl?"

Donovan said nothing. Gunderson already knew the answer.

"I thought so. So drop the nine or the bitch goes out gasping."

Donovan hesitated. If he dropped his weapon, Gunderson would have a free and clear shot at him. But was Gunderson stupid enough to take him out right here in front of Fogerty's men and a team of federal agents? Donovan didn't think so.

In the corner of his eye he saw movement in the shadows. The cops were slowly closing in on them. Carefully avoiding potential booby traps.

"Tick tock, Jack. She's losing precious time."

Donovan waved an arm at the approaching cops. "Fall back!" he shouted. "The situation's under control!"

The movement slowed, then stopped.

"Nicely done," Gunderson said. "Now put your weapon down and come on over here."

Keeping his eyes on Gunderson, Donovan crouched and dropped his Glock to the ground. He wasn't dealing with a moron like Willie Sanchez. No last-minute surprises would help him here. His only choice was to play along until he found out where Jessie was buried.

He stood up again, started toward Gunderson.

"Damn it, Jack, I'm close to tears. You really do love your pumpkin." Gunderson's smile widened. "It warms my heart to see that some of us haven't lost our sense of family val—"

A shot rang out and Gunderson's face went slack. His chest exploded as a bullet ripped through him, the force knocking him backward.

Before he could completely comprehend what had just happened, Donovan sprang forward, catching Gunderson, blood streaming from his chest and mouth.

"Jesus," Donovan muttered, clamping a hand over the wound to stop the flow of blood. But it was pointless. The wound was fatal. Whoever had fired that shot had done exactly what he'd set out to do. The life in Gunderson's eyes was sifting away fast, and Donovan had precious seconds to get what he needed.

"Listen to me, Alex, you've gotta listen to me. Tell me where she is. Where's Jessie?"

Gunderson focused for a moment, moving his mouth, but nothing came out.

"For God sakes, *tell me!*"

Gunderson's mouth moved again, blood flowing, his voice barely audible.

Donovan leaned in close.

"Forget God," Gunderson croaked, the words coming out in bubbly gasps. "This isn't over yet. It's very far from . . ."

And then his eyes went blank, his body limp in Donovan's arms.

He was gone. Finished.

Dead.

Donovan sat there, staring into those eyes, the shock that had threatened him earlier now creeping up again, crawling through his bloodstream, leaving him numb.

There was movement all around him, cops shouting as they approached, but Donovan had no idea what they were saying.

After a moment, he looked up to see Fogerty's bulk emerge from the shadows of a train car. Fogerty holstered a Smith & Wesson, a big shit-eating grin on his face. "Looks like CPD's gonna have to take credit for this one, boys."

And before anyone could stop him, Donovan was on his feet and pouncing at Fogerty. With an angry roar, he knocked him to the ground and hit him over and over again as the fat man squealed like a motherless child.

It took four uniformed cops to pry Donovan away.

24

The news coverage was merciless. Networks broke into their regularly scheduled broadcasts—pissing off more than a few sitcom fanatics—to tell the country about the federal agent and his kidnapped daughter and the savage but clever fugitive struck down by police gunfire.

The moment Donovan was pulled off Fogerty, the leaks had begun, and soon the sky above the train yard was filled with those dreaded news-copters, their pilots dutifully reporting the massive sweep for land mines.

Three cops were dead and the girl was still missing, and none of it looked good for the grieving father and the ATF. Donovan was painted as a rogue agent. Fogerty was considered by some to be a hero, and by others to be a complete idiot.

Reporters were waiting for them both outside the train yard, where uniformed cops did their best with crowd control. Donovan had no comment, but Fogerty, playing it up for the cameras as he was loaded into the back of an ambulance, shouted that he was just doing his job and would be speaking to his attorneys tomorrow.

Somewhere in the suburbs, the families of slain security guards Walter O'Brien and Samuel Kingman thanked God for answering their prayers.

But how sad about the little girl . . .

25

Rachel knew she wouldn't be going home tonight. No way she'd walk out that door knowing what Jack was going through.

Two years working for the man wasn't the only thing that kept her here. She felt his hurt. In the pit of her stomach. Like a mother feels the hurt of a child. Or a wife the hurt of a husband.

Sure, they all felt it. But not like Rachel.

She stood in the doorway of the Situation Room, watching Jack struggle to contain his torment. He stared down at a conference table covered with the contents of Gunderson's train car: guns, knives, convenience-store receipts, Polaroids, a half dozen cartons of Marlboros, an assortment of candy bars, pamphlets touting antigovernment propaganda, a handful of battered-looking books on metaphysics and cult religions.

The yard had been thoroughly searched, a dozen or more land mines uncovered and diffused by the CPD bomb squad. But there'd been no sign of Jessie anywhere, and none of the items on the table gave them the slightest indication of where she might be.

The oxygen tank from Gunderson's train car had been traced to a recent warehouse theft at Clayman Medical Supply. Seven portable E cylinders had been stolen, containing about 680 liters of oxygen each. The manager of the supply house estimated that, depending on the rate of intake and barring any leakage, each tank could last between five and ten hours. If Gunderson had used the remaining six tanks rigged to an automatic switchover system, the most optimistic projection gave Jessie approximately 60 hours of air. Two and a half days. And the clock had already started.

An eternity for Jessie.

But for Jack . . .

He was trying to cover, but Rachel could see the look of hopelessness in his eyes as he stared down at the evidence spread across the table.

"This is it?" he said, speaking to no one in particular. "This is all we've got?"

He was surrounded by most of his team: Sidney, Al, Darcy Payne, Franky Garcia. A.J.'s absence was a palpable, living thing dulled only by shock and disbelief.

"CPD's still looking for the Suburban," Sidney said. "Maybe they'll get lucky."

"I don't want lucky, Sidney, I want results." Donovan looked around the room now. "Has anybody bothered to contact A.J.'s folks?"

"I talked to Bill Klein in Austin," Rachel said. "He's on his way over right now."

"What about my ex? Has she been notified?"

"The Caymans are in the middle of a level-three hurricane. Phones could be down for days."

"Son of a bitch!" Donovan exploded, sweeping an arm across the tabletop. Weapons and evidence flew everywhere. The agents around the table jumped back to avoid the debris, staring at Jack in stunned silence.

After a moment, Rachel crouched down, gathering up a handful of books and returning them to the table. *The Book of Changes. Metempsychosis in the Modern World. The Doctrine of Eternal Life.* Gunderson's choice of reading material was interesting, to say the least, an odd counterpoint to his public persona.

It also, strangely enough, reminded her of her grandmother, a woman who took great stock in ancient folklore and the promise of eternal life. She could just imagine the conversation the two would have. . . .

Among the litter were a half dozen washed-out Polaroid photos, shots of Gunderson and Sara standing in front of the Lake Point Lighthouse.

Funny, Rachel thought. She'd never really looked at them as normal people. Yet here they were, happy and smiling like a pair of love-struck high school kids on an all-day field trip.

Setting the Polaroids on top of the books, she looked at Jack. His eyes were bloodshot.

"Maybe you should take a break," she said.

Donovan glared at her. "Why are you even here, Rachel? You're off the clock."

Heat rose in Rachel's cheeks. The words stung and Jack knew it, but at the moment he didn't seem to care. She'd seen him in a dozen different moods, but had never known him to be cruel. She felt tears coming on and held them back.

Be tough, Rache. He didn't mean it.

She wished she could say something to him, something that would ease his mind—a bit of Grandma Luke's wisdom, perhaps. But she came up empty.

Lowering his gaze, Donovan stomped past her and exited the room.

She found him in his office, sitting at his desk, head slumped forward, eyes closed. The newspaper clippings, police reports, and photographs that normally covered one wall had been ripped down and scattered across the floor.

Rachel looked at them, then at Donovan.

She closed the door behind her.

"Jack . . ."

He didn't open his eyes. His voice was soft, faraway. Filled with regret. "What the hell have I done, Rache?"

"Don't start thinking like that. This is all Gunderson."

"Is it?" He looked up at her now. "I knew what he was. I should've protected her. If I was any kind of father . . ."

"Stop," Rachel said. She moved around to his side of the desk, perched on the edge. "Let's just concentrate on finding Jessie." She reached over and squeezed his shoulder, a gesture of comfort, but somehow more than that. "You *will* find her."

Donovan nodded absently, but she could sense that he didn't quite believe it.

"When I was in that train car," he said, "Gunderson asked me how it felt knowing I'd abandoned my own daughter. What do you say to a question like that? Truth is, when Jessie needed me most, I let her down. Made her feel like she didn't matter."

"For God sakes, Jack, quit beating yourself up. You've changed things, you've tried to make up for it. None of us can claim sainthood."

He stared at her a moment, offered her a wan smile. "Guess I'm way beyond grumpy now."

She returned the smile, held his gaze.

He didn't look away.

Then the door flew open and Sidney Waxman burst in, flushed with excitement. "We just got a call from CPD."

They both looked up.

"They found the Suburban."

26

It was raining when he got there. The weather reports had promised a presummer storm, but nobody had believed it until the first drops started falling.

By the time Donovan was on the road and headed across town, his wipers were churning full blast. He couldn't help feeling as if he'd stepped into an old movie, where the weather always served to underscore the main character's mood. All he needed to top things off was the plaintive wail of a jazz trumpet.

The Suburban was parked at the side of a narrow, two-lane road about fifty yards from a highway underpass. It sat next to an empty parking lot that was surrounded by a chain-link fence. A faded, rain-drenched banner across the fence said ALL DAY PARKING—$6.50.

The other side of the road held a couple of forties era Quonset huts with roll-up doors: JUNIOR'S AUTO BODY. A handful of cars in various stages of disrepair were parked out front.

Before the night was over, someone from the Chicago Police Department would be contacting both the parking lot attendant and Junior's team of fender pounders to check if anyone had witnessed the Suburban being dropped off. There was only a thin hope they'd have anything significant to offer, but it had to be done.

The street itself was crowded with patrol cars and cops in yellow rain slickers, the crime-scene carnival at full tilt. The Suburban sat with its doors hanging open, protected from the rain by a canvas canopy, as forensic technicians went through it with meticulous care.

Donovan watched them as he pulled up, knowing they wouldn't find much. A few cigarette butts, a couple of stray candy-bar wrappers. Judging by the litter in Gunderson's train car, he'd been addicted to both chocolate and nicotine, two demons Donovan himself had never fallen prey to.

He killed his engine and got out. A uniformed cop stood nearby, clutching a handful of leashes, straining to hold back a pack of search dogs.

A voice called out behind him. "Agent Donovan?"

Donovan turned as a lanky plainclothes detective carrying an umbrella approached.

"Ron Stallard," he said, shaking Donovan's hand. "Just heard about A.J. Can't believe it. Under any other circumstances I'd be celebrating Gunderson's send-off with an Irish coffee and a big fat cigar."

Donovan nodded, involuntarily summoning up the image of A.J.'s mutilated corpse. It was an image he'd just as soon relegate to a part of his brain he never used, but he knew it would take him a while to get it there. In the meantime, he had no desire to talk about it, even if Stallard did. Better to stick to the business at hand. "You got anything for me?"

Stallard seemed to sense Donovan's mood and didn't push it. Reaching under his raincoat, he brought out an oversized evidence bag containing a blue cardigan sweater. A machine-stitched Bellanova Prep logo was visible beneath the plastic. "Found this in the Suburban. Your daughter's?"

Donovan nodded again. The first time he'd seen Jessie wearing it, he'd complained that it was half a size too small, a comment that had provoked an exasperated sigh.

"Rain's a bitch," Stallard said. "But it looks like the dogs've managed to pick up the scent."

Donovan felt his heart accelerate. "So what the hell are we waiting for?"

The dogs led them straight to the underpass. They barked and whimpered, dragging their handler behind them, as Donovan and Stallard followed. The underpass was high and twice as wide as the road, a nice respite from the rain. Its cement walls were scarred by graffiti—names, gang symbols, and crude drawings of male and female genitalia lit up by their roaming flashlight beams.

Traffic crawled by overhead, stalled by the sight of all the cop cars and flashing lights below. Horns honked, echoing faintly through the underpass.

The men said nothing as they walked. Donovan's heart pounded in his chest, anticipation pumping through his veins like a hit of speedball. Could it be this simple? Could Jessie really be here somewhere?

They were nearing the middle of the underpass when Waxman and Cleveland caught up to them, raincoats dripping.

"Where you been?" Donovan asked. "I thought you left right after me."

Waxman grunted. "A coupla honchos from D.C. showed up just as we were about to leave. Making a lot of noise."

"What kind of noise?"

"The kind you don't need to hear right now."

"Give me a little credit, Sidney."

Waxman sighed. "They wanted details on what happened between you and Fogerty. Had questions about your state of mind."

"And?"

"I get the feeling they're thinking about putting you out to pasture on this. They even brought a Bureau psychologist along."

"Jesus," Donovan said.

"For what it's worth," Stallard told him, "you're quite the celebrity back at the house."

"Meaning?"

"The tune job you did on Fogerty. That's something a lot of us have wanted to do for a long, long time."

The dogs came to an abrupt stop at a large manhole, barking and sniffing and scratching at the cover. Stallard gestured for the dog handler to back off. The cop jerked their leashes and led them away.

Donovan gestured to Waxman and Cleveland. "Give me a hand with this."

The three men crouched and tugged at the manhole cover, but it was wedged in tight and refused to budge.

"Anybody got a pry bar?" Waxman asked.

Cleveland grunted. "What d'ya bet we'd find one in the Suburban?"

"Fuck that," Stallard said, joining in. They kept at it, huffing and straining until the cover finally scraped free. They dropped it to the black-top, the heavy clang bouncing off the underpass walls.

Donovan shone his Mini-Mag into the hole. A rusted metal ladder disappeared into blackness.

He knew exactly where it led.

"Freight tunnel," he said, then slipped the flashlight into his coat pocket and climbed onto the ladder. "You boys wait here."

"Easy," Cleveland told him. "If Gunderson was down there, it could be booby-trapped."

"I'll take my chances."

Donovan started down, then stopped a moment to look up at Waxman. "Tell your buddies from D.C. if they think they're getting me off this, *they're* the ones who need that psychologist."

The Chicago tunnel system was built in the early 1900s, when the country was in the midst of a great electric-railway boom. Sixty-two miles of intersecting tunnel and track were laid forty feet below street level in hopes that businesses citywide would utilize the system to haul coal, ashes, mail, and assorted dry goods. Pint-size locomotives ran day and night, chugging beneath the city like worms in dirt.

It was, however, an interesting idea that never quite worked, largely because getting the freight into the tunnels in the first place was a labor-intensive pain in the ass. It made more sense to throw the freight onto a truck and *drive* it across town. . . .

The Chicago Tunnel Company teetered on the verge of bankruptcy for several decades until it finally gave up and abandoned the tunnels in 1959.

Since then, a handful of the drifts had been refurbished and used by ComEd to stretch electric cable to its customers. The rest were left to neglect. Access to the system was restricted and scattered throughout the city, mostly via manhole, but here and there you'd find a building that had a freight elevator connected to the tunnels.

Donovan knew this because one of his first assignments as a uniformed cop was to patrol certain accessible sections of the tunnels to make sure no trespassers were skulking around.

It didn't surprise him that the trail from the Suburban led down here. He was convinced that Gunderson and his crew had used the tunnels to avoid capture after the Northland First & Trust robbery.

The ladder descended into the blackest darkness Donovan had ever known. Dropping to the ground, he silently cursed as he sank ankle deep into icy water.

Scavengers had long ago stripped the tunnel system clean, taking the much needed reciprocating pumps along with them. Without the pumps, rain and river water had seeped into several of the drifts and remained there, stagnating.

The water sloshed, echoing through the darkness, as Donovan turned and took his Mini-Mag out, flicked it on.

He was in middle of a grand union, a three-way intersection of tunnels. The tunnels were no more than seven feet high, probably less than that in width, and made of nonreinforced concrete.

The question was, which one to take?

His shoes sucked mud as he moved. Lifting a foot out of the water, he shone his light on it, wondering if this was where Gunderson had picked up the mud on his Doc Martens. Could he have been making preparations down here before he grabbed Jessie?

The mud might explain the boot prints on the bus—but what about the fertilizer? Where had it come from?

Maybe A.J. had been right, maybe Gunderson *had* been cooking up a combustible, and Donovan wondered if he should take Al Cleveland's warning a little more seriously. Like the train yard, this place might be booby-trapped.

Yet, as he moved forward, fanning the narrow beam of his flashlight over the seamless tunnel walls, he felt no threat. Except for the mud and the water and the missing trolley wire that had been stripped away by scavengers, the place seemed undisturbed. He doubted much had changed down here since the system was abandoned. And despite Gunderson's love of explosives, the idea of a booby trap just didn't feel right.

Not here, at least.

So what, then, was this all about? Why had the scent from Jessie's sweater led him here? Gunderson had told him that she was buried somewhere. Had he been speaking only figuratively? If so, forty feet below street level would certainly qualify.

But what about the oxygen tanks? The air down here was cool and a bit musty, but plentiful enough to keep someone alive. So why had Gunderson warned that Jessie would soon be gasping for breath?

It didn't make sense.

As Donovan stood there, trying to puzzle it out, the slosh of the murky water gradually subsided and he thought he heard a sound.

He stood perfectly still. Listened.

Yes.

It was faint and muffled, coming from somewhere far off. It sounded like . . .

Like someone crying.

Donovan's heart kicked up a notch. Jessie?

He wanted to move, to spring into action, but the noise of the splashing water would make it impossible to determine which direction the sound was coming from.

He shone his light toward the two adjoining drifts, wishing he had the dogs down here to pick up Jessie's scent. Listening intently, he tried to trace the source of the sound and finally settled on the tunnel to his left, knowing he could double back if he had to.

He pressed forward, traveling several yards into it, feeling the floor beneath him angle downward. He sank deeper into the water as he progressed, until it was nearly at waist level. The crying grew louder with each step.

It was Jessie. He was sure of it.

Who else could it be?

The burial, the oxygen tanks, were a lie. Gunderson had been playing him, that's all. Instead of putting her into the ground, he'd left Jessie alone down here—cold, frightened, and unable to find her way out in the dark.

The crying was still muffled, but he was close enough to recognize her voice.

"Jessie!" he shouted, sweeping the flashlight beam wildly.

The crying continued unabated.

"Jessie, it's me! It's Dad! Can you hear me?"

No answer. Just the crying.

Donovan tried to pick up speed, but the water was like a living force, slowing him down. He half expected something dark and malevolent to reach up and grab his legs.

Then all at once he was at the end of the tunnel, blocked by a concrete bulkhead. The bulkhead housed a steel door that looked like something from a German U-boat. Doors like this had been placed in the drifts that dipped under the river. A safety precaution in case of a collapse.

The crying came from beyond the door.

"Jessie, can you hear me?"

No response.

"Jessie?"

She was probably in shock. Possibly drugged.

"Hang on, kiddo. I'll have you out of there in a heartbeat."

Clenching the Mini-Mag between his teeth, Donovan gripped the wheel mounted in the center of the door and—

—Al Cleveland's warning flashed through his mind again:

Booby-trapped.

What if the thing was booby-trapped?

He froze, stopping just short of turning the wheel. Grabbing the Mini-Mag, he shone it along the seam of the door, looking for telltale wires.

Nothing.

The lower half of the door was submerged in at least three feet of water. Popping the flashlight between his teeth again, he crouched, sinking to his shoulders, a pungent stench filling his nostrils as he ran his hands along the seam.

No wires. No molded bits of plastique. No signs of anything unusual. Satisfied, he stood up, his clothes now plastered to his skin, the chilly air enveloping him.

Jessie's sobs continued unbroken.

"I'm coming, kiddo, I'm coming."

Donovan shivered. There was a chance that Gunderson had rigged the other side of the door, but he decided to trust his initial instincts.

He grabbed hold of the wheel.

It groaned as he spun it three-quarters of a turn, then a latch clicked and the seal was broken.

So far so good.

He pulled on the door and the water around him began to swirl, shifting toward the adjoining tunnel, where it remained at waist level.

Jessie's sobs were much clearer now. Very close.

He shone the Maglite into the darkness. "Jessie?"

Still no response.

As he crossed the threshold, his left foot got caught something solid and he stumbled, plunging face-first into the murky liquid. Momentarily seized by panic, he did a quick half twist, then found the floor and stood up, drenched now from head to toe.

Sonofabitch.

The flashlight flickered, threatening to go out. Donovan banged it against the heel of his hand, brought it back to life.

Jessie's cries were behind him now.

Turning, he shone the light back the way he'd come. "Jess, where are you?"

The crying continued.

He swept the beam from side to side. The walls were rougher here, still bearing the impression of the wooden arches that formed the tunnel, as if the final coat of cement had never been applied.

Jessie was nowhere in sight, yet the crying continued.

"Talk to me, Jess. Say something."

Still nothing.

"Goddammit, Jessie, where the hell . . ."

Then it struck Donovan. Now that he was this close, now that he was past the barrier that had muffled Jessie's sobs, there was something odd about the sound.

An unreal, hollow quality.

The bulkhead door clanged shut and he immediately shot the Mag beam toward it, saw a flash of blue and white just above it: clothing hanging from a rusty piece of trolley wire.

A skirt and blouse.

The rest of Jessie's uniform.

Donovan pushed toward them and ripped them free, feeling something hard and weighty as the blouse fell into his hands. Jamming his fingers into the pocket, he brought out a portable minidisc recorder, the kind reporters use for on-the-spot interviews—the kind with a built-in microphone and speaker.

Donovan shone his light on it. The tiny LED readout said it was set to repeat mode. Jessie's sobs rose from the speaker, vibrating against his hand.

Heart sinking, he felt something else in the pocket and dipped his fingers in, bringing out a single Polaroid photograph.

It was Jessie, naked, feet and hands duct-taped, staring into the camera with wide, terrified eyes. She was lying inside a crude wooden coffin, an oxygen mask covering her nose and mouth.

And written on the narrow border of the photograph in neat block letters were the words:

NICE TRY, HOTSHOT
NO CIGAR

27

Wake up, Jessie.
Jessie . . . wake uhhh-up.
. . . Jessie?

She awoke to rain.

It was faint, but unmistakable—even through the wood and God knew how many layers of dirt piled on top of it: the muffled, but steady tattoo of water against—what?

Metal of some kind? Aluminum, maybe.

It didn't matter. It was raining and she could hear it, and that one small link to the real world was enough to make her realize that she was still alive, still had a chance. She just hoped the water didn't seep down here. She was already shivering.

Then she thought about how thirsty she was and changed her mind. Any kind of liquid would do right now. Even dirty rainwater.

Jessie had lost count of how many times she had drifted in and out of sleep. Her consciousness seemed to float on the same aimless current as her emotions. Awake. Asleep. Hysterical. Calm. Somewhere in between.

She usually came awake seized by a sudden rush of panic, but for the moment she was okay. She was Jessie Glass-Half-Full. And she knew that sooner or later someone would find her and take her out of this horrible place. Someone would save her.

The angel had told her so.

But she also knew that Jessie Glass-Half-Empty was lurking just around the corner, waiting to pounce. Then the tears would come—as they always did—and all hope would be abandoned to the dark demons gripping her soul.

How long had she been down here?

Hours? Days?

She couldn't even begin to guess. She had no real point of reference to latch onto. Her memories were a blur of disjointed events, like keyframes in some whacked-out animation timeline.

Focus, Jessie. Focus.

But it was hard, really hard. And before she could rein herself in—

—she was undressing in the back of the Suburban, the man with the ponytail watching her in his rearview mirror, his gaze crawling over her as she stripped down to her bra and panties. She hesitated, but he waved the gun at her. Wanted it all off. She swallowed, tears falling, then reached back and unhooked her bra. The panties came next. And after she stepped out of them, she felt more naked—more exposed—than she'd ever felt before.

Humiliated. That was the word.

His gaze continued its slow crawl, watching her instead of the road, and she was sure he would crash, she *wanted* him to crash, and—

—then she was in back of a cab again, the driver looking at her as if he'd never seen a girl in a school uniform and—

—wait, what was that? Gunshots?

—a hole the size of a dime opened up in the neck of a man in a Megadeth T-shirt, followed by the screams of the passengers. Or were they *her* screams? Someone grabbed her hair and pulled her toward the front of the bus and—

—now she was zipping up her backpack, Matt Weber glancing at her as he walked by, and before she could return the look, before she could smile—

—tape was wrapped around her hands and ankles, the man with the ponytail smiling at her as he lowered her into a narrow wooden box—only she wasn't quite sure, was it Mr. Ponytail or Matt who was doing all that smiling?

Or maybe it was the angel. The one who came to her as she slept.

The angel had called her Jessie Glass-Half-Full.

"It's okay, Jessie. Everything'll be okay."

Then she came awake to the mask cutting into her face and the cool rush of air streaming into her nostrils and the faint stench of fertilizer and the deadly silence, and she realized she had zoned out again and nothing had changed. She was still trapped in this godforsaken box, still buried beneath the earth, still thirsty, and, most of all, hungry.

She screamed and cried and bucked and kicked and tried desperately to loosen the tape around her wrists—

—and then she remembered the rain.

Her only link to the real world.

Had she already said that?

Focus, Jessie, focus. Gotta stay in focus.

. . . Jessie?

Shhhh. Don't bother her.

She's sleeping.

28

Donovan had never been a religious man. Despite his Irish roots, he had been raised a Methodist, apparently a compromise between his father's dubious Catholicism and the strict Southern Baptist upbringing his mother had been forced to endure. He and his sister had attended church and Sunday school as children, but no one in the family had ever taken their religious activities seriously, and their attendance had tapered off over the years.

Donovan's tenuous belief in a higher power had been hammered out of him after his sister's suicide and his days working Special Crimes. The evil he'd regularly witnessed had convinced him that no God could possibly be watching over us. The Founding Fathers had been right. Mankind had long ago been abandoned and left to fend for itself.

Yet, as he sat behind the wheel of his Chrysler, clutching the Lisa Simpson key chain, watching rain splatter the windshield, he sent up a prayer.

"If you *are* there," he said quietly, "bring her home to me. Please bring her home."

Leaning back in his seat, he closed his eyes to make it official, but he heard no voice in return, was given no sign that his message had been received. Despite the effort, his heart didn't fill with joy or hope or the promise of a new day.

Which didn't particularly surprise him.

What kind of God would let an innocent fifteen-year-old be snatched away like this? What Benevolent Power would stand idly by as a good, honest man was ripped to shreds by a land mine? What Heavenly Father would let a jackass cop destroy the only chance they had of finding a little girl?

Donovan felt nothing but fury. Toward himself, toward Gunderson, Fogerty, and toward a neglectful God who would never answer his prayer.

He sat up and started the engine, resisting the urge to jam his foot against the gas pedal and plow through anything that got in his way. There was a tap on the passenger window and Sidney Waxman stood outside, gesturing for him to roll it down.

Donovan did.

Sidney leaned in, dripping rain. "CPD's been all over those tunnels. We got bupkis." He paused. "You alright?"

Donovan just stared at him.

"Okay, dumb question. What's our next move?"

"Pray forensics finds something in the Suburban," Donovan said. "In the meantime, get CPD and the team topside, walking a grid, six-block radius, then expand from there if you have to."

"What exactly are we looking for?"

"Any patch of earth you can find that's big enough to hold a coffin. And don't stop digging until you're sure you've come up empty."

"That's a pretty tall order, Jack, especially in this rain. We're gonna get a lot of flak."

Again, Donovan just stared.

"Okay, okay." Waxman raised his hands in surrender. "Anybody complains, I'll break his balls."

"See that you do."

"And while I'm having all this fun, what'll you be up to?"

"Driving," Donovan said, and popped the Chrysler in gear.

So he drove, and drove fast, knowing that on these rain-slicked streets, every turn was an invitation to disaster. But driving was his therapy, always had been, even with cases that weren't so personal. He'd reach a dead end in his mind and feel compelled to jump behind the wheel and drive for hours, endlessly circling the city as he worked the puzzle, looking for the break that eluded him.

But this time he had no desire to sift through evidence. All he wanted was to make his mind a blank, to forget he even existed in this screwed-up world where Evil was the true God.

He took a sharp right, splashing through a puddle, hearing the shouts of a cluster of angry streetwalkers as water sprayed over them. Traffic had slowed up ahead—late-night partyers on the way home—so he took another turn, a left this time, and found himself on long, empty stretch of road; a stretch of road that would allow him to pick up speed.

He punched the gas pedal, the Chrysler's beefy engine roaring. A VW Bug turned off a side street and pulled in front of him, going way too slow, and he swerved around it, angrily honking his horn.

He knew this was wrong, knew that he had to regain control of himself, but the fury he felt wouldn't allow for compromise. All good sense had been abandoned to raw emotion.

Despite his best efforts to make his mind a blank, thoughts of Gunderson and Jessie continued to tumble through his head.

Taking out his cell phone, he speed-dialed Rachel's direct line.

After two rings, she answered.

"It's Jack."

"Oh, God, I heard. I'm so sorry. I don't know if Sidney told you, but a couple of guys from Washington have been hanging around and—"

"I know all about it. Right now I need your help."

"Anything."

"Transfer the Gunderson files to my laptop and meet me at my apartment in twenty minutes."

"Why? What are you looking for?"

"Something we missed. Gunderson was smart, but he wasn't exactly tight-lipped. Somebody else knows about Jessie, and that somebody is in those files."

"I hope to God you're right."

"Twenty minutes," Donovan said, and hung up.

He took another turn, onto four-lane highway that stretched back toward the Chicago River. A sea of taillights confronted him, but he didn't slow down. Instead, he weaved in and out of traffic, making a game of it.

A woman with one face-lift too many throttled the horn of her BMW as he breezed past her and cut in, narrowly missing her front bumper. Another driver showed him the finger as Donovan switched lanes and cut him off, kicking back a torrent of rainwater.

No matter how he tried, he couldn't get the image of that Polaroid out of his head—Jessie looking so helpless, so vulnerable. The sight of her lying there exposed to Gunderson's camera made him sick to his stomach. What kind of animal would subject a child to that?

What kind of devil?

Snapping to attention, he realized he was coming up fast on a lumbering SUV. He braked and looked to the right, but the lane was jammed tight. No way to force himself in. Craning his neck, he looked to the left, past the SUV, checking the opposing lane for a break in the oncoming traffic. The river was directly ahead now, cars braking slightly as they approached the bridge that spanned it.

But again Donovan didn't slow down. Spotting his break, he whipped the wheel, cutting across the double yellow line, letting his fury blind him to the risk he was taking. Picking up speed, he pulled onto the bridge, rainwater spraying out from beneath his tires as he again tried to block the image of Jessie from his mind.

Then, without warning, a large container truck changed lanes up ahead and barreled straight at him, headlights blazing. Donovan gripped the wheel, ready to cut back to his side of the road, but there was no room—he hadn't yet cleared the SUV.

The truck was coming up way too fast. Donovan hit the brakes and—

—there it was, a gap in his lane—

—but just as he turned the wheel, the bottom seemed to drop out of the Chrysler. It hit a puddle and hydroplaned, sending him into a rudderless swerve.

The truck's horn blasted mournfully as Donovan pumped his brakes and fought the wheel. He struggled to regain some traction, but the street below him seemed to have vanished.

The Chrysler washed diagonally across the oncoming lanes. A chorus of horns blasted through the rain as Donovan spun toward a guardrail. Seeing what was coming, he threw his arms up as if to ward off evil spirits. With a deafening, metallic crash, the Chrysler smashed through the rail and plummeted.

The next thing Donovan knew he was vertical, headed nose first toward the icy blackness of the Chicago River. The surface of the water rose toward him like a wall of cement, shattering the windshield as he hit.

Donovan had just enough time to suck air into his lungs as what felt like subzero water flooded in, hammering him mercilessly. He fumbled for his seat belt, struggling to unhook it as the Chrysler sank like a brick in a well.

A final tug and the latch clicked open. Freeing himself from the harness, he kicked back against the seat, then shot forward through the window frame and swam, his legs and arms pumping furiously toward the surface.

But his lungs could only hold so much air and they were on fire.

Hold on, Jack, hold on. You can make it.

But could he? Not with this current tugging at him. Not with this freezing water slicing deep into his bones, numbing his arms and legs to the point of uselessness.

Not with his lungs about to burst.

He fought with every bit of strength he had, but he knew it wasn't enough. Not even close.

He'd once read that Harry Houdini had conditioned himself to hold his breath underwater for a full five minutes. But Donovan was no Houdini, and he'd be doing pretty good just to hold his breath for *one* minute, let alone five.

Sixty-three seconds after the river crashed through his windshield, a final, searing jab of pain claimed Donovan's lungs, feeling much like Willy Sanchez's knife to the kidney . . .

Then everything went black.

part three

DARKNESS

29

If you had asked him before this moment what he thought about life after death, he would've told you it doesn't exist.

Death, he would have said, is a dark vacuum where all memories cease and all senses are cut off as cleanly and abruptly as the power company switches off electricity to your home.

He had never held the illusion that there was something waiting for him in the great beyond. Heaven and hell were fairy tales, a promise and a warning, created by superstitious men. Religion was nothing more than politics dressed up with symbols and sacraments—and too often used as justification to conquer and control.

He lived in a world where evidence was king, and the promise of life after death had not lived up to scrutiny.

Faith was a sucker's bet. A fool's game.

And while he certainly wasn't perfect, by any means, he'd never been a fool.

Or had he?

When he opened his eyes, he was standing on the bridge.

The container truck was gone, as were the cars. And the people driving them. The sky was dark and restless, but the road was dry, no sign of the rain that had washed him away.

The only sound was a distant, howling wind.

In front of him stood a mangled mass of steel that had once been a guardrail, sporting a huge gap where the Chrysler had crashed through.

But if the Chrysler was down there . . .

. . . how did he get up here?

Had someone pulled him out?

Moving closer to the gap, he stared at the black river and watched as a body crested the surface of the water like a fishing bobber. Somewhere in the distance, a boat horn gave off three short blasts. A distress signal.

Jesus, he thought, that guy looks dead. I hope they get to him soon.

Then, just as he began to realize, with growing anxiety, that it wasn't just *any* body floating in the water—but was, in fact, *him*—a sudden rush of wind enveloped him and a black, turbulent wormhole opened up overhead.

Something grabbed him by the shoulders and yanked him upward. In a few short seconds, both bridge and river were little more than pinpricks below as he was sucked into an endless, swirling corridor of light and sound.

Fear blossomed in the pit of his stomach as a surreal barrage of images hurtled toward him at lightning speed, much too fast to decipher. He sensed that he was seeing his life play out before him, some sort of high-speed chronicle of where he'd been and who he'd known in his thirty-nine years. His parents, his sister, his marriage, Jessie—

Gunderson. . . .

Above him, at the far end of the corridor, a bright circle of light flickered.

Was it a star of some kind?

All he knew was that there was something compelling about it. And soothing. His fear and apprehension suddenly sifted away as an odd sense of warmth vibrated through his body—

—a warmth like nothing he'd ever felt before.

There was no pain, no pleasure, just—and this seemed strange, considering the frenzied activity swirling around him—just calm.

Then, the faint murmur of voices filled his head, calling his name, beckoning to him.

Were they coming from the light?

He couldn't be sure.

Before he had a chance to find out, invisible hands took hold of him again and yanked him toward a shadowy fold in the corridor wall.

He found himself lying on a small patch of earth, staring into darkness.

Pulling himself upright, he looked around, waiting for his eyes to adjust. After only a moment, he could make out the vague shapes of other human beings, their faces gradually becoming clear, full of shell-shocked confusion—a look he was certain reflected his own.

They were surrounded by rocky terrain. The distant mountains looked as sharp and impenetrable as razor wire, and the sky was not simply restless, but somehow threatening. Hungry.

Yet the others seemed oblivious to it all.

Oblivious to *him*.

He watched as those around him began to rise and migrate, shuffling off toward a narrow pathway in the distance as if herded to the spot by a phantom wrangler.

He didn't hear the call, didn't feel compelled to follow, but he stood up anyway.

What, he wondered, was drawing them?

Had the Roman Catholics gotten it right? Had the penitent come here to be purged of their sins before ascending to . . . wherever?

The gathering crowd began to shift and change shape, forming a ragged line that funneled deeper into the darkness toward an unknown destination.

He remembered, with sudden clarity, what Gunderson had said back at the train car, about the ancient Egyptians and the Fields of Yaru. Were these the newly dead, lining up to be tested? Did that narrow pathway lead to a world of boiling swamps and venomous serpents?

The answers were beyond his grasp. He had no idea what any of it meant.

For him, or for Jessie.

His presence here seemed like some kind of sick, cosmic joke—a metaphysical monkey wrench—and he wondered if he was to be forever anchored to this strange place while his daughter slowly suffocated in a crude wooden coffin.

She was alone somewhere, alone and frightened, calling for him.

Help me, Daddy. Help me.

He had to find her. He couldn't let her die.

Wouldn't let her.

Yet, what could he do? There were no bus stops here. No waiting trains to take him home.

Searching the bleak landscape, he saw nothing to give him hope. It was, he imagined, much like the moon, or some far-flung asteroid. An unforgiving place that held no promise of escape.

The crowd continued its march toward whatever that pathway offered. What did they see in the darkness there? Was it a way out?

Help me, Daddy.

Feeling a sudden sense of urgency, he moved forward, catching up to the crowd, then searched the landscape beyond, looking for some kind of opening. Jessie was back in the real world, calling to him, and all he could think to do was to find the nearest exit sign and flee this place. But as he tried to work his way into the throng, they closed ranks, blocking his passage.

He pushed forward, trying to shove his way in.

"Let me through!" he shouted, but they ignored him, refusing to budge. "Move, goddammit! Let me—"

"Easy, Jack."

It was barely a whisper, right next to his ear. He felt the heat of the speaker's breath.

He whipped around. Saw nothing. No one.

Then the wind kicked up and he froze in place as a fold in the darkness opened up before him.

A familiar figure stepped out of the shadows.

Donovan stumbled back, jolted by what he saw, a mix of emotions flooding his mind: relief, joy, disbelief.

"Sweet Jesus," he said.

It was A.J.

A.J.

Alive and whole and vibrant.

30

Tears filled Donovan's eyes, and before he knew it, he had his arms wrapped around his partner, hugging him.

"My God," he said, pulling away to look him over. "Is it really you?"

A.J. was silent for a moment, then nodded and said, "I'm here, Jack, I'm with you." There was a calmness to his voice that was almost unsettling. "But what you see comes from inside. Your mind is filling in the gaps to help you process what's happening to you."

"What do you mean? Like a dream?"

"More like window dressing. The only thing that exists in this place is thought. Pure thought. Our minds supply the props we need in order to cope. But I'm real, Jack. Very real. Just not in a way you can fully appreciate right now."

Donovan shook his head. This *was* a dream. It had to be. Any minute now he'd wake up and find himself neck deep in freezing river water, thankful to be alive.

He tried to remember some of the more vivid dreams he'd had in his lifetime, but none of them came readily to mind.

A.J. offered him a benevolent smile, looking for all the world like a guardian angel, his eyes bright and clear and full of quiet wisdom. For a moment Donovan felt like a four-year-old looking into the eyes of his father.

Then A.J. squeezed his shoulder. The hand felt warm. Alive. Would it feel that way if he was dreaming?

"She's waiting for you, Jack. Go back and find her. It's what you were meant to do."

Then the smile faded and the darkness opened up again, swallowing A.J. whole.

Donovan blinked. "A.J.?"

He searched the darkness, raising his voice. "A.J.?"

But there was no sign of him.

Donovan stood there, not quite sure what to do with himself, A.J.'s words still banging around inside his head:

Go back and find her.

It's what you were meant to do.

But no matter how much he tried to convince himself that A.J. was real, he couldn't quite believe it. This wasn't death at all, it was nothing more than a hallucinatory episode brought on by severe trauma.

How could it be anything else?

His mind was playing tricks on him, that's all. He was alive and floating on the surface of the river, and any minute now, the paramedics would drag him out to safety and wake him from this terrible nightmare.

Yet, despite his protests, something in his gut told him he was wrong. No hallucination, no dream, could be as alive and as palpable as this. The corridor, the murmuring voices, the crowd of walking dead—these weren't things the mind made up out of whole cloth, were they?

Backing away from the crowd, he turned and again searched the darkness, hoping to find a fold in the fabric, the same fold A.J. had disappeared into.

Then, another whisper tickled his ear:

"This way, Jack."

For a moment he wasn't sure whether he'd actually heard the words or had only imagined them. Then he noticed a flash of movement in the corner of his eye.

"This way."

A dark figure darted into the crowd, weaving through it. He followed, the crowd yielding passage this time, as the figured bobbed in and out of view. Abruptly turning, it broke away from the line, heading across the landscape toward an outcropping of rocks.

Donovan moved after it and picked up speed, the air around him growing colder with each step. The figure disappeared behind the rocks and Donovan quickly circled around them—

—only to find himself alone.

In almost total darkness.

The faint wind howled, like the distant cry of a tortured beast. A shiver snaked up his spine, accompanied by an almost overwhelming sense of dread.

"What's the matter, hotshot? Lose something?"

A fold in the fabric opened up and—

—Alexander Gunderson stood before him. Smiling. Malevolently.

Donovan stared at him. Stunned.

"I'll bet you thought you'd seen the last of me," Gunderson said. He leaned forward, forcing Donovan to take a step back. "I told you it wasn't over."

Donovan stood immobile, felt frozen to the spot. Was this really happening?

Without warning, Gunderson reached up and clapped his hands on either side of Donovan's face.

"Give us a kiss," he said, and planted his lips on Donovan's. A reptilian tongue slithered between them, forcing its way deep inside his mouth.

Donovan gagged and pushed at Gunderson, struggling to break free as white heat burrowed deep into his chest and squeezed his heart.

Then, all at once, Gunderson collapsed in on himself and dissolved into vapor.

Recoiling, Donovan fell back, unable to breathe, his lungs once again on fire. A fierce wind kicked up from out of nowhere and swirled around him.

In a far corner of his brain he heard voices, distant voices, speaking a language he didn't quite understand.

A code of some kind.

Someone shouted, "Clear!" and the fierce wind enveloped him completely, a thousand invisible hands reaching out to grab him as a massive whirling wormhole opened up overhead . . .

And swept him away.

31

The sunlight hurt his eyes.

It wasn't much more than a pale, watercolor wash of gray slanting in through the window from an equally gray sky, but in those first few moments after he awoke, it hurt to keep his eyes open.

He felt drugged; was vaguely aware that he was in a hospital room. His lungs ached. As if they'd been scraped out with the dull edge of a spoon. In fact, his entire body ached more than he could ever remember. Even worse than those long-ago academy days, after the first hours of intense physical training, when walking took Herculean effort.

A cool stream of oxygen flowed through plastic tubing in his nose. An IV tube was taped to the back of his left hand, its needle implanted in the flesh, and deeper, into a vein, stretching it just enough to be uncomfortable. His chest was heavy with wires and a Walkman-sized heart monitor. Another monitor was clamped over his right index finger.

Somewhere nearby a machine beeped, its pattern erratic, reacting to every tiny move he made.

He turned his head slightly, saw that he wasn't alone. A petite figure was curled up in a nearby chair, and it took him a moment to realize who it was.

Rachel. Fast asleep.

He lay there quietly, waiting for his head to clear, not wanting to disturb her. He had no idea what time he'd been brought in here, but figured she must've spent the night.

She looked peaceful, knees tucked to her chest, head resting lightly against the wall. He watched her sleep, wishing this were a different time and place, a time and place where he could act on these feelings he'd been harboring for so long.

Then he cursed himself for even thinking such a thing. He needed to clear his head, focus on the present.

Jessie. What was the news on Jessie?

As if sensing his turmoil, Rachel opened her eyes and blinked at him. Then she smiled, her voice thick and drowsy: "Welcome back, stranger."

Donovan opened his mouth to speak and discovered his throat was scratchy. ". . . What happened?"

Rachel uncurled her body and sat upright. She wore jeans and a T-shirt with a dark wool sweater pulled over it. He wasn't used to seeing her in such casual attire.

"You went for a swim last night," she said. "Only you forgot to get out of your car first. Fortunately there was a police boat nearby. They dragged you out."

She paused a moment, looking as if she wasn't quite sure she wanted to continue. "They told me you were dead, Jack."

"Dead."

"The paramedics. They don't know how long. Your heart stopped. They had to pump a ton of water out of your lungs."

Dead, Donovan repeated to himself, his thoughts drifting to the dim memory of a dark, faraway place.

A.J. had been there.

And Gunderson.

And he vaguely remembered being . . . kissed.

But it all felt so distant. Dreamlike. Do the dead dream? he wondered. Does the mind remain active even after the body ceases to function? He thought about Sara Gunderson lying in a coma—what some called the sleep of the dead—and wondered what she saw.

Had she, too, been kissed?

Rachel got to her feet, moved close to the bed. "You don't look so good. Maybe you should go back to sleep."

He didn't feel so good, either, but he had other things to worry about. "How long have I been here?"

"They brought you in about three this morning. You spent the first few hours in intensive care." She checked her watch. "It's just past noon."

Noon? Jesus. Sixteen hours since Gunderson was shot. Sixteen long hours—most of them wasted now. Was it too late? Had it been too long? He was almost afraid to ask the next question.

"What about Jessie?"

Rachel's expression darkened. "Nothing yet."

"Son of a bitch . . ." Donovan sat up, his body groaning in protest. Wires shifted and the Walkman-like heart monitor tumbled to the floor.

Rachel put her hands on him. "Jack, no. Sidney and the others are working nonstop. They'll find her."

Donovan pulled away from her and yanked at the wires, popping them off the electrodes stuck to his chest. The machine beeped wildly in response and he knew it was only a matter of moments before a herd of nurses came barreling through the door.

"What do you think you're doing?"

"Getting out of here."

"Dammit, Jack. You need rest."

"I'm fine," he said. He wasn't by a long shot, but the first step toward defeat was admitting the possibility even existed. Grabbing the IV needle in his hand, he jerked it out. Blood spurted from the open vein. He clamped it with his right hand, then swung his legs around and touched his bare feet to the linoleum.

Rachel eyed the blood. "This is crazy."

Maybe, Donovan thought, but he ignored her and stood up anyway, feeling the world tilt sideways. He struggled for balance. Cold air sliced through the open back of his hospital gown. "Where are my clothes?"

Urgent shouts echoed through the hallway just outside his room. A Code Blue was in progress and he was the target.

"You're not doing Jessie any good in this condition."

"Where are my clothes?"

Rachel sighed, then crossed to a plastic bag on the floor next to her chair. "I brought you some fresh ones," she said. "And a toothbrush and razor."

Donovan managed a smile. "What would I do without you, Rache?"

32

"What exactly are you looking for?" Rachel asked. The tone of disapproval had been there since they'd left the hospital.

"I'll know when I find it," Donovan told her.

He sat in the passenger seat of her cramped Celica, working the keys of his laptop as she drove. The back of his left hand displayed a nasty black-and-purple bruise, the tiny IV needle-prick caked with dried blood.

The S.A.R.A. file filled his computer screen. A digitized photo stared up at him, Gunderson's cruel eyes mocking him. He hit another key and the *Known Associates* list popped up.

Gunderson had made a truckload of friends and acquaintances over the years, most of the major players listed here. In the weeks after the attack on Northland First & Trust, Donovan and his team had repeatedly scoured this list, hauling in Gunderson's buddies one by one for questioning.

Donovan had spent hours in the interrogation room grilling car thieves, drug runners, and suspected arms dealers, many of whom spoke openly until Gunderson was mentioned. The mere utterance of the name froze them up, as if they were afraid the man himself might break into the room and tear their heads off.

Rachel glanced over at the screen. "Sydney's been through that list half a dozen times since yesterday."

"There's something here," Donovan insisted. "There's gotta be. Gunderson couldn't have pulled off the kidnapping alone. He was too hot. He needed a front man. Someone to gather supplies and information and funnel it back to him."

"What about Nemo?"

"Too much of a wild card," Donovan said. "Nemo's loyalty depends on his mood and the time of day. What Gunderson needed was a foot soldier. Somebody who did what he was told and didn't ask questions."

The image of a large man in a ski mask filled Donovan's head. He remembered watching the guy stagger toward the overturned news van, blood dripping from a nasty gash in his left forearm. Despite considerable effort, Donovan's team had never managed to identify the guy, and that anonymity would surely be attractive to Gunderson.

"Besides," Donovan continued, "Nemo already served his purpose last night."

"Meaning what?"

"Getting us to that train yard."

Rachel frowned. "You think Gunderson *wanted* you there?"

"There were enough explosives in that yard to take out half the Chicago Police Department. Gunderson was a showman. He thrived on attention. And he knew Nemo would crack under the right amount of pressure."

"I don't think the show ended quite the way he expected it to."

"Or anyone else," Donovan said.

He hit the *PgDn* key and studied the list, running the possibilities through his mind, dismissing each name as he came to it. Gunderson's man would have to have the freedom to move without fear of arrest. Contacts and money wouldn't hurt either.

The image of Ski Mask continued to plague Donovan, but as he scrolled down to the *R*'s, a name jumped out at him like a slap to the face, and another image took center stage.

Reed. Tony Reed.

Sara's brother. Part-time video director, full-time rich boy. Except for a minor pot bust when he was seventeen, Reed's record was clean. Despite this, Donovan had managed to get warrants to search both of Reed's houses, had even hauled him in for questioning, but came up empty each time.

Even though Reed was clearly distressed over the condition of his sister, he'd somehow managed to come across as a personable, even likable guy. Sure, he'd cop to occasional phone conversations with Sara—she *was* family, after all—but he claimed no knowledge of Gunderson's activities.

"I like his politics even less than I like him," Reed had said.

Still, Donovan had sensed a nervousness beneath the surface that reminded him of the hundreds of suspects he'd interviewed over the years. At the slightest provocation, this guy would bolt. No question about it. Politics or not, he knew a lot more than he was willing to say.

Donovan remembered standing in Reed's living room a few days after the robbery, leg bandaged and throbbing like a mother, thinking, *He's been here.*

Gunderson's been here.

He'd just never been able to prove it. Two weeks' worth of surveillance turned up nothing, and Donovan had reluctantly closed the book on Reed. But now, as he punched a button and Reed's profile filled the screen, he wondered if he'd been too hasty.

A shot of Tony from *Rolling Stone* accompanied the profile. Rachel glanced at it skeptically. "Him again? He's too good-looking to be a bad guy."

"You've said that more than once."

"It bears repeating."

"Careful, Rache, your hormones are showing."

Rachel gave him a good-natured scowl and returned her attention to the road. She did, however, have a point. With his wiry, rock-star good looks, Reed didn't strike the casual observer as a threat, and he certainly didn't fit the physical characteristics of Ski Mask. But what if Ski Mask was a red herring? Every case had its share of those.

"Got your cell phone handy?"

Rachel gestured to the floor near his feet. "Purse."

Donovan snatched it up, dug around until he found the phone, then dialed Sidney's number.

Waxman picked up after two rings.

"Hey, Sidney."

"Jesus Christ, Jack, I just got a call from the hospital. What the hell are you up to?"

"I'm en route to Reed Communications. I want you to meet me there."

"The brother? How many times have we talked to that idiot?"

"Doesn't hurt to try again."

"Come on, Jack, do you have any idea what's going on out here? That little aquatics demonstration you pulled didn't exactly convince the boys from D.C. you're firing on all cylinders."

"Fuck 'em," Donovan said. "I don't have time for their bullshit. Now get your ass in gear and meet me at Reed Communications."

Waxman sighed. "You're killing me, kemo sabe. Why the hell aren't you still in bed?"

"Would you be?"

A momentary pause, then Waxman said, "Point taken," and hung up.

Donovan snapped the cell phone shut, turned to Rachel. "Make a left at the signal."

33

Reed Communications was housed in a large, weathered warehouse smack in the middle of an industrial side street. The front of the place was crowded with cars, equipment-laden pickup trucks, a catering van, and a big-rig tractor-trailer with the letters *RC* discreetly painted on the side.

Rachel and Donovan pulled to the curb directly across the street and waited a full ten minutes before Sidney showed up in his tan Buick. As Waxman pulled in behind them, Donovan popped the door, turned to Rachel.

"Go on home. I'll catch a ride with Sidney."

Rachel shook her head. "We came to the party together, we leave that way."

"I'm fine, Rache. Go home."

"You look like hell," she said, and Donovan knew it was true. Rachel never pulled punches. "You go on in there, do your thing, and I'll be waiting for you when you're ready to go back to the hospital."

"That could be a long time."

"I'm a patient woman. Don't you know that by now?"

Donovan wasn't entirely sure what she meant by that, so he just shrugged and started to climb out of the car. He was halfway to his feet when he realized he was still a little light-headed.

Rachel grabbed his hand, squeezed it. "Careful," she said.

He looked in at her, saw the concern in her dark eyes. Two years together and this woman was still a mystery. He promised himself that when all of this was over and done with, he'd take some time to explore that mystery.

He squeezed back, then got out and shut the door. He trudged toward Waxman's car as Sidney climbed out and looked him over.

"Don't say a word," Donovan told him.

They heard the faint sound of music as they approached the warehouse. More of a vibration, actually. A deep bass. A driving beat.

Donovan felt naked without his Glock. He'd lost it to the river and hadn't thought to have Sidney bring him a spare. There was no reason to think he'd need it here, but he felt vulnerable.

The guy posted at the side entrance wore blue jeans and a flannel shirt, but there was no question that he was a guard. When he noticed Donovan and Waxman headed his way, he came to attention and ditched the cigarette he'd been sucking on. "Can I help you boys?"

Waxman showed him his badge. "We're here to see Tony."

The guard unclipped a radio from his belt and was about to flick the call button when Waxman grabbed his wrist.

"No need to announce us." He twisted the radio out of the guard's hand and dropped it in his pocket. "You'll get it back when we leave."

They pushed past him, pulled open a heavy, padded door, and were immediately buffeted by a dark wall of noise, an industrial-techno beat and gut-chugging guitars that, to Donovan, felt more like nails being pounded into his head than music. Unused theatrical flats formed a makeshift corridor just inside the doorway, flickering light playing at its far end. They navigated the narrow space and moved toward the light.

For a moment, Donovan was transported to another place and time, an odd sense of déjà vu overcoming him. Vague images formed in a corner of his mind but refused to surface. A sickly sense of trepidation rolled over him.

Had he been here before?

He shook off the feeling and forced himself to concentrate on the matter at hand. The flats narrowed at the far end, and he and Sidney continued single file, Sidney in the lead. A moment later, they emerged to find—

—a vision of hell.

On a raised platform at the center of the cavernous warehouse was a scene straight out of Dante's inferno: a network of shadowy caves, intermittent bursts of fire. Sweaty female bodies, in torn fishnet and skintight leather, shook and shimmied to the driving beat, as a guy strapped into a Steadicam rig lovingly recorded them with his Arriflex. Strobe lights flickered, giving the entire scene a kinetic hyperreality.

In the middle of it all, a bare-chested, leather-clad rocker with tousled dark hair—and horns—thrust his hips to the beat of the music as he mouthed the brutish and not particularly inspiring lyrics that played over a loudspeaker:

Give me what I want, baby
Give me what I need
Do it till we burn, baby
Do it till we bleed

He was simulating sex with a diaphanous, winged beauty on her hands and knees in front of him, her wings fluttering with each and every thrust.

Donovan and Waxman exchanged glances.

This was certainly a first.

Sidney leaned in close. "Reminds me of college," he said, and the warm breath against Donovan's ear pulled him away again, churning up something he couldn't quite put words to.

Something dangerous.

When he looked again at the scene before them, he was jolted by what he saw:

The rocker was *Gunderson,* eyes black as death, a malevolent smile fixed on his face as he assaulted the angel in front of him.

He turned those eyes on Donovan, the smile growing wider, the forked tip of a serpent's tongue flicking between his teeth. For a moment, Donovan felt as if he were staring into a fun-house mirror. Somewhere in those black eyes, he could see himself.

Give us a kiss, Gunderson mouthed.

Donovan sucked in a sharp breath as the squawk of a megaphone sliced through it all.

"Cut! Cut! Kill the music! Give me some light!"

The music abruptly stopped as a bank of overhead lights came on, and before Donovan could blink—

Gunderson was gone. History.

The rocker was just a rocker. A tousled-haired punk drenched in sweat.

The residue of that brief moment, however, spread through Donovan's body like a malignant growth and settled in the pit of his stomach—hard and sour, a terminal case of acid reflux.

Then Tony Reed stepped out from behind a towering light stand, the megaphone tucked under an arm. "As much as I appreciate the sight of a very lovely nipple," he said, loud enough for his entire cast and crew to hear, "the key phrase is Standards and Practices, folks, and I doubt very much that MTV will be as appreciative as I am."

The cast and crew chuckled obediently. Tony gestured to a mousy woman on the sidelines, then pointed to the nameless supermodel who played the part of the angel. The model's left breast was in full view, its containment apparently hampered by her costume's shortcomings and her enthusiasm for the part. Looking down, she sighed and popped the offending orb back into place.

"Sorry," she said, offering Reed a wan smile.

"Maggie," Reed said to the mousy woman, "do us all a favor and break out the duct tape."

Tony Reed considered himself a patient man, but that patience was wearing thinner with each and every setback he was forced to endure. Sure, an exposed tit was nothing to cry about, but this was merely the latest in a long string of screwups that had made this shoot nearly unbearable.

The band he'd been hired to immortalize—a neophyte group of techno-metal punks who called themselves Scream, of all things—had about as much talent as Justin Timberlake's evil twin. The song they'd chosen for their debut video was a weak imitation of Nine Inch Nails—as was their entire act—and Tony had little tolerance for imitators, no matter what style they chose to rip.

But, as usual, the record company embraced such larceny as if it were the second coming of Nirvana. The publicity machine had been pumped up so hard and high that it would be nearly impossible for the band to recover from the inevitable letdown of their first release. By this time next year, they'd be back at their jobs painting cars or rehauling transmissions or doing whatever the hell it was they did before fate threw them a nice, juicy bone.

While Tony didn't care about the band or their music, he did care about his vision. Working with new, untested acts like this one allowed him greater creative freedom than he'd get with older, established artists. Now, if he could just keep the screwups to a minimum—which had so far proved impossible—and get this thing on film, he could retire to his office where the real creativity was born: in the editing room.

Summoning up every bit of patience he had left, he waited as Maggie crossed to Naomi with a roll of duct tape and got to work. He had no doubts that when Maggie was finished, the game of peekaboo would be over, but he couldn't help wondering what the next screwup would be.

"Hey, Tony."

Swiveling his head, Tony looked off toward the left side of the warehouse where the flats were stored and saw two familiar figures walking toward him.

Oh, goody. Agents Donovan and Waxman.

What an unexpected thrill.

"You got a minute?" Waxman was doing the talking, which wasn't surprising. Donovan looked like he'd been stomped on, then run over by a truck. Tony had no idea what had happened to the guy, but he thought about Sara chained to those machines in Saint Margaret's Convalescent Center and sent up a silent thank-you. At least somebody had gotten it right today.

"We need to chat," Waxman said.

Tony sighed and threw a forlorn glance at his assistant director, who stood nearby, jotting something on a clipboard. "Take ten, Jimmy."

The AD pulled his own megaphone out from under his arm and repeated the command to the rest of the crew.

Tony smiled at the two agents. "Let's go to my office."

On Reed's office wall was a framed poster for Francis Ford Coppola's *One From the Heart,* an obscure little gem that few people had ever heard of. In some circles it was believed to be a cinematic masterpiece. Donovan had seen the movie with his ex-wife, Joanne—Jessie's mom—who had promptly labeled it a pretentious piece of crap.

He could clearly remember her saying this with a dour look on her face that, in later years, was as permanent as her smile had once been.

He also remembered being dazzled by the film, but would now be hard-pressed to tell you what it was about. It was *different,* he knew that much. And he figured the poster on Reed's wall was a way of saying, I'm different, too. I'm an independent.

Joanne would undoubtedly label Reed a pretentious piece of crap as well.

This all, of course, shot through Donovan's mind like grease through a hot pipe as Reed escorted them into the office. Donovan was still reeling after that moment of darkness he'd encountered back on the soundstage. The blackness of Gunderson's eyes haunted him, along with the feeling that—for just an instant—he had been staring at himself.

Where the hell had *that* come from?

Reed crossed to a refrigerator in the corner of the room and grabbed a can of Coke. He didn't offer any to Waxman or Donovan.

"Look," he said, popping the top. He was trying for nonchalance, but the undercurrent of nervousness Donovan had sensed in their previous encounters was still present. "I realize you gentlemen have a job to do, but I'm in the middle of a bitch of a shoot right now, so why don't we cut past all the crap and get to the point?"

"You first," Waxman said.

"I haven't seen him, I don't know where he is, and I don't expect to hear from him anytime soon." He took a sip of Coke, smiled at them. "Anything else you need to know?"

"We're still waiting for you to cut past all the crap."

"How many times do I have to tell you, I barely know the man. Met him, what—twice? And that was before he made the transition from annoying to homicidal. Marrying my sister doesn't make him my best friend."

"Uh-huh," Waxman said, unimpressed. "You happen to watch TV last night or read the papers today?"

"Are you kidding? Who has time?"

"Get any calls from friends or relatives?"

"I told you. I'm in the middle of a shoot. That pretty much takes up every second I have. And you two aren't helping much."

"Then I guess you haven't heard."

"Heard what?"

Waxman looked at him. "Your brother-in-law is dead."

Dead, Donovan thought, Rachel's words drifting back to him. *They told me you were dead.*

He watched Reed, looking for a reaction to Sydney's news. All at once Reed's nervousness drained away. His whole body relaxed. He set his Coke on a desktop and sank into a leather executive's chair. He didn't have to say a thing to communicate exactly what he was feeling.

"You don't seem very broken up about it," Donovan said.

Reed looked at him. "Name me three people on this planet who would be."

"Sara, for one."

"Leave her out of this."

"She's smack in the middle of it, Tony. Whether you like it or not. Always has been. And I think it's time you told us the truth."

"About what?"

"Alex came to your house, didn't he?"

"I already told—"

"Come on, Tony, we both know it's true. Right after the crash. He sat in your living room watching CNN. And when they showed Sara in a coma, and me being rushed to the hospital, Alex turned to you—looked right at you—and said, 'I'm gonna put that motherfucker away, and you're gonna help me.' Isn't that how it went, Tony?"

Reed was trying hard not to show it, but every word Donovan said had hit home. Donovan couldn't explain it, but he knew—he *knew*—that that was exactly how the scene had played out. In a corner of his mind he could see Gunderson sprawled on Reed's living room sofa watching television while Reed paced nervously. He didn't know where this image was coming from, but there it was.

"Well, Tony?"

"I want a lawyer," Reed said.

"Christ on a cracker," Waxman muttered.

"We don't have time for lawyers," Donovan said, feeling his adrenaline rise. "Just tell us where she is."

Reed gave him a puzzled look. "Where *who* is?"

Donovan had had enough. Grabbing a handful of Reed's shirt, he pulled him out of the chair, slammed him against the wall. The framed *One From the Heart* poster rattled, threatening to fall.

"Don't fuck with me, Tony." His head was starting to throb. "I'm very short on patience right now."

Waxman moved toward them. "Easy, Jack. Take it easy."

"Stay out of this, Sydney." Donovan kept his eyes on Reed. "Where *is* she? Tell me now or you'll be directing videos from a wheelchair."

"Come on, man, I don't even know who *she* is."

Adrenaline buzzed through Donovan's body, his head pounding now. He spun Reed around again and shoved him back into the leather chair. The force sent Reed toppling to the polished wood floor.

Donovan started toward him, but Waxman blocked his path. "That's enough, Jack. Take a couple of deep breaths."

"He knows. He's hiding something."

"He ain't Nemo. And this isn't gonna help."

"You have any other suggestions?" Donovan pushed past Waxman and moved toward Reed again. "Your sister's in a coma because of me, Tony. At least that's what your buddy Alex thought. Maybe the two of you didn't share a whole lotta burgers and beers, but Sara's something you had in common."

"Fuck you," Reed said.

Donovan reached down, grabbed him again. "Where is she, you little turd?"

He was about to lift him up off the floor when Reed threw his hands up in surrender. "Alright, alright!" he shouted. "I'll tell you what I know!"

Donovan let him loose, backed off. Reed took a breath and climbed to his feet as they waited.

"Here it is, no bullshit: Alex did come to my house. And he *did* say something about you. But all he wanted from me was money. That's all they ever wanted. He and Sara. I was their personal bank account, whether I liked it or not."

"What about Jessie?"

"I swear on my sister's life I don't know who the hell you're talking about. I haven't seen Alex in weeks."

Donovan stood there, wanting to pound the crap out of Reed, wanting to make him squeal the way Fogerty had. But something clicked in his brain, and in that instant he knew this was a waste of time.

Reed was telling the truth.

Donovan relaxed, turned to Waxman. "Let's get the hell out of here."

"Huh?" Waxman said.

"He's clueless. Let's go."

Waxman looked as if he'd just dropped in from another planet and couldn't quite fathom the behavior of this alien beast. "Did I just miss something?"

A guy with a clipboard appeared in the office doorway. One of the crew members they'd seen earlier. "Hey, Tony. The creep's back."

Reed's face went pale. "What?"

"I told him you were in a meeting, but I don't think—"

A deep baritone cut him off: "Hey, asshole, you trying to hide from me?"

All at once the doorway filled with a hulking mass of muscle in a Gold's Gym T-shirt, his fierce gaze directed at Reed. "I need cash, man, and I need it now."

Donovan's own gaze dropped immediately to the hulk's inner left forearm. A long, puckered, pink scar ran the length of it, bearing all the earmarks of a homemade stitch job.

Donovan's heart skipped.

Holy shit. Ski Mask.

At that instant, the hulk's head swiveled in Donovan's direction, the eyes going wide. Without missing a beat, he grabbed Tony's crew member by the shoulders, hurled him at Donovan and Waxman, then turned on his heels and ran.

34

He was already across the warehouse by the time Donovan reached the stage floor. Coming around a corner, Donovan heard the echo of a door banging open and saw a blast of sunlight, the hulk's massive frame silhouetted against it as he darted outside.

Cutting a diagonal path toward him, Donovan plowed through a gaggle of cast and crew members milling around a catering table. The angel let out a shriek, wings fluttering, as he swept past her. He brushed against a light stand and it toppled over with a loud crash, more shrieks and cries of alarm rising behind him.

Somewhere in the confusion he heard the sound of Waxman's voice, shouting for people to "Move!" There was another loud crash and Waxman let loose a flurry of profanities that would make a truck driver blush.

Donovan ignored the commotion. Reaching the door, he slammed through it and found himself in a parking lot, pale sunlight glinting off the windshields of a dozen or more cars. Squinting against the light, he quickly scanned the lot, his pulse up, heart pounding in his ears, head now feeling as if he'd been worked over by a jackhammer operator on a vicious amphetamine high.

Across the lot, the hulk was about to climb behind the wheel of an F-150, but quickly abandoned that idea when he saw Donovan coming his way. Taking off on foot, he cut across a narrow side street, blew past a forklift operator unloading rolls of carpet from a container truck, and headed into an alley between two warehouses.

Donovan followed, the thud of his heart growing louder with every step. As he neared the alley, the forklift operator swung into a reverse arc, warning beeps shrieking. Donovan veered around him and reached the mouth of the alley just as the hulk made an abrupt left turn at the far end.

Donovan felt his chest seizing up but pushed himself, picking up speed. As he moved deeper into the alley, its walls seemed to close in on him, that odd sense of déjà vu sweeping over him again. For just a moment, he felt separated from his body, as if some dark part of him were being sucked away. The faint whisper of voices filled his ears.

Donovan shook off the feeling and continued forward, bad leg throbbing, lungs scorched by every ragged intake of breath. Reaching the end of the alley, he turned left and saw a vacant lot up ahead, its far end bordered by a chain-link fence.

The hulk was halfway across it.

Relying on pure adrenaline, Donovan willed his feet to move even faster. He knew he'd pay for this, probably wind up right back in the hospital, but he couldn't give up. Not now.

But as the hulk neared the chain-link fence, the pounding in Donovan's head grew so fierce it overrode everything else. He was suddenly deaf to the world, his vision narrowing, a circle of light the size of a penny pulsing like a tiny sun spot between his eyes.

The hulk was halfway up the fence now, limbs moving furiously as he scrambled up and over it. Beyond it was a steep, grassy embankment that sloped downward toward a highway. Midafternoon traffic streaked by.

Donovan's vision continued to narrow, the sun spot growing bigger and brighter with every step he took. A nickel. A quarter. A half-dollar. He felt his body beginning to give out on him, the chain-link fence within his reach but at the same time seeming miles away.

Then, inside the circle, he saw it: a face. Nothing more than a fleeting glimpse, a quick flash of sense memory. Dark eyes, malevolent smile, reptilian tongue flicking between the teeth.

Gunderson.

Donovan hit the fence hard and collapsed against it, fingers caught in its wide mesh, the circle of light widening as Gunderson's grin flashed at him again.

Give us a kiss.

Donovan willed the vision away, trying desperately to see past the light toward the embankment below. But everything outside the circle was a blur.

Was the hulk down there?

Legs collapsing beneath him, he felt himself falling. He scrambled for purchase, trying and failing to hang on to the fence. After a moment of blackness, he realized he was on his back, staring up at the pale afternoon sky.

His head continued to pound, but his vision had cleared, and now sounds of traffic filtered in, horns honking, angry shouts. Ski Mask had undoubtedly reached the bottom of the embankment and was either getting away or would soon be roadkill. But Donovan couldn't move. Could barely breathe.

A voice called out to him. "Jesus, Jack, you got a friggin' death wish or what?"

A moment later, Waxman crouched next to him, out of breath, fingers pressing Donovan's neck, checking his pulse. "You are one dumb motherfucker."

Struggling for air, Donovan tried and failed to get some words out, offering Sidney little more than a wheezy grunt.

"Don't worry," Waxman said. "I called it in. He won't get far."

But Donovan had something else on his mind, trying again to get it out. Another wheezy grunt.

Waxman leaned in closer. "What?"

". . . It was real . . . ," Donovan said between breaths.

Waxman frowned. "Real? What are you talking about?"

". . . the dream."

The frown deepened. "Sorry, old buddy, you lost me."

"A.J. . . . Gunderson."

"What about them?"

"They were there," Donovan said, knowing that where he'd gone when he'd hit that black river last night was as real as the ground beneath him, and the gray sky above.

The netherworld.

Purgatory.

The road to Yaru.

It didn't matter what the name was. He'd been there, and it was real. And he remembered it all.

He looked up at Waxman, at the puzzled expression on his friend's face.

Then he said, "I saw Gunderson."

35

Rachel checked her watch and discovered it had stopped: 1:28 p.m. About the time she and Jack had left the hospital.

They'd lost another hour since then, maybe more, and Jessie was only a stone's throw away from what most people in law enforcement considered the cutoff point between hope and despair: the twenty-four-hour mark.

The majority of children abducted by strangers wound up dead within the first three hours. The rest rarely made it past twenty-four.

And even if Jessie *was* being kept alive by those stolen oxygen tanks, there was no telling how much longer they'd last.

But Rachel wouldn't allow herself to give up hope. Not yet, at least.

She had been waiting here for what seemed an eternity, listening to the radio until a song came on that reminded her of her ex.

The Eagles. Tequila Sunrise.

Two bars into the thing, she jabbed the off button with such ferocity she almost broke a nail.

No point in reliving that nightmare.

But then it was too late, and all the memories came crashing back, all the times she'd spent behind the wheel of a car very similar to this one, a four-year-old Toyota she and David had scrimped and saved to put a down payment on. And what she remembered in particular were the late nights after David and his buddies from the muffler shop had poured their paychecks down their throats and she was dragged out of bed by a drunken phone call.

Then it was into that Toyota and out to McBain's. Rachel's taxi service.

"Best goddamned driver in the state," David would say with a wheezy chuckle. His breath stank of cigarettes and Jose Cuervo and God knew what else as he staggered out of the bar and climbed in next to her. "How much I owe you, babe?"

More than you'll ever know, Rachel thought.

The next day, she'd give him holy hell while he cradled the toilet bowl in agony and promised never to take another drink. Ever.

But a few days later, Rachel's taxi service was back in business— surprise, surprise—the sober nights becoming fewer and far between.

Then the abuse started, the smacks across the face when she talked back to him.

"Stupid Chink bitch!" he'd scream, showing her the back of his hand, cocked and ready to fly. Despite her fear, Rachel thought the epithet a little wacky, because David himself was half-Chinese.

She called it quits the night he dislocated her jaw. Called a *real* taxi service and got the hell out of there.

She moved in with Ma and Grandma Luke, into their cramped little apartment in Chinatown. She stayed there nearly a year, thinking she was a failure because she hadn't been able to keep her husband from self-destructing.

That first night, Grandma Luke had traced a finger along Rachel's swollen jaw and told her, in quiet broken English, not to blame herself. David was *kai dei,* a bastard, who didn't deserve to occupy even a small place in Rachel's heart.

Rachel hadn't bothered to tell her grandmother that her heart was as cold and dead as an old car battery. She knew it would be a long time before someone came along to give it the jump start it needed.

Then she met Jack.

It was a humid Friday afternoon and traffic was a bear, but she had managed to make it to the Field Division office relatively dry and on time.

Deena Crane, an ATF support staff supervisor, was impressed enough by Rachel's test scores (and a three-year stint at the legal aid clinic in Chinatown) to usher her straight into Jack Donovan's office. The bureau was gearing up a new task force, for which Jack had been named lead agent, and they desperately needed help to reduce the clutter they'd already accumulated.

This was close to a year after her divorce. The only thing on Rachel's mind was finding a job that paid enough to get her out from under Ma's and Grandma Luke's feet. During that year she'd had to endure the Wrath of David, at first begging her to come back, then later threatening her. Always drunk, of course.

Every other week she'd find him waiting on the narrow steps that led up to her mother's apartment, which was located above Ling Su's, a popular seafood restaurant. She remembered the pungent kitchen smells mixing with the heat and the stench of tequila on David's breath as he professed his undying love. The waves of revulsion had nearly smothered her.

Despite David's proclamations, there was that oh-so-familiar fury in his eyes, and she wondered what had happened to the fresh-faced college boy she'd fallen for. Was he still buried in there somewhere? Driven into retreat by whatever demons haunted him?

These were questions she had asked herself over and over in the last months of their marriage, but she'd never found a satisfactory answer.

Maybe there wasn't one.

A request for a restraining order was filed and granted, but David routinely ignored it. His job at the muffler shop long gone, he was living on the streets now, spending most of his time with a group of newfound friends in the parking lot of a 7-Eleven just a couple blocks south of Chinatown. That put him within walking distance of her doorstep. She called the police a few times to shoo him away, but a week or so later he'd show up again, looking gaunt and filthy.

And dangerous.

Then the investigative analyst position at the bureau opened up and Rachel met Jack and dreamed of escape. A better-paying job, a place of her own, and hopefully no more David.

When Deena first ushered her into Jack's office, Jack had been brusque and preoccupied, searching for something he'd misplaced on his desk. But when he finally raised his head and took a good look at her, he paused, his eyes clear and direct and pleased by what they saw.

Then the look passed and he avoided her gaze as if he'd been caught in some forbidden act, busying himself with his search until he uncovered a copy of the *Chicago Tribune,* folded to the crossword puzzle. Picking up a stubby pencil, he told her to have a seat and sank into his own chair.

"Congratulations," he said. "You're the first to make it through that door."

"She has all the qualifications," Deena told him. "And a solid ninety-eight on the written exam. That puts her at the top of the list."

Jack nodded and looked at Rachel. "You have any idea what you're getting yourself into?"

My own apartment, Rachel almost said, but resisted the urge. "I've seen my share of cop shows."

Lame, she thought, immediately regretting it.

Way to kill 'em, Rache.

Jack looked at her as if he wasn't sure if she was joking, then dropped his gaze to the folded newspaper in his hands.

"Tell me this," he said without looking up. "What's a six-letter word for German mythological protector?"

Now it was Rachel's turn to wonder. Was he serious?

She thought a moment, reaching back to a class she'd once taken in college. World Mythologies. She'd always been good at retaining trivia (most of it about as useful as her degree in art history) and she was pretty sure she knew this one.

Mentally counting the letters, she shrugged and said, "Kobold?"

Jack's eyebrows went up and he put his pencil to work, filling in the appropriate squares.

Then he smiled.

Rachel thought it looked good on him. Maybe too good. As their eyes met, a spark of electricity stuttered through her dormant heart.

"Welcome to the fun factory," he said.

The incident that really warmed her to Jack happened one afternoon several weeks later. She was living the dream by then—the new job, the upstairs floor of a duplex in Bridgeport that she was just able to afford—and, miraculously, no sign of David in over a month.

Until that afternoon.

She and Jack and some of the crew were in the middle of a working lunch at Boysen's Deli, just across from the federal building, when the door burst open and David staggered in, drunk and disorderly, a filthy, disheveled mess. His angry eyes searched the place until they locked on Rachel.

"Fuckin' bitch," he muttered, his voice slurred. "You think you can sneak out on me?"

Rachel felt her scalp prickle and her cheeks get warm as she shot up out of her chair. Jack was on his feet, too, and so were A.J. and Sidney, all three threatening to make a move toward David. But she waved them off and went around the table to where he was standing. The eyes of everyone in the restaurant were on her as she approached him.

"David, please," she said, taking his arm. "Let's go outside."

But David recoiled at her touch and swung his free arm, backhanding her. She yelped and stumbled into the table as David clenched his fists and staggered toward her.

A.J. was the first to reach him and wrestled him to the floor. David hit it hard, grunting, resisting with everything he had—which wasn't much. And as A.J. held him there, David let his body go limp and started to cry. Buckets.

Rachel felt a hand at her elbow and turned to find Jack. He guided her into a chair, his grip firm and sure and welcome, steadying her not just physically, but emotionally as well. The shame and anger and embarrassment she felt quickly drained away, and as she watched David cry, nothing remained but pity.

Jack brushed her hair aside and studied her cheek, which felt as if it were on fire. "You'll be wearing that for a while," he said. "You okay?"

Rachel nodded.

"I assume this guy is your ex?"

Another nod. "He's had a little trouble accepting it."

"What do you want me to do?"

Rachel looked at David for a moment. His shoulders shook as he sobbed. Then she said, "Let him go."

Jack nodded and gestured to A.J. "You heard her."

A.J. was panting and his face was red. "Are you fucking kidding me?"

"Do it."

A.J. frowned, then reluctantly rose and stepped away as Jack bent and grabbed David's arm, helping him to his feet. David's eyes were red and rimmed with tears, but he didn't look at Rachel.

She watched Jack guide him out the door and onto the sidewalk. Watched them through the front window, Jack's body language revealing only patience and authority as he sat David at the curb. He said something and David reacted visibly, looking up sharply, then slumped his shoulders in resignation as he did what he'd never done with Rachel: listened.

Jack continued talking, took out a business card, scribbled something on the back, and handed it to him. David nodded and glanced back toward the deli. Wiping his eyes with his shirtsleeve, he got up and shuffled away, heading down the street.

"Jesus Christ," A.J. said, storming toward Jack as he came back inside. "You're really gonna let that scumbag skate?"

Jack patted his shoulder. "Go buy yourself a cup of coffee."

Later, when she and Jack were alone in his office, she asked him what he had said to David.

"I told him he was lucky," Jack said.

"Lucky?"

"Lucky he'd had the time he had with you, lucky you were the forgiving kind, because his luck is wearing thin."

"And what makes you think I'm so forgiving?"

"Because you didn't make a scene, you treated him with a dignity he clearly didn't deserve. Even when he gave you that knot on your face, you were more concerned about him than yourself." Jack looked at her. "Am I wrong?"

Rachel shook her head, knowing that most men—men like David— would never have been able to read her so effortlessly. Something about this new boss of hers, something that went much deeper than his good looks and easy smile, set him apart from the men she'd known.

Anyone else in that restaurant would have taken David down for what he did—A.J. was practically frothing at the mouth. But instead of using his fists, Jack had counseled David. A move that was as unexpected as it was noble.

She later learned that what Jack had written on the back of his card was the name and number of an alcohol treatment facility. She wished she could say that David had used it, but she was pretty sure he never had.

But he didn't bother her again. Not even a phone call. And that was the last time she saw him.

She and Jack had worked together for two years, their relationship close, sometimes moving right up to the water's edge. But neither had ever taken the plunge.

There was the job. And office protocol.

And the timing just never seemed right.

Besides, maybe she was fooling herself. Maybe Jack didn't feel the way she did. She had given him all the signals without actually throwing herself at him, but he had never quite responded the way she'd hoped he would.

So she waited. Because that's all she could do.

And here she was, still waiting, sitting behind the wheel of another Toyota thinking about David and Jack and of the events of the last couple of years. And the last several hours.

Hope and despair.

Was she witnessing another self-destruct?

Jessie was missing. The man who'd taken her was dead. How long could Jack keep going before he folded under the weight of it all?

And what if they never found her? What then?

Before she could even allow herself to think that far ahead, an ambulance streaked by, siren screaming, then tore around the corner past Tony Reed's warehouse.

Knowing this couldn't be anything but bad, Rachel flew out of her car and ran across the rutted blacktop. Following the path of the ambulance, she rounded the side of the building just in time to see Jack and Sidney emerge from a nearby alley, Sidney struggling to keep Jack upright as the ambulance came to a stop and two paramedics jumped out.

Barely able to walk, Jack waved them away. The paramedics ignored him and took over for Sidney, guiding him to the rear of the ambulance. Throwing the doors open, they sat him down on the lip of the doorframe as one of the paramedics pressed a stethoscope to his chest.

Rachel just stood there, holding her breath, wanting to shoot him. Kick him.

Punch him, at the very least.

Maybe he wasn't technically her responsibility, but he might as well be, because she wasn't about to waste all this anger on anyone else. He was her jump start, goddammit, and two years exchanging glances and quick smiles and tucking away her feelings was two years too many.

Screw the job, screw office protocol.

Screw the waiting.

And despair need not apply. Only hope.

Hope was essential.

They would find Jessie and things would change—oh, boy, would they change.

That is, of course, if she didn't kill the bastard first.

36

Donovan wasn't about to go back to the hospital. Not a chance.

His heart was still doing a dance inside his chest, but it had started to slow and he could already feel his strength returning. Another trip to the hospital would only be wasted time—time he couldn't afford.

As he sat at the back of the ambulance, arguing this point with Waxman and the paramedics, Rachel walked up and joined the chorus. She looked upset, and Donovan felt a twinge of guilt. But he didn't back down.

"Look at yourself," Rachel said as she angled one of the doors to show him his reflection in the window. "You think you're doing Jessie any good in this condition?"

Donovan was surprised by what he saw. Skin pale. Dark circles under his eyes. Pupils dilated. He looked like a skell, a hype. One fix away from the graveyard.

They told me you were dead.

A whisper of voices cascaded through his already crowded brain, and before he could stop them he was thinking about where he'd been and what he'd seen. He closed his eyes for a moment, willing the thoughts away, and when he opened them again, Rachel was staring at him, full of concern. Waiting.

"It's almost twenty-four hours," he said. "If I give up now—"

"For God sakes, Jack, nobody's asking you to give up. Just get some rest. Let Sidney take over for a while."

"You don't understand. There are things going on here. Things I can't explain."

"What things?"

"Oh, brother, here we go again," Waxman muttered.

Rachel glanced in his direction but he looked away, studying the ground. Frowning, she returned her gaze to Donovan, concern giving way to puzzlement.

"*What* things?" she repeated.

At the periphery of his brain, Donovan saw a turbulent sky, dark craggy mountains. A crowd of people marching like lemmings into the darkness.

He considered telling her about it, but held back. He didn't want her looking at him the way Waxman had. What little he'd related to his friend had been greeted with a heavy—and entirely reasonable—dose of skepticism.

Actually, that was putting it mildly.

Waxman thought he was nuts.

"Later," he said. "Right now we've got a suspect to track."

Rachel started to protest, but he cut her short by turning to Waxman and gesturing across the street to the parking lot. A small group of people were gathered outside Reed's warehouse door, watching them. Reed's cast and crew.

"Get a canvass started. See if somebody knows that asshole's name. And get Al working the F-150. Maybe the guy was stupid enough to drive his own truck."

"Wishful thinking," Waxman said, pulling out his cell phone. "You see Reed over there?"

Donovan squinted at the crowd and shook his head. "Nope."

"I'll check inside."

"Wait for me." Donovan got to his feet, but his legs were as weak and rubbery as month-old celery sticks. He grabbed the door to steady himself.

Rachel took his arm. "Jack, let Sidney handle this."

"I'll be fine."

"Not if you keep going at this pace." She clearly wasn't happy, but he wasn't about to budge, either. She sighed. "At least let me get some food in you. You haven't eaten since yesterday."

She was right. He hadn't even thought about food. Now that he *was* thinking about it, he realized he was famished. The tap dance in his chest had nearly subsided, but a bit of nourishment might make him feel better.

"She's making sense," Waxman said. "You keep running on empty, sooner or later you won't be running at all."

Donovan felt the heat of Waxman's gaze, judging him, the flicker of doubt in his eyes.

He wanted to resist, but he knew full well that Waxman could handle Reed as well as he could. Probably better at this point.

It was his turn to sigh. "Someplace close," he said to Rachel. "A quick refuel and that's it."

She squeezed his hand and started across the street. "I'll get my car."

Donovan watched her go, feeling as though he'd just escaped a lynching. She was as stubborn as he was.

"You sure you're okay?" Waxman asked.

Donovan looked at him. "I know you think I've lost it, Sidney, but I saw what I saw."

"I don't doubt that, old buddy. But you *are* under a lot of stress."

"Just get me a goddamned name."

Waxman nodded. "Consider it done."

They found a deli about three blocks over.

Donovan thought the short ride might rejuvenate him, but when he stepped onto the curb, the world started to sway and he nearly lost his balance.

Rachel came around the car, took his elbow, and guided him inside to a table.

"Déjà vu," she said as she sat him down. "Only in reverse."

Donovan had no idea what she was talking about and didn't have the energy to try to figure it out, so he forced a chuckle and left it at that.

She waved a hand toward the menu mounted over the counter. "What are you hungry for?"

Donovan scanned it. "Pastrami. Mile high."

Rachel mumbled something he didn't catch and headed for the counter where a stout, round-faced woman waited to take their order. It was long past lunchtime, but still too early for dinner, and the place was nearly a ghost town. All but two of the remaining tables were empty.

Donovan watched as Rachel put in their order, but his mind was on a different plane, thinking of Waxman and Reed and Ski Mask.

And the dark place. The road to Yaru.

He thought about the stark landscape, remembering what A.J. had told him. That we bring our own baggage to the place, our minds filling in details to help us cope with something we don't yet understand.

Did this mean that some of the walking dead found themselves in a field of lilies or on a beach at sunset? Were others cruising through a Vegas casino, slot machines spitting out shiny silver dollars?

What did it say about Donovan's state of mind that *his* chosen deathscape was as bleak and as cold as the far side of the moon? Had the dark world he'd conjured up always been there at the periphery of his brain?

He thought about the job, and about the death and destruction he'd witnessed over the years. He thought about his parents, both gone, lost to a plane crash in the Bahamas just months before his divorce.

And he thought about his sister. The *other* Jessie.

Jessica-Anne Donovan, as smart as she was artistic, a scholar, a painter, a terrific pianist—and a victim of suicide just three days before her nineteenth birthday. She had suffered a nervous breakdown during her freshman year at Sarah Lawrence and come home to recuperate. A week later, Donovan—still in high school—trudged in from a long afternoon of football practice to find her hanging from a ceiling beam. A lavender robe tie was cinched around her neck, her once beautiful face an unnatural shade of blue.

Donovan was devastated, but he wasn't surprised. Nobody was.

No matter how cheerful she might have pretended to be, Jessie-Anne had always worn sadness like an accessory. It shaded her eyes. Colored her speech.

And Donovan had never known why. Wasn't sure *she* had, either.

All these years later, he didn't often think about her. He usually pushed such distractions aside, refusing to allow himself to succumb to sentiment. And to the guilt he felt, the feeling that if only he'd come home earlier he could have stopped her.

Maybe he had paid for that. Maybe he was a fraud. Maybe, like his sister, he had never been as happy or content as he pretended to be. Could her death be the reason he'd so often ignored his wife and kid in favor of work? Was he afraid to get too close?

That bleak world he'd visited last night might well be a reflection of a bruised and battered soul. And now, with Jessie gone—*his* Jessie—he wondered if he'd ever have a chance to heal.

Rachel came back from the counter and sat across from him, her eyes immediately registering concern, as if she sensed the depth of his mood.

"What is it?" she said.

Donovan shook his head, dismissing the question, afraid to say anything. Afraid she, too, would think he was nuts. But what was the point? Sooner or later he'd have to spill it. Better for her to hear his version now than Sidney Waxman's later on.

"Tell me something," he said. "You ever think about life after death?"

Rachel looked surprised. "Maybe you should ask my grandmother. She's got a whole boatload of theories on the subject."

"I'm asking you."

Rachel sobered. Touched his hand. "Jack, if this is about Jessie, you can't start thinking like that."

"This is about me."

"What are you saying?"

Donovan shook his head again, having second thoughts. "You'll just think I'm crazy."

"And that would be different how?"

Vintage Rachel, he thought, but it sounded forced. Unnatural. She shifted in her chair, but he sensed her discomfort was more than physical.

At the table next to them, a man in a gray suit was finishing up the last crumbs of a corned beef on rye as the fingers of his free hand toyed with the seal on a pack of Marlboros. The guy was obviously trying to quit and couldn't decide whether to succumb to his addiction.

"Jack?"

Donovan returned his attention to Rachel, but said nothing.

She prodded. "Earlier you told me there were things going on. What things? What did you mean?"

Donovan hesitated, glancing again at the pack of Marlboros. Fingers scraped the cellophane. "You remember what the paramedics told you at the hospital? That I was dead?"

"You think I'd forget?"

He thought he saw a flicker of dread in her eyes, as if she was anticipating where he was headed and wasn't quite sure she wanted to go there with him.

"I wasn't just floating in the river, Rache. I went somewhere."

"Went somewhere," she repeated.

"At first I thought it was just some screwy dream, but now I know it was real. As real as you are. And this place."

"You're telling me that when your heart stopped . . ."

She didn't finish, so Donovan finished for her. "Tunnel, bright light— the whole ball of wax. And that wasn't the end of it."

Rachel fell silent for a long moment and he was sure that once she'd processed his words, she'd give him that same look Waxman had. Then her gaze steadied and she reached across the table and grabbed both of his hands, holding them between hers.

"Tell me everything," she said.

Twenty minutes later, her cell phone rang.

Donovan was halfway through his story, delivering it in fits and starts, remembering new details as they came to him, and hoping she wouldn't run screaming from the place once he'd finished. At one point, the stout woman brought their sandwiches over, but Donovan barely noticed her.

Rachel answered the phone, listened a moment, then passed it across to him.

It was Waxman.

"The F-150's a bust," he said. "Stolen off a dealer's back lot. They didn't even know it was missing until we called them."

"Wonderful. What about Reed?"

"Turns out our boy's been riding his ass for weeks. Reed's so terrified of the guy, he threatened to lawyer up and take his chances. Once I promised him a night in a cell with Bobby Nemo, he got very cooperative."

"A name, Sidney. Give me a name."

"Luther Dwayne Polanski. Like the movie director. Twenty-eight years old, did a six-year stint at Danville Correctional for armed robbery and aggravated assault."

"Let me guess. He was there the same time as Gunderson."

"Their sentences overlapped by about a year. Luther was released six months ago."

Donovan thought back over the weeks immediately following the Northland First & Trust heist. Gunderson's sheet had revealed a short stint at Danville for weapons possession, and Donovan and A.J. had been out there a half dozen times, looking for possible associates of Gunderson's. Neither the warden nor the guards had ever mentioned the name Polanski.

"I talked to his PO," Waxman said. "Says Luther's been a model parolee. Shows up twice a week like clockwork, has a job washing dishes at a place called Millie's Diner. They told me he hasn't been to work for a couple days."

"Where's he living?"

"His mother's house in South Deering."

Donovan stood up, feeling the room sway only slightly this time, the news giving him a renewed sense of energy.

At the table next to them, the man in the gray suit crumpled his napkin, then rose and headed for the door, leaving the unopened pack of Marlboros behind.

Attaboy, Donovan thought. He'd never been a smoker himself, but at this moment he could almost understand the guy's reluctance. There was something alluring about that little red-and-white box. Something . . . familiar.

"Jack? You still there?"

"I'm here," Donovan said. "Give me the address."

37

They sat on the house for close to an hour before they saw any sign of life.

It was typical South Deering working-class, a two-story, rust-colored box with a neatly trimmed yard surrounded by a waist-high chain-link fence. An old Chevy Nova sat on blocks in the street out front, looking as if it hadn't gone anywhere in decades.

Marilyn Polanski hadn't either. According to Luther's parole officer, his mother had been living in the place since the late seventies. A single mom, she'd been witness to the gradual change in the neighborhood makeup, from predominantly white to black and brown and even a few Vietnamese.

Luther had grown up in the house and immediately come home to roost after his stint at Danville. But unless the guy was a complete fool, Donovan didn't figure he'd be returning anytime soon.

Unfortunately, the house was all they had.

They were parked half a block down, Waxman behind the wheel, Donovan riding shotgun. Al Cleveland and Darcy Payne—the lone female agent on his team—were nested in their beige sedan across the street.

Donovan had sent Rachel home. He didn't want her in the line of fire in case things got hairy. She'd agreed, reluctantly, but insisted on getting their sandwiches to go and left them both behind for Donovan.

One veggie, one turkey breast.

Not a pastrami in sight, mile high or otherwise.

Donovan devoured them both, feeling like Popeye sucking down a gal-
lon of spinach. As usual, Rachel had been right. The food was a tonic, a
cure-all that pulsed through his body like an electric charge. The legs that
had been so rubbery an hour ago suddenly couldn't stay still. They felt
cramped inside the car, wanting to *move*.

Add that to the ticking clock in his brain, the constant reminder that time
was wasting, that those cylinders of oxygen Gunderson had buried along
with Jessie could only last so long . . . and Donovan was ready to scream.

Waxman, however, had other things on his mind. Eyeing the half-
crumpled take-out bag, he said, "You got any more of those?"

Before Donovan could answer, his radio crackled. Cleveland's voice.
"We may have movement inside the house."

Donovan flicked his call button. "What, exactly?"

"Front window. Drapes. Maybe somebody peeking out."

"Maybe?"

"I saw *something* move. Could be the family pet."

"You're killing me, Al."

"Hey, I'm doing the best I can, here. Wait—there it is again. Definitely
somebody at the window."

Donovan turned to Waxman. "What do you think?"

"Your guess is as good as mine."

Reaching for the holster on his hip, Donovan pulled out the Glock that
Cleveland had brought him. The clip was full.

It felt good in his hand. Weighty.

The radio crackled again. "Car coming," Cleveland said. "Older white
broad. Could be the mom."

"If it is, let her go in. We don't want to tip our hand too soon."

"I don't know, Jack. Sounds a little iffy to me."

"Trust me," Donovan said. "If things go bad, he's not gonna shoot his
own mother."

"Then he's got a lot more willpower than I do." Cleveland clicked off.

Waxman turned, the hint of a smirk on his face. "Not gonna shoot
his own mother? How the hell you know that? You some kind of sooth-
sayer now?"

"Don't start, Sidney."

"No, really," Waxman said, enjoying this. "Your little trip to the other side turn you into Uri Geller?"

"Careful," Donovan said. "I've got a weapon in my hand."

Waxman grunted, turned his attention to the house. The car, a gray Buick Regal, pulled to the curb behind the Nova. The woman at the wheel put it in park, set the brake, opened the door, and stepped out.

She was about sixty, tall and well built, but with a weariness in her eyes and a tautness of skin that reflected a hard life. She wore a tight-fitting gold-and-white waitress's uniform that screamed coffee shop.

"What do you bet she works at Millie's Diner?" Donovan said. He had the glasses on her, watching as she approached the door, saw it swing open just before she reached it.

Someone inside. Nearly lost in the shadows.

Donovan lifted his radio. "Is it him?"

"Can't tell," Cleveland said. "Too dark in there."

The woman stepped into the doorway and kissed the dark figure on the cheek as the door closed behind her.

Donovan lowered the glasses.

"It's him," he said, but he wasn't sure. Maybe he just wanted it to be. Either way they had no choice. Time to move.

He clicked the call button again. "Okay, this is it. No mistakes. I want this guy alive and talking. Franky, you awake?"

Franky Garcia sat in a postal truck about three blocks down the street. "Standing by."

"Time to deliver the mail."

As mandated by the Justice Department, every incoming agent of the Bureau of Alcohol, Tobacco, Firearms and Explosives receives intensive training in tactical entry and suspect apprehension. Despite the thoroughness of the training, however, every good team likes to develop its own techniques, based on the strengths and weaknesses of each of its members.

Because of his small size and nonthreatening appearance, Franky Garcia often took on the role of decoy, posing, for example, as a delivery boy during the successful apprehension of Bobby Nemo. The maneuver had been improvised when the real delivery boy had showed up, and because Garcia was often mistaken for Asian, the switch had worked out well.

The crew called him Franky the Chameleon, telling him he'd missed his calling, that he should be strolling the red carpet at the Academy Awards instead of taking down perps. They'd even presented him with a gold-plated Oscar replica after a particularly successful bust. The caption read, "Best Performance by a Decoy."

What Franky didn't dare tell them was that he was secretly taking an acting class. Two hours, every Saturday morning. The highlight of his week. He figured if cops like Eddie Eagan or Dennis Farina could make the career transition, why not him? And these little decoy jobs were excellent preparation.

This time around, Franky was playing the part of mailman. Nothing groundbreaking, sure, but he liked to think he handled it with a subtle authority.

A minute and a half after Donovan's call, he nosed a regulation postal truck to the curb in front of the target's house and hopped out, a package marked EXPRESS MAIL in hand.

Moments before, Donovan and the others had exited their vehicles and vaulted the chain-link fence surrounding the house, the pale sky offering them no protection whatsoever from prying eyes. Cleveland and Payne headed toward the rear of the house as Donovan and Waxman crouched near the bushes out front, weapons drawn, awaiting Franky's approach. Franky could only hope that no one inside was watching, because his butt would be the first to go down.

Whistling softly, he threw the gate open, sauntered up the walkway to the front porch, and knocked.

There was no immediate answer, so Franky knocked again, then found the bell and rang it. After a moment, the door opened a crack and an attractive older woman peaked out.

"Yes?"

"Afternoon, ma'am. Got a package here for"—he glanced at the label—"Luther D. Polanski."

"Who's it from?"

Franky played his part, glanced at the label again. "Danville Correctional Center."

The woman frowned. She seemed distracted, glanced over her shoulder into the house. "Just leave it on the porch."

"Gonna need a signature," Franky said, flashing a smile.

The woman sighed and pulled the door wide, stepping into the doorway. She was wearing a short terry-cloth robe, cinched at the waist, showing a hint of cleavage. Franky had to admit she looked pretty good for her age. The way she was dressed, he wondered if he had interrupted something.

"Let's make it quick," she said, not bothering to hide her irritation. "I've had a long day."

"It's best if I get the recipient's signature," Franky said. "Is Mr. Polanski in?"

"No, and I don't expect him anytime soon, so either let me sign or bring it back tomorrow."

Testy old broad. Now he was *sure* he'd interrupted something. Time for a little attitude adjustment.

Keeping his voice low, he said, "I've got a better idea. How about if you step outside for a moment?"

The woman's face took on the universal what-the-fuck? expression that Franky had seen a thousand times before. "What did you just say?"

Franky smiled and lowered the package to reveal the Glock 20 in his right hand.

"I think you heard me."

Donovan was the first one through the door.

As soon as Garcia got the woman outside, Donovan radioed an urgent "Go!" then cleared the bushes and shot forward through the doorway, knowing Waxman wasn't far behind. Cutting to the right, he moved into a crouch and scanned the room for any sign of a threat.

Nothing. Just a dimly lit, standard-issue living room with doilies on the furniture.

With a quick hand gesture to Waxman, he pushed forward toward a narrow hallway as Waxman split off and headed for what looked like a basement door.

There was a crash somewhere at the back of the house. Footsteps on stairs. Cleveland and Payne, headed to the second floor.

The sound was clear notification that the place was under siege, and if Luther had a weapon within reach, things could get nasty. With surprise no longer a factor, their only advantage was speed.

Keeping his Glock raised, Donovan moved sideways down the hallway, his back against the wall. Halfway down on the opposite side, was a closed door with a faded Ozzy Osbourne poster taped to it. Donovan quickly approached it. Bringing his leg up, he kicked it open and immediately ducked away, anticipating a barrage of gunfire.

Nothing came.

A quick scan revealed what looked like a teenager's bedroom: baseball memorabilia on the shelves, a set of barbells tucked into one corner, an unmade bed, closet hanging open with dirty clothes on the floor. It had to be Luther's, but Luther himself was nowhere to be found.

Pressing on, Donovan approached an open bathroom, which was small and cramped and empty.

Then he heard a scream above him.

Donovan shot through to the back of the house to where a narrow set of steps led upstairs. Taking them two at a time, he reached the second floor, barreled through the hallway, and found an open door, Darcy just inside, in shooting stance. Her weapon was pointed at a large, short-haired woman who sat shrieking in the middle of a queen-size bed, sheets clutched to her ample bosom.

"Hands!" Darcy shouted, her voice cutting through the din. "Show me your goddamn hands!"

The woman's eyes were nearly as wide as her open mouth, but the shrieks caught in her throat as she let the sheet drop and threw her hands into the air. Tears streamed down her cheeks.

"Luther Polanski," Darcy demanded. "Where is he?"

"I-I don't know," the woman blubbered. "I don't live here. . . . I . . . I haven't seen him in days."

Donovan moved to a nearby closet door, threw it open, found only a neat row of blouses, carefully arranged by color. An adjoining bathroom was also empty—except for the gold-and-white waitress's uniform hanging on a hook next to the shower.

Christ, Donovan thought, shifting his gaze to the foot of the bed where a pile of clothing lay. Pants, blouse, bra. He looked at the woman, hands still in the air, tears rolling off her chin onto her bottom-heavy breasts.

Was this who they'd seen in the doorway? The recipient of Marilyn Polanski's kiss?

Donovan heard a noise and spun. Al Cleveland in the hallway. Cleveland's eyes immediately went to the half-naked woman on the bed. "Second floor's clear. No sign of him anywhere."

"Son of a bitch," Donovan said, then jabbed the call button on the radio clipped to his belt. "Sidney. Give me some good news."

The radio crackled in response. "Sorry, Jack. Basement's clear. Same with the first floor. We got bupkis."

38

Marilyn Polanski was refusing to cooperate.

Sure, she told them, Luther had gotten into some trouble when he was younger, but he was a good boy, sucked in by the wrong crowd. He'd done his time and he was clean now—just ask his parole officer. So if they wanted any help from her, forget it. She'd said all she was going to say.

Her girlfriend, Barbara Watkins, a beautician who had met Marilyn at the Cuts & Curls Beauty Salon just three weeks earlier, knew less about Luther than they did.

Sniffing back tears, she told them she was humiliated and embarrassed by this whole situation and was seriously considering a lawsuit against the ATF, the Treasury Department, and the Attorney General's Office.

It was all background noise to Donovan, a jumble of high-pitched voices drifting in his general direction as he stepped into Luther's bedroom for a closer look around.

The room had been seized by a severe case of arrested development. Next to the baseball memorabilia on the brick and plywood shelves were two Monsters of Hollywood models of Dracula and the Mummy. Next to them, a camouflage-garbed G.I. Joe was twisted strategically to suggest doggy-style sex with the Barbie doll beneath it.

A Polaroid camera sat on the dresser. Pulling open the top drawer, Donovan found socks and boxers, all neatly stacked and folded. There was a precise, anal-retentive feel to the arrangement, and judging by the un-made bed and the clothes strewn on the closet floor, Luther wasn't the culprit. Twenty-eight years old and Mommy was still doing his laundry.

Donovan formed an image of him in his mind: a huge, muscle-bound galoot with limited brainpower and an overbearing mother. A grown man trapped in adolescence who liked to think he was independent, but could be twisted and manipulated as easily as the G.I. Joe on his shelf.

He was the perfect target for a guy like Gunderson.

Donovan could see them in the prison yard, Luther bench-pressing an easy two hundred, Gunderson spotting, sucking on a Marlboro as he worked Luther like a hungry politician, recruiting him for the cause—whatever that might be. The image was so clear in Donovan's brain that he had to wonder where it was coming from.

Earlier, in Reed's office, he had pictured Gunderson sprawled in Reed's living room watching TV. But now that he thought about it, when he *really* concentrated on the moment, he wasn't quite sure he'd seen Gunderson at all. The guy had been there, all right, but he was little more than a gesture of the hand, a crossing of legs, a reflection in a window.

It almost felt as if these images were coming from Gunderson himself.

Like . . . memories.

"Find anything?"

Donovan looked up from the drawer. Waxman stood in the doorway.

"Luther has little sea horses on his boxers."

"Cute," Waxman said, stepping into the room. "The Dynamic Dykes ain't giving us squat. Cleveland and Payne volunteered to sit on the house, but I don't think Mama's little troublemaker'll be coming home anytime soon."

"What about his file? We need that list of known associates."

"Danville Correctional is faxing it to the command center, same for the CPD." Waxman frowned and nodded to the open drawer. "What's that?"

Donovan followed his gaze and found a corner of white plastic peeking up from beneath the edge of the drawer liner. He pulled the liner aside to reveal at least a dozen Polaroids lying facedown at the bottom of the drawer.

Gathering them up, he thought about the photo of Jessie he'd found in the tunnels. His stomach tightened as he turned them over in his hand.

The first one featured a girl of about twenty, naked and smiling at the camera, her legs parted in invitation. She was in this room, sprawled on Luther's bed. A defect in the emulsion made it impossible to identify her, but the next photo left no doubt about who she was.

This time she had a hand between her legs, playing with herself, as the other hand hooked a finger at the camera, beckoning to the photographer.

It was Sara Gunderson.

The third photo introduced a new player to the scene, Luther Polanski in all his glory, standing next to Sara with an erection so large it nearly dwarfed her face. She was smiling up at him, mouth slightly open.

The fourth and fifth photos showed Sara engaged in the inevitable, and thoroughly enjoying herself. Then they were both on the bed, Luther taking her in various positions as the photographer snapped away, getting it all down for the scrapbook.

"Energetic little minx," Waxman said, moving in for a closer look. "Any guesses who's manning the camera?"

Donovan didn't have to guess. He *knew* who it was, could feel it. Could see it plainly in the part of his brain that seemed to be reserved for Gunderson's point of view. He felt the weight of the camera in his hands, heard the familiar *click-wrrrr* as each new Polaroid slid out of the box. Voices echoed in his head, the faint sounds of sex, the grunts and groans of intense pleasure.

Then he was there in the room with them, watching them writhe on the bed, legs wide, hips thrusting, Sara looking over Luther's shoulder, looking straight into the camera, sweat glistening on her forehead, lips twisted into a smile as she slowly mouthed the words *I . . . love . . . you . . .*

"Jack?"

Donovan blinked. Looked at Waxman.

Waxman was frowning again. "Thought I lost you there for a minute. You okay?"

No, Donovan almost told him, I'm very far from okay. Something strange is brewing in your old buddy's brain.

But he held back, knowing that Waxman's reaction was bound to be less than sympathetic. Sucking in a breath, he returned his attention to the Polaroids.

The next couple shots showed more of the same, culminating in the expected conclusion. Then the scene shifted.

The last three photos were part of the set they'd found in Gunderson's train car: typical tourist shots of Sara standing in front of the Lake Point Lighthouse.

The final photo featured all three of them smiling for the camera, Sara, Luther, and Gunderson, arm in arm, taken by an unknown photographer.

Donovan stared at Luther's image for a long moment, then shifted his gaze to the camera atop the dresser. He'd lay odds it was the same one used to snap Jessie's picture. Which meant that Luther and Gunderson had been in contact since the kidnapping.

"He's the link, Sidney. He knows where she's buried."

"You don't have to convince me," Waxman said.

39

Wake up, Jessie.
Jessie . . . wake uhhh-up.
. . . Jessie?

Jessie opened her eyes, stared into the darkness. Every time she drifted away like that it got harder and harder to come back. Sleep always tugged at her, dragging her eyelids shut, making it soooo easy to give up and let the dreams take over.

This last time, she and Lisa Simpson had been playing hopscotch on the sidewalk in front of Lisa's house, while Bart watched them from an upstairs window. Jessie had felt uncomfortable under Bart's gaze, but Lisa had told her not to sweat it.

"He's just jealous," she'd said. "Nobody wants *his* key chain."

Then the angel called to her and Jessie woke up.

She lay there, thinking of the dream, feeling the angel's warmth soak through her body and shield her from the cold of the box.

Without the angel she'd be dead. Jessie was sure of it.

Her protector. Her savior. That's what the angel was. Always pulling her back from the brink whenever she drifted off too far. Because if she drifted off too far, she'd never come back.

Ever.

At first, the angel was nothing but a voice. A sweet, melodic whisper that filled her dreams, telling her not to give up. Help was coming.

"I know it looks bad," the angel sang, "but the glass is half full, Jessie. That's something you always have to remember. You're Jessie Glass-Half-Full."

The voice grew stronger over time, louder, but no less melodic. A sweetness that soothed the soul.

But this time, it was more than just a voice. Jessie had seen a face to go with it.

She was playing with Lisa, worrying about Bart, when the sky grew dark and a full moon lit up the street and a face appeared on the side of the moon, a pale but beautiful young woman with melancholy eyes.

Wake up, Jessie.

Jessie . . . wake uhhh-up.

Jessie had stared at her, thinking, I've seen you before. Where have I seen you?

Then her eyes opened and the face was gone, and the darkness of the box spilled into her consciousness and she was once again alone and frightened and wanting to cry, but at the same time feeling that she *wasn't* alone, that the angel was watching over her.

Glass half full, Jessie thought. Glass half full.

Then she remembered where she'd seen the angel's face, and she knew, with irrefutable certainty, that everything would be alright. The glass wasn't just half full, it was filled to the brim and spilling over. Two, three, four glasses couldn't contain the optimism that flowed through her veins.

But as soon as she thought this, Jessie Glass-Half-Empty reared her ugly head again like some horror-movie demon who can't be killed. No matter how many times you strike her down, she rises up, over and over, stronger and more determined than ever.

Don't waste your energy, kid. Hope is for fools.

Nobody's gonna find you, not way down here. There's only so much oxygen in those tanks and sooner or later it'll all be gone and then what are you gonna do? Huh?

You're gonna die, that's what.

Die, die, die.

Hell . . . you're already dead.

40

Donovan and Waxman were coming out of Luther's bedroom when Darcy Payne approached, a sour look on her face. She nodded toward the open front door. "We've got company."

A government-issue sedan sat outside, a quartet of suits emerging from it. In the lead were Alan Doyle, Donovan's immediate superior, and Joe Robledo, head of the local Field Division. Robledo rarely left his desk, and his presence here was nothing but bad news.

"Oh, Jesus," Donovan said, thinking of Jessie.

"Easy, Jack," Waxman said. "It's not what you think. I called them."

Donovan turned. "You?"

"We've been keeping the lines open ever since you went off the bridge. They insisted."

It was a standard enough request, but bypassing Donovan was a blatant breach of protocol. Donovan was the task force leader.

Waxman raised his hands in defense. "You didn't have time for their bullshit, remember?"

Not then and not now, Donovan thought. But for Waxman to go behind his back like this was disconcerting at best. How much had he told them?

Donovan felt like a bug under a magnifying lens, and the heat was rising.

Sensing his discomfort, Waxman nodded toward the approaching quartet. The two in the rear were unknowns, probably from Washington. "They just want to talk," Waxman said. "Get a reading on the situation."

"Sure," Donovan told him. "That's why they came all the way out here. To talk."

Robledo was the spokesman, and like many agents at his level of command, he was an officious, smarmy prick. "First, Jack, let me say how sorry we are about this whole situation."

It was clear to Donovan that they already thought Jessie was a lost cause. They'd never admit this, of course, not even to each other, but it was in their eyes, and in the tone of their voices. The twenty-four hour mark had officially passed, and everyone knew what that meant.

Donovan resented them for it.

No, scratch that.

He wanted to *hurt* them.

They stood in Marilyn Polanski's kitchen, the five of them, away from the civilians and Donovan's team. The two unknowns had been introduced as Crow and Panitch—both, as Donovan had suspected, from D.C. They looked like twins, with their close-cropped haircuts and charcoal gray suits. Pursuant to departmental mandate, they oozed superiority.

"And I assure you," Robledo went on, "we aren't here to muck up this investigation."

Muck? Donovan thought. Who the hell says muck? "Then why *are* you here?"

Doyle took his turn. "We've given you a lot of leeway, Jack. Let you run with the ball even when there was a clear conflict of interest."

"Conflict of interest?" Donovan said, his voice rising. "Is that what you're calling this?"

Now Crow chimed in. "With all due respect, Agent Donovan, there's no need to be argumentative."

Donovan turned. "How's this for argumentative," he said. "Fuck you."

Then he lost control.

Grabbing Crow by the lapels, he jerked him forward. Crow's eyes got big and the others were on top of Donovan in a flash, hands locking onto his arms, dragging him toward a chair, Robledo shouting, "Whoa! Whoa! Whoa!" as Donovan struggled to break free.

They sat him down, hard, the chair groaning beneath him, and somewhere in that moment he found his balance and immediately stopped struggling.

"Alright, alright!" he said. "I'm okay."

They released him, breathing hard, suits rumpled, ties askew.

Crow carefully straightened his jacket, then cleared his throat. "Feeling better now?"

Donovan looked up at him. "Why don't you ask Sidney? He seems to have pretty good handle on my state of mind."

Quick glances around the room.

"I think you've already answered any questions we might have," Crow said.

"What's that supposed to mean?"

Now Panitch spoke up, delivering what sounded like a well-rehearsed speech. "The bureau has specific standards and procedures, Agent Donovan, and you've violated a number of them. First, you assault a suspect, then a police officer, then you drive so recklessly you almost get yourself killed—"

Not almost, Donovan thought.

"—and now you attack a superior officer. We understand that you're under a lot of stress. Anyone in your position would be—which is why we're willing to overlook a few transgressions. But policy clearly dictates that we do what we should have done hours ago and remove you from this case."

"In short," Crow said, delivering the final, unnecessary blow, "you're relieved of your command until further notice."

The four men braced themselves for Donovan's reaction, but he surprised them by not reacting at all. He just sat there, numb.

So there it was.

He'd known this was coming. Had known it even before he saw them getting out of their car. Before Waxman had taken it upon himself to call them.

And none of it mattered.

Did they really think that relieving him of his command would make a difference? He was a father first, a federal agent second—a sentiment he might not have agreed with a couple of months ago. Now, there was no doubt about it, and shunting him aside would not keep him from doing what had to be done.

"I know this is tough," Doyle said, putting a hand on Donovan's shoulder, face full of brotherly concern. "Nobody likes to do this to a fellow agent. But you've got to have faith in us. We have people coming in from all over the country to help us find your daughter. You're not alone by any stretch of—"

"Shut up, Alan," Donovan said. "Do us all a favor and just shut the fuck up."

He was on the sidewalk and halfway to the car when Waxman caught up to him. "Jack, wait."

"I've got nothing to say to you, Sidney."

"You think I wanted this?"

"I don't know *what* to think," Donovan said, picking up speed. "Congratulations on your new command."

"Come on, Jack, that isn't fair and you know it."

Donovan stopped, turned. "Fuck fair, Sidney. Who gives a damn about fair?" He could feel the heat rising in his cheeks. "My daughter's missing and all these chowderheads care about are a couple of bullshit procedural violations."

"They're just following protocol."

"You think that makes it go down any smoother? I don't exactly get off on being looked at like I'm some kind of freak."

"What the hell are you talking about?"

"I'm sure you all got a nice big laugh over Wacky Jacky's adventures on the other side."

"Jesus Christ," Waxman said. "You think I'm that big of a fool? Tell 'em something like that and they'll be sizing us *both* up for straitjackets."

Donovan glared at him, then continued toward the car.

Waxman moved after him. "Jack, come on."

Donovan reached the driver's door, threw it open, and climbed in.

Waxman caught it before he could close it. "What do you want from me? You want me to say I'm sorry? Then I'm sorry."

Donovan looked up at him. "Screw the apologies."

"What, then?"

"It's simple. Either you bend a few of their precious rules and work with me, or you waste another twenty-four hours getting jerked off by a bunch of desk jockeys who couldn't find their asses in a bathtub with two flashlights and a pair of goggles." He started the engine. "The choice is yours."

Waxman sighed. Donovan knew he was considering the effect this might have on his career, but he wasn't sure what the problem was. This was about Jessie. Either you do the right thing or you don't.

He was about to give up on him when Waxman sighed again and said, "I suppose you have some plan of action in mind?"

Donovan killed the engine. "Don't I always?"

41

"Mr. Nemo?"

The guy behind the glass was either a spic or a Jew, Nemo couldn't figure which. He was short, had a faggy little goatee and wire-rim glasses. When Nemo took a closer look, he'd swear there was a bit of slant to the eyes behind them.

The guy was a mutt, no doubt about it, but that didn't matter. Nemo wouldn't trust him if he was Idaho white.

It was close to 6 p.m. on Nemo's second day in custody and they were sitting in the reception room of the U.S. marshals' lockup, where he'd been staying ever since that crazy motherfucker Donovan had stuck a gun up his nose.

The reception room wasn't particularly receptive—a couple rows of cubbyholes that faced each other with a giant window of safety glass between them. Prisoner and visitor spoke over phones, a scene Nemo had watched at least a hundred different times on television—and replayed a few himself.

The guy behind the glass was waiting for a response. When he didn't get one, he said, "You are Robert Nemo, aren't you?"

"You asked for me, didn't you?"

"Uh, yes. Yes, I did."

"So who the fuck else would I be?" Nemo had no patience for retards.

The guy took a business card from his breast pocket and pressed it up against the glass. "Simon Escalante," he said. "Your attorney?"

Nemo squinted at the card, saw the name above the words ASST. FEDERAL PUBLIC DEFENDER, and groaned inwardly, thinking, now I'm fucked. Another shit-fer-brains mouthpiece who couldn't make it in the real world. The last public defender he'd had managed to get him five years in stir.

Escalante returned the card to his pocket. "You did request an attorney, didn't you?"

"Yeah," Nemo said with a decided lack of enthusiasm. "I just didn't think anyone was listening."

"Guess you were wrong about that. I may have some good news for you."

"Oh?" Nemo figured this probably meant he'd get chocolate pudding on his dinner tray tonight, because on every other level he was about as fucked as you can get. Not even the late great Johnnie Cochran could change that.

"Do you know anything about federal criminal law, Mr. Nemo?"

"What's to know?" Nemo said. The way he saw it, the only difference between a state and a federal rap was the color of your jumpsuit. The bunks in the marshals' lockup were just as uncomfortable, and you still had to watch your backside in the showers.

"Title Eighteen, Section Five, of the criminal code prohibits holding a suspect in custody longer than twenty-four hours," Escalante said. "Seems the Feds dumped you in here, then promptly forgot about you. That, coupled with the testimony of two eyewitnesses who say they saw you grievously manhandled by federal agents, makes a compelling case for your immediate release."

Nemo stared at him. Somebody had actually seen those assholes attack him in the alley? "You gotta be shittin' me."

"I shit you not," Escalante said, and smiled. "I've asked the court for a hearing, and I expect to be in front of a judge within ten minutes."

"Isn't it a little late for court?"

"This is an emergency situation. All I need is your signature."

"Signature?" Nemo said, balking. "I'm not signing any friggin' confession, if that's what you're thinking. Nice try, asshole."

"Please, Mr. Nemo, I'm on your side. And if I have anything to say about it, there won't be a single confession in your future. What I need you to sign is a waiver."

"What the hell's a waiver?"

"A simple document that says you waive your right to appear in court this evening."

Nemo frowned. "Why would I want to do that?"

"Because," Escalante said, "if you insist on being present for the hearing, the marshal will have to prep you for delivery to the courtroom and delay the proceedings for an indeterminate amount of time. If it takes too long, the judge may postpone until a later date—and I'd like to get you out of here as soon as possible."

The guy was still smiling. Nemo studied him a moment, thinking there was something wrong with this picture. He was up for bank robbery, aggravated assault, and multiple murder charges. And hadn't the Feds just told him they considered him some kind of homegrown terrorist?

Nemo might not know much about federal law, but he'd watched enough Fox News to know that thanks to a bunch of towel-heads on crack, the Feds routinely locked up terrorism suspects and threw away the key—all without charges or even the benefit of some retard lawyer. So what made Robert Edward Nemo so friggin' special?

Escalante said, "You're probably a little wary, Mr. Nemo, and I can understand that. But it turns out the Feds have made some major mistakes in handling this case and the lead investigator has just been relieved of his command."

"What?" Nemo wasn't sure he'd heard him right. "Jackass Donovan?"

"I believe his legal name is John," Escalante said.

Yessss, Nemo thought, feeling a sudden surge of triumph. Make that motherfucker skip recess and stand in a corner.

"Since Agent Donovan is the only eyewitness who can connect you to the Northland First and Trust incident, the Department of Justice is in a bit of a bind."

Holy Jesus. The ski masks. Nobody but Donovan had seen him without that sweaty-assed ski mask. Thank yoooou, Luther, you big, ugly bastard. The masks had been his idea.

"Needless to say," Escalante continued, "they're scrambling to cover their asses."

"Meaning what?"

"They're fighting very hard to keep you in custody. Fortunately, the law's on our side. I don't think I'll have much trouble convincing the judge to cut you loose."

"What about the MP5?" Nemo said.

"The what?"

"The weapon they found."

"Ahh," Escalante said, nodding. "It seems their warrant only covered you and not Ms. Devito's apartment. Any weapons they recovered were the fruits of an illegal search and, as such, can no longer be used as evidence against you."

"Halle-fuckin-lujah," Nemo said.

"Don't start celebrating too soon," Escalante warned. "You're not completely out of the woods. If the Feds can put together a strong enough case, you could be back in here as early as tomorrow afternoon."

Jeez, Nemo thought, that doesn't leave much of a window. If these idiots were stupid enough to let him out, he didn't plan on giving them a chance to take it back.

One of the deputies had told him about Alex last night. How the cops had shot him down in cold blood, the stupid twit. That was the thing about Alex. Always letting his ego get the better of him, especially after Sara took her nosedive. Alex had been out of control.

Nemo, on the other hand, was only interested in two things: cash and pussy. And he'd be damned if he'd wind up facedown in a rat-infested train yard all because some rich bitch got her brain fried.

Instead, he'd do what he should have done two months ago and hop a bus to Ensenada. Plenty of pussy there. All those tight little Mexican *chochos*.

Caliente, baby, *caliente.*

Now all he needed was cash.

"Well, Mr. Nemo?"

Escalante was unfolding a sheet of paper with official-looking writing all over it. Nemo stared at it, thinking, *the guy's serious. This is the real thing.*

"You tell these crank-yankers to get me a pen," he said, "and I'll sign whatever you want."

You think he swallowed it?" Donovan asked.

"Like a twenty-dollar whore," Waxman said, his voice distorted over the cell line. "He's being processed as we speak."

"And you're sure he didn't recognize Franky?"

"Even *I* barely recognized him. Put on a fake beard, glasses, did a whole number on the moron. Cited some bullshit criminal code and even made him sign a waiver—you believe that?" Waxman laughed. "This thing pans out, we'll have to give Franky another trophy."

"Or a ticket to Hollywood," Donovan said.

Despite what Waxman thought, Bobby Nemo was no moron. If they had simply let him go, he was bound to be suspicious, and sending the Chameleon in with an appropriately long-winded cover story was designed to allay those suspicions.

They had discussed coming down hard on Nemo, the way they had before, but if it backfired, if Nemo clammed up this time, then where would they be? Better to make him think he was in control rather than take it from him.

And the next step was key.

Donovan just hoped it would work.

He sat behind the wheel of his sedan, parked across the street from the U.S. Marshals Office, which occupied the lower floor of the federal building. It was just past 7:30 p.m., and the streetlight above his car was burnt out, offering him an extra layer of darkness as protection.

"You sure you don't want me along?" Waxman asked.

"I can manage." It would be hours before the brass figured out what they were up to, but Donovan had decided it was best to err on the side of caution and handle the surveillance duties solo while Waxman played lead agent.

"What about the woman? You talk to her?"

"She's on board," Donovan said. "Not that she's happy about it, but she'll come through."

"She'd better or we're screwed."

"We're screwed no matter how you look at it," Donovan said, then clicked off.

Once word got upstairs that Nemo had been released, about two tons of shit would hit the fan, but neither Donovan nor Waxman had bothered to think that far ahead. They'd weather that storm when it blew in.

Donovan tapped his fingers on the wheel, feeling the jumpiness in his legs, as if an alien life force had crawled into his body and was struggling to take control. His head had started to throb again and he wished he had a couple of Advil and a nice cold Coke to wash them down.

Ten long minutes later, the lobby doors of the federal building swung open and Bobby Nemo and a little guy with a goatee emerged. The Chameleon. Franky Garcia. And Waxman was right, he was barely recognizable.

Garcia handed Nemo a business card along with a few bucks in cash, then shook his hand and headed off toward the parking lot. Nemo kept his eyes on him a moment, then glanced around as if he suspected some-one might be watching. Then, turning his attention to the street, he waved a hand at an approaching cab.

The cab sliced across a couple lanes of traffic and pulled to the curb. Nemo jumped in the back, made a gesture, and the cab took off again, tooting its horn as it merged back into traffic.

Here we go, Donovan thought, then started his engine and pulled out.

42

Nemo told the driver to drop him off near the alley behind the Pussy Palace, a narrow strip of urine-streaked asphalt that led to the back-stage door. He'd been tempted to have the guy take him straight to the Greyhound station, but there were a couple of snags in that plan.

First, he was horny as all hell. As much as he'd like to save it up for the Mexican hotties, he'd never had a lot of willpower when it came to women. His five-year drought at Danville had been pure torture (he'd never fancied himself a butt pilot), and he'd been making up for it ever since. As far as Nemo was concerned, a day without tang was like a day without sunshine.

Second, the only cash he had on him was the twenty bucks Escalante had given him, and half of that went for the cab. With what was left, he could probably afford a decent sub sandwich and a soda. If he counted pennies.

That was where Carla came in.

Not only was she a Grade A piece of ass, the twenty or so grand he'd managed to pocket during the Northland First & Trust heist was stashed in her apartment.

She didn't know this, of course. Nobody did. Nemo figured if the Feds had found it, either Donovan or the lawyer would've mentioned it, but neither had.

After Tina had crashed the news van, he'd always felt a little sick about leaving all that bank loot behind. But when you're running from the cops, dragging a couple of fifty-pound duffel bags behind you is usually a bad idea. Fortunately, he'd had the foresight to fill his pockets in the vault.

Luther had seen him, shaking his head in disgust. "When Alex finds out, he won't like it."

"He's not gonna find out, is he?"

"Not from me," Luther said. "But Alex has the power. Knows all, sees all. And I think maybe Sara's got it, too."

Nemo looked at him, continuing to stuff his pockets. Luther was definitely a dim bulb in a dark room. "What Alex has is a smooth line that only suckers like you fall for," Nemo said. "As for Sara, don't get me started. She's got rich relatives and a nice ass. That's about it."

Luther scowled at him then. Nemo knew the dimwit had tapped Sara's ass a couple times himself, knew that he and Alex and Sara had a freaky little threesome thing going on, but that had been more about control than anything else. Alex playing puppet master, Sara the willing apprentice. Luther was either too stupid or too horny to realize he was being managed.

Nemo was his own man, thank you, and Alex or no Alex, he figured it never hurt to carry some insurance. Unfortunately, his pockets could only fit so much.

Two days after he'd moved in with Carla, he had removed her toilet tank, punched a hole in the wall behind it, stuffed the cash inside, and replaced the tank. Nice and neat. His own personal bank vault.

Now all he had to do was make a withdrawal.

Escalante had told him that no charges were brought against Carla, that the Feds had released her shortly after he was taken into custody. He supposed he could just head over to her apartment and grab his stash, but why not take a few minutes for a proper goodbye? After a couple days in stir, he figured he deserved it.

He stepped over a fresh stream of urine and crossed the alley to the backstage door. Faded letters across it read TALENT ONLY. He pounded on the door and waited. A moment later, it creaked open and music spilled out, a guy in leather pants frowning at him. "What the fuck you want?"

"I'm looking for Carla."

Leather Boy nodded toward the door and started to pull it shut. "Read the sign, asshole."

Nemo caught the door with his right hand. "I forgot my glasses."

"Look, you wanna see the show, go around front like everybody el—"

Nemo swung his left hand up between the guy's legs and grabbed his balls, applying just enough pressure to send a clear message.

"Carla," he said. "She here or not?"

Leather Boy's eyes bulged, his whole body going stiff. You could almost see his brain working, trying to figure out how to extricate himself from this delicate situation without getting his nads crushed. "Uhhh," he said involuntarily.

Nemo applied more pressure. "What was that? I didn't hear you."

"S-she won't be in tonight," Leather Boy croaked. "Called and said something came up."

"She say what that something was?"

Leather Boy's face had lost all color. He looked and sounded like a guy passing a gallstone. "That's all I know, man. I swear."

Nemo released him and Leather Boy stumbled back, gasping, grabbing his package to make sure everything was still in one piece. "Asshole," he muttered.

"Strike two," Nemo said, then stepped inside, grabbing him by the shirt. An imitation-silk number.

He spun the guy around and slammed him against a wall, pinning him there. "Now give me twenty bucks. I need cab fare."

When the knock came on the door, Carla Devito sucked in a breath and let it out again. She hadn't been this nervous since she'd turned her first trick.

Not that Bobby made her nervous. He had a temper, sure, but he could be tamed the way most men could, a lesson Carla had learned when she was thirteen years old.

It was the situation that was getting to her. The Fed showing up at her doorstep, telling her what a badass Bobby was—like that was news— saying she'd better cooperate or she'd be facing charges of obstruction and harboring a fugitive and God knows what else.

The Fed had looked sick, all pale and stuff, with dark, crazy-looking eyes. He was one of the ones who'd come busting in the day before, the one in charge, and Carla didn't doubt he meant business.

He'd told her that Bobby was getting released from jail and would probably come knocking before the night was over. And, sure enough, here Bobby was, standing at her door, looking kind of small and distorted through the peephole, but still sexy as hell.

Carla sucked in another breath, then flipped the latch and yanked the door open, hoping she could pull this off, knowing she had to, because jail was not an option.

"Ohhh, my God," she said, putting it on extra thick.

Bobby smiled, looking her over. She wore a tight black T-shirt and a tiny lavender thong, and he seemed to like what he saw. "Hey, baby."

"Oh my God," she repeated, then threw her arms around him and pushed her face into his. She found his mouth and sucked his tongue between her lips, pressing up against him, feeling his hands crawl over her, feeling him grow hard against her thigh.

Pulling him inside, she shut the door. "They told me I'd never see you again."

"I ain't no ghost," Bobby said.

And then she had his pants undone and his zipper down and Bobby's beast in her mouth, Bobby moaning, "Oh, yeah, baby," and before she knew it, they were on the floor, Bobby yanking the thong aside, using the Beast like a weapon, impaling her, radiating heat like she'd never felt it before, radiating it right up into her brain. The pressure built and built and *boom*, there it was, firecracker number one, and then *boom,* firecracker number two, followed by a whole series of firecrackers popping off inside her head.

But deep down, all she could think about was how nervous she was and how sad she felt, because she was about to betray the best damn thing she'd ever had.

I gotta piss," Bobby said.

They were in bed now, round three and counting, the sheets all torn up and soaked with sweat. Feeling both whipped and wired, Carla realized that this was her cue.

"Do it in the shower," she said, the nerves coming back, a knuckle of tension in her stomach.

Bobby frowned at her. "What the hell for?"

"Toilet's broke."

He got up on his elbows. "What do you mean, it's broke? Broke how?"

Carla hesitated, wondering again if she could pull this off. "There's something I gotta tell you, Bobby. Something bad."

And then he was sitting upright, the frown deeper, his eyes starting to cloud. All of a sudden she wanted to dump this whole scam and tell him the truth. But that would mean jail time, and despite her past, Carla had never done a day of jail in her life. Not one.

Sensing her hesitation, Bobby was out of bed before she could say anything more, crossing toward the bathroom, his beautiful bare ass flexing as he walked.

The moment he stepped through the doorway, he made a sound, something guttural and unpleasant, and she knew he was staring at the hole in the wall—the hole that had been hidden by the toilet tank that now sat off to the side—the hole she hadn't known about until she'd come home last night and found it just like the Feds had left it: empty.

When she'd gone to pee, she'd had to squat over the shower drain like some third world orphan. Her landlord was missing in action and she sure as hell didn't know how to put a toilet back together. Then the Fed showed up and told her what was what. Now all she wanted to do was crawl under the bedsheets and stay there.

When Bobby came out of the bathroom, he had a look on his face she'd never seen before. A heat in his eyes that had nothing to do with sex or desire. "Where the fuck is my money, bitch?"

Bobby may not have made her nervous, but now he was scaring her, so much so that all the details of the story she'd been rehearsing suddenly vacated her brain.

His skin was two shades darker, a deep crimson stain spreading all the way down to the Beast, which seemed to be twitching with an anger all its own.

He moved toward the bed, hands grabbing for her, and Carla tried desperately to remember the name the Fed had told her to use, knowing that if she blew this, jail would be the least of her worries.

For some reason an image of Superboy popped into her head, the one from TV—Superboy and his cute bald friend—just as Bobby hooked her forearm and yanked her toward him.

"Luther!" she shouted, suddenly remembering.

The name must've meant something to him, because he stopped just short of hitting her, the heat in his eyes replaced by bewilderment. "What?"

"He was here . . . a little while ago. Pushed his way in, threatened to hurt me." She hoped she was getting this right. "I wanted to tell you right away, but I was scared."

"Are you fucking kidding me?" Bobby shook his head as if he were trying to clear some cobwebs from his brain. "A big guy? Scar on his arm?"

"That's the one," Carla told him. "He took it. He took your money. Said you wouldn't need it where you're going."

"Motherfucker," Bobby muttered, releasing his grip on her arm. *"Muuu-ther-fuuucker."*

In that moment, Carla began to believe in the devil, because he was surely lurking behind Bobby's eyes. She was sitting upright, as naked as a newborn, and despite spending a large portion of her life in this state, she suddenly felt exposed and vulnerable. The urge to blurt out the truth washed over her again.

You stupid jerk, she wanted to tell him, the first place they look is the behind the toilet. They found your stash ten minutes after they hauled us out of here.

But she resisted. Hard.

Keep going, she told herself. Finish what you started.

"There's more," she said. "I-I think the cops are after him. He said something about getting out of the city. That's why he wanted your money."

"Sonofabitch." Bobby said. He searched the floor, then grabbed his pants and jerked them on. "That fucker is toast."

"He's leaving *town,* Bobby. How you gonna find him?"

"I don't know if you noticed, cupcake, but Luther ain't exactly a wattage hog when it comes to brainpower." He slipped his shirt on, started buttoning it. "He's the kind of guy always needs somebody to tie his shoes for him. And if the cops are after him, I've got a pretty good idea where he'll go."

"Where?"

Bobby glared at her. "Why do you care? You fuck him or something? Looking for a repeat performance?"

"Jesus, Bobby, what do you think I am?" They both knew the answer to that, but that was beside the point. "I'm just curious, is all."

Bobby snorted, shoving his feet into his shoes. "Curiosity's overrated," he said, then snatched her car keys off the dresser and headed for the bedroom door.

"You're taking my car?"

"Don't worry, you'll get it back."

"And what am *I* supposed to do?"

Bobby paused in the doorway and looked at her, his gaze sliding over her body. "You just keep shaking those tits, baby. That's what you're good at."

43

When he heard the front door slam, Donovan pulled his earpiece out and shut off the receiver. It had been a while since he'd done his own wire work. He usually let the techs handle the job. Yet, despite his lack of practice, the signal had come in crisp and clear. Especially the transmitter in Carla's bedroom.

He had hoped Carla would be able to draw Nemo out a bit more, get him talking about Luther's whereabouts, but at least the bastard was pissed off and on the move. That's all that really mattered.

Parked across from Carla's apartment house, a newly renovated, twenty-story pile of glass and stucco, Donovan kept his gaze on the underground parking ramp, waiting for Nemo to ride the elevator to the garage. His concentration, however, was wavering. The headache that had started earlier had blossomed into a full-fledged brain-banger, and his recently recharged batteries were steadily draining.

Craving a cigarette, he reached into his coat pocket and brought out a pack of Marlboros. The wrapper was halfway off before he realized what he was doing.

A faint whisper of voices skittered through his brain like rustling leaves.

He'd never smoked a day in his life.

Suddenly uneasy, he flashed back to the deli and the man in the gray suit who'd left his cigarettes behind. He remembered staring at the red-and-white box, feeling an odd kind of attraction to it.

But when had he picked it up? And why?

Not only had he never smoked, cigarettes disgusted him. He hated the smell, the smoke, the sickness they caused. He was the poster boy for a cigarette-free lifestyle.

Yet here he sat, holding a pilfered pack of Marlboros, feeling the urge to shake one out and fire it up. The thought of taking smoke into his lungs soothed him, even made the pounding in his head subside for a brief but welcome moment.

Then the headache was back with a vengeance, accompanied by a sick, sinking feeling in the pit of his stomach.

What was happening to him?

Before he could even try to make sense of it, Carla Devito's emerald green Honda Del Sol rolled up the parking ramp and onto the street, Bobby Nemo behind the wheel.

Snap out of it, Jack. Time to move.

Tossing the box and all of the questions it raised aside, Donovan started the engine, then waited for Nemo to turn a corner before pulling out after him.

He was still craving a cigarette when they reached the expressway.

Fifty miles south, however, a cigarette was the last thing on Donovan's mind.

All he could think about was the pain.

He hadn't had a migraine since he was twelve years old, a condition his doctor had insisted was brought on by childhood anxieties, yet this head-banger certainly qualified as one. His skull felt as if it might burst apart at any moment, unable to contain the throbbing, swollen mass that used to be his brain.

It was raining again, coming down light, but threatening to get nasty. The view beyond his windshield was a blur of taillights in the darkness, the Del Sol's distinguishable only because of their lower proximity to the road. Half-blinded by pain, he did his best to keep them in sight while maintaining a discreet distance from the car, careful not to tip Nemo to the tail.

Five minutes later, Nemo took the Fredrickville turnoff, splashed through a fresh puddle of rain that had formed at the bottom of the ramp, then headed west toward the battle-scarred signs that advertised Motel Row.

Fredrickville was a small, forgotten town that wore its failed economy on tattered storefronts and pockmarked streets. Motel Row was no exception. Three motels lined a narrow road just off the expressway, a pathetic, ramshackle collection of flophouses located within a few hundred yards of each other, looking more like tenement homes than overnight lodging.

Despite their proximity to the main thoroughfare, travelers tended to stay away, leaving the sagging mattresses and dingy sheets to the handful of drug addicts, prostitutes, and petty criminals who chose anonymity over hygiene.

Donovan watched through his haze of pain as the Del Sol rolled past the first two motels and pulled into the parking lot of the third, the Wayfarer Inn.

Pulling into a gas station, which was apparently closed for the night, Donovan doused the headlights, but kept his wipers going. Popping open the glove box, he grabbed his field glasses and trained them on the Del Sol as it angled into a slot near the motel's front office. The magnified image intensified his headache, sending a wave of nausea through him.

Lowering the glasses, he closed his eyes, wondering again what was happening to him.

Was it fatigue? Hunger?

Or was there something more sinister at work?

He knew he should open his eyes and concentrate on Nemo, but keeping them shut seemed to soothe the pounding in his skull. A moment of sleep wouldn't hurt would it? Just enough to feed the migraine and recharge the double A's.

Feeling himself about to slip away, he snapped his eyes open.

Concentrate, Jack. Think about Luther. He's your only link to Jessie.

Donovan raised the glasses again. The Del Sol's door flew open and Nemo climbed out, a deep scowl on his face. He crossed toward the office, which was encased in battle-scarred glass and lit up by harsh fluorescent light.

Yanking the lobby door open, Nemo approached an overweight, slope-shouldered counterman in a paisley shirt, who was working on a slice of pepperoni pizza that he clearly didn't need.

Their exchange did not look friendly.

Feeling the need to get closer, Donovan set the glasses on the seat and took hold of the wheel. He was about to shift into gear when needle-sharp pains pierced his skull. A burst of hot, white light blinded him.

For a moment he saw Jessie, lying in the coffin—not the Polaroid version, but a live, moving rendition—looking up at him with terrified eyes as the lid of the coffin slammed shut, hiding her from view.

He cried out her name as a fresh burst of pain assaulted his senses like the sudden and unexpected flash of a camera bulb.

Then it was dark.

44

When the knock came on the door, Luther Dwayne Polanski rolled off the bed and grabbed the Smith from atop the nightstand. It wasn't much of a weapon, just a funky old spare Charlie had kept in a drawer under the counter in case his SIG went south. He'd insisted that Luther take it.

That was the thing about Charlie. Always looking out for Luther. And his friends, too. After the bank heist, when things got too hot at Tony Reed's place, Charlie had cleared a room for Bobby, letting him stay rent-free for nearly two weeks, bringing him food and whatnot while he waited for the news stories to die down.

Funny thing was, Charlie didn't even like Bobby. Had warned Luther that he and Alex were a couple of psychos who couldn't be trusted.

"Why you hangin' around with those turds, man? You know how much trouble you're in if the Feds find out about you?"

"No reason they should," Luther had said.

"Yeah? One of these assholes gets his head in a vise, ten to one your name's the first thing pops out of his mouth."

Maybe, Luther thought. But what Charlie didn't know was that if it hadn't been for Alex, he probably wouldn't have lasted a week at Danville. In the short time their sentences had overlapped, Alex had taught him a lot about prison life and how to survive.

"Never show weakness," Alex said. "Never show fear. Take a cue from the samurai. Operate like you're already a dead man and that'll keep you alive."

After Alex was released, he kept in touch with Luther, telling him about all the plans he had, how he wanted to build his own army, make Luther his first lieutenant. Luther had liked the sound of that. It gave him hope. Something to think about other than the shithole he was living in and how much he missed his mom.

Then, when Luther got out, Alex was the first one there, waiting at the bus stop, sweet little Sara on his arm. Sara had been a gift from Alex that night, his welcome-home present. Took him places he hadn't been in six long years.

So maybe Charlie was right about Bobby, but he didn't know shit about Alex. Alex had been a true friend. Sara, too. Now, one was dead and the other one might as well be.

And Luther was on the run.

The knock came again. "Hey, Dumbo, open up." It was Charlie. Charlie always called him Dumbo. Ever since they were kids. Luther never really knew why. It wasn't like his ears were any bigger than normal. "Come on, man, I got the pizza."

Luther relaxed, stuffing the Smith into his belt. He was starving. All he'd had to eat was a half-melted candy bar that Alex had given him yesterday when he'd picked him up at the bar. He'd found it in the glove compartment of the F-150 this afternoon and scarfed it down right before he'd gone in to see Tony. He'd practically chucked it up again when the Feds tried to chase him down.

Fuckin' Feds. All he'd wanted from Tony was a little something to supplement his income, and what did it get him?

Jackass Donovan.

After he'd hopped the fence, he'd wanted to run straight home and hide in his room. But he knew the Feds would put pressure on Tony and his days of anonymity were over.

So he'd found a pay phone and called Charlie, asking him for help. Charlie, his lifelong buddy. They'd known each other since they were ten years old, back when their moms had had a little lesbo fling, and they got stuck together playing Nintendo in Charlie's room.

Charlie even let him win sometimes.

When Charlie had answered the phone, he'd sighed and said, "What'd you get yourself into this time? Don't tell me you're involved in that thing with the kid?"

"You know about that?"

"Jesus Christ, Dumbo. What'd I tell you about that psycho?"

"Alex needed my help."

"Yeah, and now he's off in la-la land and you're headed down the crapper, you big, stupid jerk."

"Jeez, Charlie, take it easy."

Charlie swore under his breath, then the phone went quiet for a long time, Luther feeling panic rise, thinking he might've been hung up on.

"Just tell me this," Charlie said finally. "You know where she is?"

"I helped him pick the spot. You remember that trip I told you about? When me and—"

"Don't tell *me*, for chrissake, tell the goddamn cops. Don't you get it? That's your out, my friend. You give her up, you're gold. She dies, forget due process. They'll fuckin' kill you."

"I don't know," Luther said. "I don't want to go back to jail."

"What're you gonna do, then? Run? You wouldn't survive ten minutes on your own."

Charlie was right. Luther wanted to keep running, but where would he go? He didn't have a clue. He'd never been real good at taking care of himself. That had always been his mom's job, and Charlie's. And Alex's.

"Get your ass out here pronto," Charlie said. "We'll figure this out together."

So here he was, locked up in this room, packing a funky old Smith for protection and wondering if he should do what Charlie had said and tell the Feds where the girl was buried. Maybe they'd cut him a break.

After all, it wasn't like he'd actually snatched her. That was Alex's thing, and Alex was dead.

The knock came on the door a third time. Loud.

"Goddammit, Dumbo. It's raining out here. Open the friggin' door."

"I'm coming," Luther said, and reached for the knob, happy to hear his friend's voice. It made him feel safe. Protected.

He pulled the door open to find Charlie standing there, pizza box in hand. He was about to break into a smile when he realized somebody else was with him, standing off to the side, the barrel of Charlie's prized SIG-Sauer pointed at his rib cage.

It was Bobby. And his eyes were blazing.

Bobby took the pizza box out of Charlie's hands. "Get inside."

Charlie complied, pushing his bulk through the doorway, forcing Luther to back up. "I told you these guys were trouble."

Luther was dumbfounded. He didn't know what to make of this. "What the fuck, Bobby? What's going on? I thought the Feds had you."

"That was then and this is now, asshole." He dropped the pizza box on the dresser, then put a hand on Charlie's back and shoved him toward the beds. There were two of them, both soft and lumpy. Unless you were too drunk to stand, getting a decent night's sleep on either one was next to impossible.

"Face down," Bobby said. "Hands in view."

Charlie did what he was told, climbing onto the bed closest to them, the box springs groaning under his weight. He kept his hands above his head, Luther watching him with his mouth hanging open, wondering how the hell Bobby had managed to get himself sprung, and what exactly the problem was.

He thought about the Smith in his belt, trying to decide whether he should go for it. Probably not a good idea. Bobby had a crazed look that made him uneasy. He'd seen that look enough to know when to tread lightly.

"What's this about, Bobby?"

Bobby turned his gaze on him. "What do you think? My money."

"Huh?" Luther had no clue what he was talking about. "How come they let you out, man? I figured you'd be locked up forever."

"I've got a better question. How'd I get tagged in the first place? You have something to do with that?"

"What?" Luther said. "Why would I do that?"

"The money," Bobby said, swinging the SIG toward him. "That a good enough reason?"

"Money? What money?"

"Cut the shit, Luther. Carla told me everything. You bust in on her like that, you think she's just gonna smile and pretend it never happened?"

"I swear to God, Bobby, I don't know what you're talking about."

Bobby swung the SIG around and shot Charlie in the left thigh. Charlie howled, grabbing the wound, blood seeping between his fingers.

"Jesus, why'd you go and do that? Charlie didn't—"

Bobby shot Charlie's right calf. Charlie screamed this time, curling up into a ball as Bobby swung the SIG around toward Luther again. "You're next, numb nuts. Give me my fuckin' money."

"I'm tellin' you, man, I don't have any money. I don't know what you're talking about."

"You're the only one saw me take it. You're the only one knew I had it. Carla tells me you bulldoze your way into her apartment for it, I got no reason to doubt her."

"She's lying," Luther said.

"Why the hell would she lie?"

"Come on, man, I-I don't even know her! I don't even know where she lives!"

"Hey, moron," Charlie groaned, staring at Bobby now, his face the color of cottage cheese. He looked like he was about to puke or pass out. "Listen to the kid. He's telling you the truth."

Bobby gestured with the SIG. "The first two weren't enough? Shut the fuck up."

Charlie winced. "It's your girlfriend, dumb ass. Don't you get it? . . . The bitch punked you."

Luther saw a flicker of doubt in Bobby's eyes, like he was thinking this over, thinking maybe it made sense. Luther thought again about the Smith stuck in his belt, wondering if he should make a move.

Charlie kept going. "She's the dancer you told Luther about, right? Probably does her fair share of hooking, too." He squeezed his eyes shut and shuddered, still leaking all over the place.

It looked like he'd pissed his pants.

"Bitch like that'll do anything for a few bucks," Charlie went on, his voice getting weaker. "You hear that, Luther? The Pussy Prince got punked by a two-bit whore."

Bobby didn't say anything, like he was still thinking it over. Maybe everything would be okay. They could call one of Charlie's paramedic connections, get him taken care of, and—

"Nice try," Bobby said. "There's just one little problem with that story." He pointed the SIG at Charlie again. "I never told her about Luther. So how the hell does she know his name?"

He pulled the trigger and the SIG coughed and the back of Charlie's head exploded. Luther felt his stomach clutch up as what was left of his lifelong friend shook like he was on one of those vibrating beds, then stopped moving altogether.

Holy Jesus.

Luther leaned over and vomited on the carpet, Bobby jumping back to avoid the spray.

"The money, asshole. Where's my goddamned money?"

Luther grabbed the dresser for support, trying to think how he was going to get out of this. He was bigger than Bobby, sure, and stronger, too, but he didn't have the stone-cold heart Bobby had, or the nerve. Or the SIG in his hand.

"Get on your knees," Bobby said.

"Huh?"

Bobby pointed the SIG at his head. "Get on your fuckin' knees. Now!"

Luther slowly sank to his knees, trying to think of something to say, some magic word that might bring Bobby back to his senses. Then a shadow fell across him, the light from the doorway blocked by someone standing in it.

"Can't leave you two alone for even a minute."

Luther looked up sharply, saw a dark figure there, rain pooling around his shoes. He couldn't make out a face. All he saw was the orange glow of a cigarette.

The voice sounded different, but the way the words were spoken was unmistakable. Impossible, but unmistakable.

". . . Alex?" Luther said.

Bobby was already spinning around, raising the SIG. The figure in the doorway stepped forward, extending his arm, then pressed the barrel of a gun against Bobby's temple and fired.

Bobby went down without a sound, blood spreading beneath him on the carpet.

Jumping to his feet, Luther stared at him in stunned disbelief. Then he looked up again, as the man with the gun took a long drag off his cigarette and stepped deeper into the room, his face finally coming into the light.

The gun was pointed at Luther now.

"Sorry, stud. I love you like a brother, but I can't risk you going to the Feds."

Luther barely registered what the man had said. He wasn't thinking about words right now, or the Smith in his belt, or poor old Charlie on the bed, or Bobby crumpled on the floor near his feet. All of that was blocked by the adrenaline rush of instinct that overtook him the moment he saw the man's face.

There was only one thing he could think to do.

Run.

45

Wake up, Jack.
Jaaa-ack . . . wake uhhh-up.
She's waiting for you. Better hurry.
Ticktock ticktock ticktock ticktock . . .

Donovan awoke to the sharp sound of knuckles on glass. "Mr. Reed?"

He opened his eyes, blinked a few times to clear them. There was a chill in the air. Pale morning sky.

Jesus. What time was it?

A woman peered in at him through a window and it took him a moment to realize where he was: lying on the backseat of the Chrysler.

"Mr. Reed?"

The woman wore white, clutching car keys, a purse, and the remnants of a sack lunch to her chest as she frowned in at him.

What had she called him?

"I'd like to go home now. You're blocking my car." Her voice was muffled through the glass. She sounded annoyed.

Donovan pulled himself upright, his body groaning. He felt something plastered to his cheek and pulled it away.

A candy wrapper. Baby Ruth.

His throat was sore. His mouth tasted like dried cow dung.

Tossing the wrapper aside, he stared out the window at the woman. She lowered her hands now, revealing a little placard on her chest that said LUCILLE BAKER, RN.

Was he back at the hospital?

"Look," she said. "I'm sorry I was so abrupt with you, but you shouldn't be sneaking into your niece's room. Rules are rules. That's no reason for childish pranks." She gestured impatiently. "Could you move your car please? Now?"

Donovan blinked again, then looked around, trying to scrape away what felt like a thick layer of scum coating the inside of his skull. The Chrysler was parked haphazardly in the middle of a rain-slicked parking lot, blocking at least three of the cars that were angled neatly in their stalls.

Across the lot was a long, squat building. A sign near the entrance read ST. MARGARET'S CONVALESCENT CENTER.

He knew this place.

It was Sara Gunderson's hospital.

"Shall I call security? Is that really what you want me to do?"

"Uhhh," Donovan managed, trying to get his mouth to form the words in his head. It wasn't working.

Lucille gave him a moment, but with nothing forthcoming, she said, "Very well, then." She opened her purse, dug around for a moment, and withdrew a cell phone.

"No, wait," Donovan said, holding up a hand, his mind on overdrive. "I-I'll move the car."

He reached across to the door release, pushed the door open, and climbed out. He felt dizzy. Grabbed the roof of the Chrysler to steady himself.

"Are you alright, Mr. Reed?"

Donovan turned. "Why do you keep calling me that?"

"I'm sorry, isn't that what you said your name was? You're Ms. Gunderson's uncle, I just assumed—"

"Uncle?" Donovan said. This was getting crazier by the minute. "What are you talking about? Where do you know me from?"

Lucille frowned. "Really, Mr.—whatever your name is—this isn't the least bit funny. I realize you're upset, but your behavior is growing quite tedious." She gestured to the car. "Now, please. I'd like to go home."

She turned abruptly, moving toward a silver Nissan, one of the cars that was blocked by the Chrysler.

"Wait," Donovan sputtered, grabbing her arm. "Who is it you think I am?"

"Let go of me."

"You said I was in Sara's room. When was I there? What did I do?"

"Let go of me," Lucille repeated, looking more scared than angry now.

Donovan released her. "I'm sorry. It's just I . . . I don't remember going in there."

Lucille waved a dismissive hand at him and continued to her car. "You need professional help, mister. If this is any indication of the kind of up-bringing that poor girl had, it's no wonder she fell in with the wrong sort."

She unlocked the door and got inside, Donovan's bewilderment quickly turning to horror. The last thing he remembered was pulling into a gas station near Motel Row.

And the headache. That terrible headache.

But how had he gotten here? And why?

It just didn't make any sense.

Lucille was sitting in her car now, tapping her fingers on the wheel, her angry eyes visible in the side-view mirror.

Climbing onto driver's seat of the Chrysler, Donovan found the keys in the ignition. He was about to start the engine when the sight of the in-dash ashtray stopped him.

It hung open, nearly overflowing with cigarette butts. Their filters were torn off.

What the hell?

Had someone else been in the car with him?

Then he remembered the craving he'd felt as he'd waited outside Carla De-vito's apartment building. The intense desire to light up a Marlboro. Judging by the taste in his mouth, *he* was the one who had smoked all these cigarettes.

But how could that be?

His cell phone bleated, startling him. Fumbling through his coat pock-ets, he found it, flicked it open. Hesitated. "Donovan."

Or should he have said Reed?

"Where you been all night?" Waxman barked. "I must've called you a hundred times in the last couple hours."

Donovan was reeling. A spike of nausea assaulted him. "I, uh . . . I-I must've turned my phone off."

"Nice going, genius. You better get your ass out here to Fredrickville, pronto. The Wayfarer Inn."

Donovan's gut tightened involuntarily. "What's going on?"

"I was hoping you could tell me."

Donovan felt like a drunk who'd had one too many on the golf course, only to wake up in a four-by-five jail cell with a fresh new shiner adorning his face. The last few hours were a complete, impenetrable blank.

"Jack? You still there? I got some news you aren't gonna like."

He wasn't liking much of anything right now. He braced himself. "What is it?"

"We found Luther. He's DOA."

Before Donovan could respond, a horn blared—a blast so loud and long it startled a flock of pigeons perched on a nearby telephone line.

Lucille Baker had lost her patience.

46

The Wayfarer Inn looked even worse in the daylight. An oblong box with peeling blue paint, a row of dilapidated doors, windows sporting stained curtains.

The parking lot was host to a Crown Victoria convention. More cars than it had seen in over a decade. Sheriff's cruisers. Unmarked federals. Coroner's van.

Donovan pulled in and found a spot near a stretch of crime-scene tape, dread bubbling in his stomach as he stared out at the mix of uniformed and plainclothes cops flowing in and out of an open doorway.

What the hell had happened last night?

He thought about the headache, and the odd, erratic glimpses into Gunderson's mind. He thought about the previous night, his plunge into the river, those few minutes that seemed like hours, stranded beneath a black, turbulent sky as Gunderson reached for him, grabbing his face.

Give us a kiss.

He remembered the serpentine tongue, the heat of Gunderson's breath burrowing deep into his chest like an invading force, an aggressive, ravenous parasite.

Could it have been more than just a kiss?

Was it possible that Gunderson . . .

No, Jack, don't even think it. That's crazy talk. Follow that whacked-out train of thought and before you know it the men in white will be scooping you up to take you straight to the booby hatch.

Wacky Jacky's adventures on the other side.

"Hey, Jack! Over here!" Waxman stood near the open motel-room doorway.

Fighting to steady his nerves, Donovan cut the Chrysler's engine and climbed out. Glancing down, he noticed his shoes were caked with dried mud.

Yet another mystery.

He tapped them against a tire to knock the mud loose, then crossed through the maze of cars. Waxman gave him the once-over as he approached. "You look like hell."

"I love you, too," Donovan said.

"Gotta make this quick. Brass could be here any minute, and if they see you nosing around, they're gonna go ballistic. As it is, our little stunt with Nemo will probably land us both on the unemployment line."

"Where's Luther?"

Waxman handed him a pair of gloves and white cotton shoe covers. "Let's go inside."

Donovan slipped them on, then stepped through the doorway to find a dingy motel room with decades-old furniture and threadbare yellow carpet, the air ripe with decay.

The place looked vaguely familiar:

Pizza box on the dresser. Carpet stained with blood and vomit.

There were two beds in the room, the far one missing a bedspread. Crime-scene techs hovered around the one closest to the door, where a man about the size of a house was curled up in the fetal position, a gelatinous mass of bloody flesh where the back of his head used to be.

Donovan recognized the paisley shirt.

"Charlie Kruger," Waxman said. "Manager and part owner of this wonderful establishment. Why he's in here is anybody's guess." He gestured to the blood on the carpet. "Looks like the assailant put a couple in Kruger's legs, then Kruger stumbled to the bed, collapsed, and got a bullet to the head for his trouble."

Donovan looked at the stained carpet, then shifted his gaze to the bed. "I don't see a trail."

Waxman shrugged. "So sue me. I'm no homicide whiz. But if that isn't Kruger's blood, we're short a body."

"What about Luther?"

"We'll get to him in a minute. First I wanna know what the hell happened with you and Nemo last night."

Donovan looked around at the crime-scene techs. Sensing his hesitation, Waxman nodded toward a corner of the room. They moved into a huddle, keeping their voices low.

"Well?"

Donovan knew he had a choice. He could tell Waxman the truth—that the last few hours had been sucked into a deep black hole—or he could lie.

"I lost him," he said.

"Lost him?"

"Everything was working like we planned. He went to Carla's apartment looking for his stash, swallowed the bait, told her he was going after Luther."

"And?"

"I started a tail, got caught by the rain, and lost him. Spent half the night looking for him, but couldn't catch a break. You and Rachel were right. I was so exhausted by then I wound up pulling to the side of the road and crawled into the backseat. That's where I was when you called me."

"Explains the suit," Waxman said. "You didn't think about clueing me in?"

"It was late and I was out of it. You may have noticed I haven't exactly been thinking straight."

"No shit, Sherlock. What was he driving?"

"Who?"

"Nemo. Who else?"

"A Honda Del Sol. Carla's car."

"You know the tag number?"

"Not offhand," Donovan said. "You're thinking Nemo did this?"

"It crossed my mind once or twice."

Donovan looked at the body, scanned the room. "Where's Luther?"

Waxman jerked his head. "Follow me."

In back of the motel was an empty lot. A patch of mud and weeds that might have been prime real estate at one time.

Those days were long gone.

A far corner of the lot was roped off with yellow crime-scene tape. A cluster of cops and technicians quietly worked the spot, their attention focused on a body lying faceup before them.

The rain-soaked earth sucked at Donovan's shoes as he walked. Remembering the dried mud he'd just knocked off, a fresh spike of nausea assaulted him.

Had he been here before?

Thoughts of Gunderson's kiss drifted through his mind again, but he immediately smothered them. Play this out, he told himself. Don't jump to conclusions.

Yet even as he pushed himself toward denial, his old friend instinct dragged him in the opposite direction, connecting the dots.

He didn't like the picture that was forming.

"Luther Dwayne Polanski," Waxman said as they reached the body. Luther's face was a death mask, glassy eyes staring heavenward. "Looks like the assailant came into the room, shot Kruger, managed to wing Luther"—he turned and gestured toward the rear of the motel where a row of windows faced the field. One of them was hanging open—"then chased him out here and put another one in his back. The impact spun him right around."

Donovan swallowed. Stared down at Luther's body. "You're talking about Nemo."

"Who else?"

"Because of the money?"

"That would be my guess," Waxman said. "You realize we're completely screwed, don't you? This is all on us. Once the brass puts it together, we'll both be lucky they don't bring us up on charges."

Donovan kept his gaze on Luther's body. "That's the least of my worries. Without Luther, I've got nothing. He was my last link to Jessie."

"You don't know that," Waxman said.

"I don't know much of anything right now, except time is running out."

And so was Jessie's oxygen.

"Maybe Nemo's been the key all along," Waxman said. "I wouldn't put it past him. He's definitely a chilly bastard."

"What do you mean?"

Waxman gestured to a nearby tech. "Hey, Joe, can I see that butt again?"

The tech nodded, then opened his forensics case and brought out an evidence bag, handing it across to Waxman. Waxman held it up for Donovan, showing him the damp cigarette butt inside.

"Son of a bitch stood here and had a smoke after he shot Luther. Mr. Casual. Flicked it onto Luther's chest. Pretty cold, you ask me." He handed the baggie back to the tech, but Donovan couldn't take his eyes off the butt inside.

The filter was torn off.

Donovan felt himself starting to teeter.

"Joe's gonna try a saliva trace," Waxman said, "but the rain probably ruined any chances of . . ." He paused, looking at Donovan, grabbing him by the elbow. "Christ, Jack, you look like you're about to keel over."

"I think I'm gonna be sick," Donovan said, then turned abruptly and headed back toward the motel.

47

He went straight to the Chrysler, shut himself inside, then closed his eyes and leaned his forehead against the wheel.

Willing himself to concentrate, he tried to remember what he'd done last night. He knew he'd followed Nemo, saw him get out of the Del Sol, go into the motel office—

—then nothing. Nada. Zip. Zero.

Now Luther was dead and Donovan had mud on his shoes. And a dull, sick ache in his stomach told him that Waxman was wrong. It wasn't Nemo who shot Luther. It wasn't Nemo at all.

Sitting upright, he reached under his coat, pulled out his Glock, and ejected the cartridge. It had been full when Al Cleveland gave it to him. Now, three rounds were missing.

Three rounds.

But that didn't add up, did it? Luther had taken one to the arm and another to the back, while Charlie Kruger took three hits, making a total of *five*.

So maybe Waxman *was* right, maybe the killer *had* been Nemo after all.

But what about the blood on the carpet?

Unlike Waxman, Donovan had spent some time with homicide, just prior to going federal, and he knew—just as the forensics techs would soon confirm—that it wasn't Charlie Kruger's blood on that carpet. Charlie was already on the bed when he was shot.

The simple process of elimination said it was Nemo's blood. It had to be.

And if Nemo had been lying on that carpet, where was he now? No way he could've lost that much blood and walked away. Besides, the stain was static. No trail to the bed, no trail any . . .

The bedspread. One of the bedspreads was missing.

Had someone used it to transport the body?

When investigating a crime, it's easy to come up with a half dozen different theories, different ways the job could have gone down. Each one is kept in mind as the crime scene is processed, but no matter how many theories you come up with, there's always one that stands out. One that makes the most sense. One that sticks in your mind even before the evidence is collected.

The one in Donovan's mind went something like this:

Nemo drove straight to the motel, which meant he'd been here before. He knew Charlie Kruger, had met him sometime in the past, and he knew that Kruger was hiding Luther. Pissed off and wanting his money, he grabbed Kruger and forced him to take him to Luther's room.

Once inside, Nemo demanded the cash, shooting Kruger in an attempt to scare Luther into giving it up.

Then something unexpected happened. A uninvited guest arrived, shot Nemo, winged Luther, and chased him through the bathroom window and onto the field.

Luther had been shot twice.

And Nemo?

Judging by the pattern of the stain, Donovan would guess he'd suffered a head wound. Probably a single shot, close range.

Which meant three rounds from the same weapon.

Nemo's head, Luther's arm and back.

Glancing uneasily at the Glock and its cartridge in his hands, Donovan shifted his gaze to the cigarette butts crowding the ashtray.

The killer had smoked a cigarette, flicked it onto Luther's chest, then calmly walked back to the motel room, grabbed a bedspread, and rolled up Nemo's body.

But why? And where had he taken it?

A sudden thought occurred to Donovan, accompanied by a surge of panic.

Bracing himself, he took the keys from the ignition, then climbed out of the Chrysler and moved around to the trunk. Shoving the key into the slot, he hesitated a moment, then slowly turned it.

The latch popped open with a loud *thunk*.

Glancing around to make sure no one was watching, Donovan carefully raised the lid, knowing exactly what was in there before he even looked inside.

To his surprise and relief, however, he was wrong. The trunk was empty. No bedspread, no Nemo.

Not that this changed anything. He had no doubt that Nemo was dead, nor did he harbor any illusions about who had pulled the trigger.

But again he wondered, where was the body?

Then he remembered the Del Sol.

He found it in the back of the gas station, only yards from where he'd parked last night. It sat in the middle of a row of cars in various states of disrepair. They looked as if they'd been there for half a decade.

The gas station was closed, just as it had been the night before, and judging by the condition of the pumps and the graffiti on the windows, it wouldn't be opening anytime soon.

Donovan exited the Chrysler and crossed toward the Del Sol, pausing when he realized the driver's seat was occupied.

Bobby Nemo.

He put a hand under his coat, touching the butt of his Glock, a precautionary habit more than anything else.

"Bobby?" he said, not really expecting an answer.

He didn't get one. Nemo didn't move. No reason he should. He was dead, the missing bedspread wrapped around him, a single gunshot wound to the right side of his head.

Donovan leaned in for a closer look and something caught his eye: a folded scrap of paper protruding from between Nemo's lips.

He hesitated. What the fuck?

With trembling fingers, he reached in through the open window and pulled it free.

There was a logo just above the fold. Motel stationery, a dozen years old, printed back in the days when the Wayfarer Inn was halfway respectable.

His name was written across it in black ink:

SPECIAL AGENT JACK

Not knowing what to expect, Donovan slowly unfolded it and found more black ink:

AUTOGENOUS WORK THAT CAN GET YOU ARRESTED
☐☐☐☐☐☐☐☐

A makeshift crossword puzzle.

Knowing he'd just stepped off a high cliff into the abyss, Donovan mulled the clue over in his mind a moment, trying to make sense of it.

Autogenous work that can get you arrested.

Autogenous.

Produced from within.

It took him a moment longer, but when Donovan finally solved it, there was no doubt in his mind who the message was from and what it meant.

Alexander Gunderson was back among the living.

48

Rachel was in the shower when her doorbell rang.

It was just past 8 a.m. and she'd already been up for hours, unable to sleep. Ever since she'd left Jack yesterday afternoon she'd felt anxious and uneasy. And at the root of it was the story he'd told her.

His trip to other side.

Rachel had never been deeply religious, but she *was* a believer. Growing up in a Chinese-American household with a grandmother who, as a little girl, had come straight from Tai Wo, Hong Kong, she'd heard her share of ancient stories. Tales of gods and goddesses, ghostly apparitions, the Ten Courts of Hell. Stories told with a quiet reverence and a conviction born of faith.

She remembered the fireworks and the colorful dancing dragons on the streets of Chinatown during the Chung Yuan Festival—Ghost Day—which celebrated the rising of souls from the bowels of hell to visit their earthly homes. Every year, Grandma Luke lit incense and set out plates full of mango, peaches, and roast duck on a card table in the living room, an offering to appease the restless spirits.

Against her family's wishes, Rachel had made the mistake of marrying David in August, smack in the middle of Ghost Month. And while she didn't exactly blame the denizens of hell for the disaster her marriage became, at times she had to wonder. Had they been cursed from the start?

Rachel wasn't a strong believer in the stories Grandma Luke had told her—every religion had its share of tall tales—but she believed enough to feel just a tickle of anxiety whenever the subject arose. That anxiety had been reinforced the moment Jack had told her about his otherworld encounter with Alexander Gunderson.

The possibility that he might have imagined it all, that his mind had conjured up some bizarre death dream, was not a thought she even entertained. She knew that what he'd experienced was all too real.

And potentially dangerous.

Now, according to Sidney, Jack had been cut loose from the investigation, asked to step aside while the fools upstairs took over the case. She understood that they were simply following procedure, that the leeway they'd given Jack was a courtesy they weren't obligated to extend. But she wondered how they could turn him away. Why deny a father access to the resources that might help him find his own daughter?

Now, with Jack at loose ends and still reeling from his encounter with death—and with time ticking at its ever relentless pace—the probability of disaster loomed large.

Jessie could die.

And a part of Jack would go with her.

Rachel was thinking about these things and rinsing the soap from her body when her doorbell rang. She quickly finished rinsing and shut the water off.

The bell rang twice more before she got to the front door, wrapped in a terry-cloth robe. Despite the perfunctory swipe of a towel, her hair was still tangled and dripping wet. She knew she looked a mess, but didn't much care. She had been waiting for hours to hear from Jack—he hadn't returned her calls—and the doorbell ringing at eight in the morning only compounded her anxiety.

Feeling like a military wife waiting for her husband to be shipped home, she pulled the door open, only to be overcome by a sudden surge of relief.

Jack was in the hallway.

Unfortunately, he looked (as David used to say on those many mornings after) as if he'd been pulled through a knothole.

"Jack, my God, what is it? What's wrong?"

"It's all gone to shit," he said, then stumbled into her arms.

Donovan knew he had no right to do this to Rachel.

Sure, there was a bond between them, had been from the moment she'd first stepped into his office over two years ago. But she didn't owe him anything. No reason she should. And throwing the weight of his troubles onto her shoulders was, to say the least, unfair.

Then again Rachel was more than just an IA who had managed to catch his fancy. She was, Donovan had come to realize, the only one he could trust.

The only one he *wanted* to trust.

When she opened the door, he had practically collapsed in her arms, raving like a street-corner lunatic. But she didn't falter. Not for a moment. She guided him to the sofa and sat him down and listened attentively as he sputtered on, telling her about the blistering headache, the night he couldn't remember, and the untimely deaths of Luther Polanski, Charles Kruger and Bobby Nemo—two of whom he was certain he had executed.

That she didn't immediately pick up the phone and call the boys with the butterfly nets was, to Donovan's mind, a testament to her strength.

Instead, she brewed him a cup of tea and sat beside him on the sofa, a gentle hand on his shoulder, lightly stroking it as he opened up to her for the second time in the last twenty-four hours.

It felt good to be with her. To share his demons. His fears. His pain.

When he told her about the note and its cryptic message, she said, "Show me."

He pulled it out of his pocket and handed it to her, watching her carefully as she unfolded it.

"Looks like your handwriting," she said. "But . . . different."

"Read it," Donovan said.

She did as he asked, reading aloud. " 'Autogenous work that can get you arrested.' " She stared at the squares drawn beneath it. "A crossword puzzle."

Donovan nodded. "Two words."

Her brow furrowed as she thought it over. Then her expression changed and she looked at him. She'd gotten it much quicker than he had.

"Inside job," she said.

Donovan nodded again.

"And you think this means you killed those men? That's ridiculous, Jack. You're not built that way. You don't have it in you."

"That's just it," Donovan said, trying to keep his desperation under control. "I *do* have it in me." He pointed to the note. "You're right about that being my handwriting, because *I* wrote it." He paused. "Only I didn't."

"That doesn't make sense."

"Inside job," he said. "Get it? It's a message. A joke. When I blacked out last night, I did things I wouldn't normally do because I wasn't in control of my own body."

Rachel stared at him for a long moment. And in that moment he thought he'd lost her. She was willing to go only so far with this stuff and now he'd crossed a line. Her hand stiffened on his shoulder, a ripple of fear just beneath the surface of her fingertips.

Then she surprised him.

"Gunderson. He's doing this." And when she said it, he wanted to put his arms around her and hold her forever.

"He's inside me, Rache. Last night he managed to take control and he wants me to know it. That's why he played hide-and-seek with Nemo's body. It's just the kind of move Gunderson would make."

It was a ridiculous notion, of course. Something you'd hear on the mental ward at Mercy Hospital. But was it any more ridiculous than what he'd been through these last couple days? Unlike Sidney Waxman, he'd already suspended any inkling of disbelief that may have plagued him.

Apparently Rachel had as well.

She stood up, heading toward an adjacent hallway. "Give me a minute to get dressed."

"Why? Where are we going?"

She turned, looking at him with concern. "There's someone I want you to meet."

49

They took Twenty-sixth out of Bridgeport and headed into Chinatown.

Rachel drove, weaving her Celica in and out of traffic with the seasoning of a pro, reminding him for a moment of A.J. Donovan watched her watch the road, the concern still in her eyes. How long, he wondered, before this steely support of hers broke down?

Chinatown was eleven blocks of gaudily painted pagoda-domed buildings, nestled among two-story walk-ups, dry-goods stores, and restaurants, plenty of restaurants. Dim sum and roast duck were the specialties, advertised on multicolored signs written in various dialects.

No matter the time of day or night, the streets always seemed to be crowded. Businessmen, shopkeepers, students, prostitutes, and just about every type of petty criminal you could name.

On its surface, Chinatown was no different from any other cultural stronghold in the city. But beneath the surface, Triad rule had wormed its way into every crevice of the small district, a fact Donovan had become well acquainted with many years ago, when he'd worked a case down here. He'd learned quickly that what happens in Chinatown stays in Chinatown.

Unlike Vegas, however, they didn't advertise.

There were no parking spaces on the street, so Rachel pulled into a public lot near the train station and they walked the two blocks to her mother's apartment.

Rachel's mother and grandmother lived in a second-floor walk-up, just above a restaurant called Ling Su's. The strong odor of clams and roasted garlic assaulted Donovan's nostrils as they climbed a dilapidated flight of stairs to a door marked 1.

Above the doorframe, a sheet of yellowed paper featuring an ornate drawing of a scowling Chinese warrior was held in place by a blue plastic pushpin.

Rachel had said little since they'd left her apartment and wasn't offering much now. She knocked, showing him a small, timorous smile as they waited for an answer.

A moment later, the latch turned and the door opened and a middle-aged Chinese woman—whom Donovan could easily have mistaken for Rachel in a dark hallway—peeked out over the safety chain.

Evelyn Wu smiled warmly at the sight of her daughter. "Rachel, honey."

"Hi, Ma."

Closing the door, Evelyn unhooked the chain, then opened it wide for them, motioning them inside. "Come in, come in. I'll make some tea."

"No, Ma, we don't have time."

Evelyn searched her daughter's eyes. "Is something wrong?"

"We're here to see Grandma Luke. Is she awake?"

Evelyn offered a short grunt that suggested this was a silly question. "You know your grandmother. Always up at the crack of dawn." She glanced at Donovan. If she was alarmed at all by his appearance, she wasn't showing it.

"I'm sorry," Rachel said. "This is my . . . my friend, Jack." Then she said something in Chinese that Donovan didn't catch and wouldn't understand if he had.

A look that mirrored Rachel's spread across Evelyn's face and she nodded, heading down a short hallway. "I'll tell her you're here."

She opened a door and the murmur of a television bled out into the hallway as she disappeared behind it.

"What did you just say to her?" Donovan asked.

"That you're battling an angry spirit."

The directness of Rachel's tone startled Donovan. He hadn't thought of it as something so simple and matter-of-fact, but what better way to explain it?

An angry spirit. Gunderson was that, and then some.

As they waited, he glanced around the room, which was small and modestly furnished. A doorway opened onto a tiny but serviceable kitchen, where an ancient refrigerator hummed noisily.

A table near the kitchen doorway held framed family photographs: Rachel as a child, clinging to the leg of a man he guessed was her father; Rachel and her mother, taken when she was still in her teens; Rachel at the prom with an unknown escort . . .

Donovan thought of Jessie and wondered if he'd ever see such a photograph in his own home.

A moment later, Mrs. Wu appeared in the doorway and nodded to Rachel, who took him by the arm and led him down the hall. They stepped into a small room dominated by a wasabi-green Barcalounger that was situated in a corner across from an old Zenith console.

The Beverly Hillbillies played on-screen, Granny wielding a shotgun.

An Asian version of Granny sat in the Barcalounger, dwarfed by the big chair, an ancient Chinese woman wearing a loose sweater over a muted gray dress. The old woman saw Rachel and spoke in her native language, holding out her arms for a hug.

Rachel obliged. "Hi, Po-Po."

Grandma Luke hugged her granddaughter, then pointed to the television and spoke again as Granny fired the shotgun into the air. Rachel laughed and Evelyn turned to Donovan, explaining, "She says Granny's a very obstinate woman."

Donovan offered a polite smile, but bristled slightly as Grandma Luke's wizened eyes shifted in his direction, assessing him. Despite her age, those eyes had a clarity and depth that was vaguely unsettling. She spoke again, her voice low and melodic, and when she was done, Evelyn reached over and shut the TV off, turning again to Donovan, her expression sober.

"What did she say?" Donovan asked.

"The look on your face," Evelyn said. "She's seen it before."

"Oh?"

"You've been to the other side."

Surprised, Donovan glanced at Rachel, but Rachel shook her head. "I haven't told her a thing."

"It's a look that only a traveler wears," Evelyn said.

Traveler, Donovan thought. Another simple, yet appropriate phrase. The Wu family's ability to cut through the bullshit was starting to impress him.

Still looking at him, Grandma Luke spoke again and Evelyn translated. "Your story," she said. "Tell us your story."

So he told them, letting it spill out of him once again, avoiding the temptation to embellish, telling it exactly as it happened.

Grandma Luke's face remained immobile throughout, but her dark eyes drew him in as he spoke. For a moment it seemed as if only the two of them were in the room, priest and confessor, mother and child. Telling his story to this old woman was an emotional cleansing that seemed to both drain him and give him strength.

When he finished, Grandma Luke spoke again and Evelyn said, "This man you saw on your journey. The one who kissed you. He died a violent death?"

Donovan flashed back to that moment in the train yard that seemed like eons ago. "Yes," he said. "He was shot."

Grandma Luke nodded.

"He is a hungry ghost," Evelyn translated.

"A what?"

"A hungry ghost," Rachel said. "It's an ancient Taoist belief. Every year, during the seventh moon, the gates of hell open and hungry spirits roam the earth in search of bodies to possess."

"Seventh moon?"

"August," Rachel told him.

"August came and went a long time ago." Donovan said.

Grandma Luke spoke once again, her words filtered through Evelyn.

"Time doesn't matter," she said. "This is a new spirit. One who found his way here before his final descent. He's the hungriest of all—and the most dangerous. That kiss he gave you opened a door into your consciousness, leaving you vulnerable to his attacks."

"Then I was right," Donovan said. "He's inside me."

"Yes," Evelyn translated. "But he failed to possess you completely. Part of his soul remains stranded in the dark world. His strength comes and goes with the ebb and flow of your own."

Donovan glanced at Rachel, saw her distress. This clearly wasn't territory she liked to explore.

"The absence of light you experienced was his way of taunting you," Evelyn continued, "enticing you to seek him out, so that the transfer of souls can be completed. He killed those men to get your attention, to force you into a confrontation."

"Confrontation?" Donovan frowned. "What kind of confrontation?"

"On the other side," Rachel said, a slight tremor to her voice.

"What?"

"He's calling you back. Challenging you to some kind of . . . metaphysical duel."

As Donovan tried to digest this, Grandma Luke spoke again.

"Ignore his taunts at your peril," Evelyn translated. "If his challenge goes unanswered, he will continue to haunt you until you either go mad or your body gives out."

"Wonderful."

"But should you choose to confront him, he will do everything he can to steal your place here on earth."

"So I'm screwed no matter what," Donovan said. "And Jessie's his trump card. If I don't accept his invitation, I'll never find her."

"You don't know that," Rachel said.

"Don't I? He's the only one left, Rache. He made sure of that when he killed Luther."

"Maybe so," Rachel said. "But how do you plan on accomplishing this little get-together? Drive off another bridge?"

Donovan hesitated. She had a point. Even if he chose to confront Gunderson, how exactly would he do it? His first trip to the netherworld had been a fluke, an anomaly. Short of putting a gun to his head, how would he get there again?

Seeming to sense his dilemma, Grandma Luke spoke.

"There's more than one way to travel to the other side," Evelyn said. "Less dangerous than what you've already experienced, but still very risky."

Grandma Luke reached to a table beside her chair and opened a battered cigar box. Inside was a collection of papers, some yellowed with age. She searched through them, found a dog-eared business card, and offered it to Donovan.

"This man will help you," Evelyn translated.

Donovan took the card.

Chinese characters.

An address printed below them.

Rachel stared at it over his shoulder. "This is crazy," she said. "Why did I even bring you here?"

Grandma Luke smiled at Rachel and spoke again.

"My granddaughter has always been a reluctant believer," Evelyn translated. "She knows this is the only way, but the truth frightens her."

"See what I grew up with?" Rachel said.

"I know you're scared, Rache, but think of Jessie. Right before he was shot, Gunderson asked me if I was willing to die for my little girl." Donovan paused, then said, "What would your answer be?"

50

It was an apothecary shop, but unless you were suffering from a serious brain-cell deficiency, you wouldn't mistake it for the local Walgreens.

A three-block walk from Grandma Luke's apartment, it was tucked into a narrow cul-de-sac as if hiding from the world, a secret to be shared with only a select few.

There were no signs advertising its presence. Only a dilapidated door and a dirty window filled with what looked like industrial-sized mayonnaise jars holding moldy powders and pickled substances of unknown origin. They reminded Donovan of the kinds of things unwitting reality-show contestants are forced to swallow as America watches. Whatever was in those jars did not look particularly medicinal.

"You sure this is the right place?" he asked.

Rachel nodded. "My grandparents used to bring me here."

"You must've had an interesting childhood."

"Life," she sighed. "An interesting life."

He knew that sigh included the current situation, and he wondered if the reluctance Grandma Luke spoke of had gotten the better of her. Was her support finally starting to waver?

He reached for her hand and squeezed it. "Don't forget," he said, "I've done this before."

The smile she offered was small, but enough to satisfy him. He reached for the door. A bell tinkled as he opened it. Stepping inside, they found a middle-aged Asian woman looking up at them from the book she was reading. "May I help you?"

She sat at a counter littered with jars of various sizes, filled with the same unappetizing substances as those in the window. The wall behind her was lined with wooden drawers, each about the size of a shoe box, which Donovan assumed held various medicinal mixes of stuff from the jars. Dried herbs hung from the ceiling, permeating the air with an almost overpowering mustiness.

Donovan ducked under something brown and approached her, handing her the dog-eared business card Grandma Luke had given him. He was vaguely aware of music. A faint strain coming from a distant room.

It sounded like Jimi Hendrix.

The woman read the card, nodded. Handing it back, she flipped the book facedown, then came out from behind the counter and moved to a curtained doorway at the back of the store.

Donovan and Rachel followed.

Pulling the curtain aside, she gestured and said, "Last door on your left."

They stepped past her, Hendrix's guitar growing louder as they navigated a corridor with faded linoleum and drab green walls that were vaguely reminiscent of a fifties-era hospital. At least there weren't any jars in evidence.

Donovan looked around. "Your grandparents bring you here, too?"

"It's all new to me," Rachel said.

The last door on the left was open just a crack, Hendrix really cranking behind it. Donovan knocked on the doorframe, but got no answer. He knocked again, louder.

Over the music, a voice called out, "Yeah?"

Donovan pushed the door open to find a twentyish, overweight Chinese-American man standing in the middle of a cluttered room. He was playing air guitar, a burning cigarette tucked into a corner of his mouth.

Donovan felt a momentary twinge. Was it a Marlboro?

Without stopping, the man said, "What can I do you for?"

Donovan glanced at Rachel. "I think there's been a mistake."

They were about to turn away when the guy snatched up a remote, silenced the music, and looked at Rachel. "You Mrs. Luke's grandkid?"

Rachel paused. "You're Mr. Wong?"

"In the flesh," Wong said, looking her over. "Where you been all my life?"

Donovan glared at him, then took Rachel's arm. "Let's go."

Wong held up a hand. "Wait a minute, wait—don't get your panties in a wad. You're the one picked up the stray hitchhiker, right?"

Donovan paused, looking at the guy. Had Grandma Luke really meant to send them to *him*?

Wong noticed the look and smirked. "What? You were expecting some wise, old kung fu master? You white boys are all the same."

Donovan didn't respond, but that was exactly what he'd been expecting.

"Sorry to disappoint you," Wong said, "but nobody's snatching any pebbles outta my hand and I sure as shit ain't gonna call you grasshopper. But I will promise you one thing: I can get you where you want to go."

He held out a hand to shake. "The name's Jimmy, by the way."

Donovan ignored the hand, taking in the clutter of the room: a desk piled with Asian girlie magazines, an ashtray overflowing with butts, a bookshelf full of hardbacks that hadn't been dusted in months.

He didn't try to hide his skepticism. "You're saying you can help me?"

"If I can't, nobody can," Wong said, withdrawing the hand. "All I need from you is the answer to one simple question."

"Which is?"

"Visa or MasterCard?"

He led them back down the hall to a set of double doors. "I inherited this place from my grandfather. My old man was a drunk, so the business skipped a generation."

He pushed open one of the doors and gestured them inside. Donovan eyed him warily and Wong grinned right back. "Don't let the youthful façade fool you. I'm an old soul."

They stepped into a windowless room with an exam table at the center. The only other furniture was a chair, a counter and sink, and a large storage closet tucked into a corner. There were more jars on the counter, containing an unappetizing array of brown and green liquids.

"Take off your shirt and shoes and hop aboard," Wong said, patting the table.

Donovan hesitated, then did as he was told, feeling a bit self-conscious as he pulled off his shirt and climbed onto the table.

Wong cracked his knuckles and rubbed his hands together rapidly, as if trying to warm them. Moving around behind Donovan, he placed his palms on his bare back and slowly worked them across it.

After a moment he said, "I've got one word for you: *chaos*. You got a lotta shit going on inside there."

No kidding, Donovan thought.

"Like I said, I can get you where you want to go . . ."

"But?"

"There's a speech my grandfather always gave his clients, full of fortune-cookie wisdom and metaphysical mumbo jumbo about chi and meridians and the manipulation of the body to release the soul . . . But the bottom line is this: I'm gonna stop your heart. And the condition you're in right now, once I get it stopped, I might not be able to start it back up."

"I knew this was a bad idea," Rachel said.

"She's right. It probably is. You sure you don't want to reconsider?"

Donovan thought about Jessie and shook his head. What other alternative was there?

"I'm sure," he said.

"You understand," Wong told him, "if you don't come out of this thing, I'm gonna be in a bit of a pickle. Cops'll be all over me and I've got a reputation to think about."

"You're backing out?"

"I didn't say that. Things get crazy, I can always tell 'em your ticker just stopped—without mentioning, of course, that I'm the one who stopped it."

"Then what are you getting at?" Donovan asked, feeling impatience bubble up.

"Another couple grand would ease the pain."

"Fine," Donovan said. "Whatever you want."

Wong grinned. "I take back every bad thing I ever thought about you."

That was when Rachel turned and left the room.

She was halfway down the corridor before Donovan caught up to her. He grabbed her arm. "Rachel, wait."

She stiffened at his touch, then turned on him, her eyes angry. "What are we doing here, Jack? This guy's a joke."

"You heard Grandma Luke."

"I know, I know. I've been hearing stuff like that all my life. But how the hell do we know what's real and what isn't?"

He took her by the shoulders. "This isn't just a grandmother's story, Rache. I've seen it. I've felt it. And right now it's the only reality I have."

"But this guy's talking about stopping your *heart,* for God sakes. Don't you think that's just a little bit nuts?"

"Then why the hell did you bring me here? Why take me to your grandmother in the first place?"

She looked at him, tears brimming. "I can't do this, Jack. I can't watch you die. When they told me you drove off that bridge, I . . ."

She let the words hang, her fear and vulnerability displayed without filters, telling him everything he needed to know. There was no mystery to solve. There never had been. All this time he'd been too blind or too stupid to see that. It was the same mistake he'd made with Jessie. And Joanne. Too self-absorbed to really see the people around him. To understand how they felt about him.

He focused on her eyes. God, she was beautiful.

Before he could stop himself, he pulled her into his arms and kissed her. She fell into it as if it was the most natural thing in the world. It lasted only a moment, but in that moment Donovan lost himself completely, feeling his own apprehension melt away.

"I need you here," he whispered.

Her arms tightened around him.

They stayed that way for a while, Rachel pressing her cheek against his bare chest, stirring something inside him that he hadn't felt in a long time.

Then, tears still clouding her eyes, she pulled away from the embrace. "I swear to God, Jack, if you don't come back, I'll kill you."

When they returned to the exam room, Wong was smoking another cigarette.

"So," he said. "Everybody on the same page now?"

Donovan shot him a look, then squeezed Rachel's hand and climbed back onto the table. "Let's just get this over with."

Wong dropped his cigarette, stamped it out, then turned to the counter and poured something green into an ornate ceramic cup.

"Drink this," he said, handing it to Donovan.

"What is it?"

"Trust me, you don't want to know. It'll help relax you."

Donovan stared at the liquid and saw what looked like flecks of dark flesh floating in it. He swirled it around a moment, then put the cup to his lips and knocked it back.

The taste was so bitter he nearly gagged. He managed to swallow, the liquid burning a trail down his throat and landing with a thud in his stomach. He instantly felt nauseous, thinking for a moment that he might throw it right back up.

"Jesus," he said, closing his eyes.

Wong took the cup. "Got a bit of a kick."

"Thanks for the warning."

Wong set the cup on the counter. "When you're ready, lie faceup for me."

Donovan waited for the nausea to subside, then opened his eyes again and saw Rachel staring at him with concern. He gave her a reassuring look, but couldn't quite fight off the feeling that the room was starting to sway. Grabbing the side of the exam table, he swung his legs around and lay back.

Wong was over at the closet now, pulling it open. "Just so you know: Before I took over the business, I spent two years as a paramedic. If things get hairy, there's always this . . ."

He reached in and grabbed hold of metal cart, rolling it out into the open. It held a bulky, premodern defibrillator. The rubber on the paddles was so worn that patches of steel shone through.

"It's old," Wong said. "But it works."

Rubbing his hands together again, he moved back to the table and stood over Donovan. "Last chance to change your mind."

Donovan felt his body starting to relax. The medicine kicking in. He glanced at Rachel and could see that she still wasn't happy with this. But she nodded.

"Do it," he said.

Wong moved to a dimmer switch on the wall. "This isn't your first trip, so I won't bother with any tour information."

He turned the dimmer, reducing the room to near darkness. "You've got about six minutes. Anything longer and your brain is toast."

He started with the soles of Donovan's feet, running his thumbs upward toward the toes, then back down again, pressing them hard against muscle, so hard it was almost painful.

Donovan felt his tension leak away and suddenly realized how tired he was. He'd been running on fumes ever since the accident. That he'd managed to survive this long was an act of sheer will.

Now Wong's magic hands were leeching the negative ions from his body, sucking the tension away. He felt himself sink deeper into the table as the hands worked their way to the tops of his feet, then on to the shins, the calves, moving upward to his thighs, thumb tips pressing into selected pressure points, each one sending what felt like a pulse of electricity through his body and straight up into his brain.

By the time they reached his shoulders, the table beneath him had melted away. He felt weightless, floating on a cushion of warm air. Wong might not look like much, might not have the most pleasant demeanor in the world, but he knew what he was doing. No question about it now.

Donovan stared up at the ceiling. After a moment it began to recede, growing smaller and smaller as his body sank into a kind of velvety darkness. Like the table, the room seemed to melt away, and he was no longer floating—

—but falling.

The sensation was so abrupt and unsettling he jerked in surprise and opened his eyes—

—only to find himself back on the table, beneath Wong's capable hands.

He hadn't even realized his eyes were closed.

His heart beat rapidly. Wong touched his chest, his voice uncharacteristically soothing. "Easy now. That's just a preview of coming attractions. You've been through it before, so just relax."

The hand moved along Donovan's chest, fingertips pressing gently into the flesh. He let himself relax again, heart beating against Wong's fingers, gradually slowing until it was little more than a lazy *thu-thump* that seemed on the verge of stopping altogether.

For some reason, the thought of that didn't concern Donovan. It felt right. Natural.

"Good," Wong whispered. "Almost there."

Then he lay one hand flat on Donovan's chest as the other cupped his chin.

"Say hello to Jimi for me." With a quick, economical motion, he pressed hard on Donovan's chest while jerking his head to one side.

Donovan felt a faint *crack* as the room instantly melted away and darkness enveloped him.

A split second later, he was gone.

51

Chaos.

Wong had been right. That was the only way to describe it.

When he opened his eyes, he found himself in familiar territory, hurtling like a rag doll through the eye of a hurricane, a whirling wormhole of light and sound, a jumble of voices murmuring incoherently in his head.

Only it was different this time.

This time there was pain. Pain so deep he thought he might scream.

It started in his chest and spread rapidly through his entire body, expanding his organs until they felt as if they were about to burst. And just when he was certain it couldn't get any worse, the pain deepened, widened, devouring him whole.

He remembered a horror movie he'd once seen, Jennifer Jason Leigh tied between two trucks as their engines revved, threatening to rip her apart. He felt as helpless as poor Jennifer, his flesh stretching, bones cracking, his ever-expanding organs ready to explode.

And then it happened. Something gave inside and he screamed, a long, agonized wail that sounded almost foreign to him.

But he wasn't the only one screaming.

Someone else was here with him. An appendage. A conjoined twin. Their interconnected bodies were ripped apart by some unseen force. Turning his head, he found Gunderson staring back at him like a mirror image, a look of pure agony on his face. His usually malevolent eyes were bright with fear.

Then, invisible hands grabbed Gunderson and yanked him into a fold of darkness—

—and it was over.

The pain gone.

His body whole again.

Hurtling though the wormhole.

Once again, there was a light at the far end. A bright, flickering bluish white light that beckoned to him, as inviting as a mother's open arms. It was a promise of safety, security, warmth.

Love.

And he knew exactly who was beyond that light. Could feel them. The murmur of their voices floated past him. *Through* him.

> *We've you*
> *missed son*
> *join*
> *Come us*

Donovan felt himself relax, letting their voices carry him ever closer to the light. It shone from a doorway of some kind, framing the hazy silhouettes of his long-dead parents.

> *We you*
> *love Jack*
> *Forever always*
> *and*

I love you too, he wanted to cry, but something held him back. As much as he'd like to be with them, as much as he wanted to feel their embrace, he knew this wasn't where he needed to go. Whatever bliss the light offered, whatever promise it held—

—it did not hold Gunderson—

—or Jessie.

And if he let himself pass into the world beyond that doorway, he knew instinctively that he would never come back. When the body on the table in Jimmy Wong's exam room opened its eyes, it wouldn't be Donovan behind them . . .

. . . but Gunderson.

Gunderson would win. He was sure of it.

And Jessie would be lost.

He tried to resist, but the light seemed to extend toward him, feathery tendrils reaching out like friendly alien visitors.

"No," he murmured, working up whatever resistance he could muster—which wasn't much.

The tendrils kept coming.

Join

us

son

"No!" Donovan shouted, trying desperately to twist away from the light. "It's not time. Not now."

The tendrils drew closer, the murmurs louder.

We love

you

Jack

Try as he might, Donovan could not turn way. The tendrils pulsed and expanded, threatening to envelop him.

"Stop, goddammit! Let me go!"

But it was too late. The tendrils surrounded him now, slithering across his body, wrapping their blissful warmth around him, sinking into his flesh and filling him with a feeling of indescribable joy—a joy so intense he thought he might cry.

Should he give in? Should he let them take him?

It would be so easy.

Soooo easy.

And what harm would it do? He would be with people who loved him.

Forever and always.

—But what about Jessie?

Where would *she* be?

Resist, Jack. You have to resist.

"No!" he shouted, arms and legs flailing against the invasion, trying desperately to break away. "Let me go! Let me find Jessie!"

And at the mention of her name, the tendrils abruptly withdrew. A roar of wind filled his ears as something grabbed him from behind—

—and yanked him into darkness.

He didn't know he'd lost consciousness. Couldn't remember exactly when it had happened.

When he came to, he expected to see the same stark landscape he'd seen before. The turbulent sky, the crooked spine of mountains that etched the horizon, the crowd of people forming a ragged line along the narrow pathway.

But no. He'd brought a new set of baggage this time.

Familiar, but different.

Instead of the purgatorial landscape, he stood alone in the middle of— it took him a moment to realize this—of the abandoned train yard.

Gunderson's train yard.

A full moon illuminated the dilapidated carcasses of a dozen or more freight cars. The remains of an old caboose, looking much like the one that had been obliterated when the land mine killed A.J., stood just to his right.

He knew exactly where he was. And something inside him, some sixth sense, told him he needed to find the passenger car. Gunderson's hiding place.

Turning, he crossed toward a gap between two freight cars, trampling the high weeds that covered much of the ground. Trudging over a set of rusted train tracks, he navigated the gap and emerged on the other side.

More of the same greeted him. Unlike the real yard, this place seemed denser, more formidable. The cars cast long shadows in the moonlight—shadows that somehow seemed alive.

He felt eyes watching him. But not the eyes of the rodents or the feral cats he'd encountered before. This was something different.

Something . . . malignant.

Fear clutched him, but he shook it off and continued forward. More train cars blocked his path, but through a narrow gap between two of them, he saw the glow of light.

He squinted, trying to make out the source of it, and as he drew closer, clearing the gap, he realized what it was.

His destination. The passenger car.

It looked much the same as before, but there were no boards on the windows. Flickering fluorescent light spilled out into the night, reminding him, of all things, of an Edward Hopper diner. Much like the rest of the yard, it seemed alive, like a pulsing organ.

As he approached, he saw that the rows of seats inside were empty and still. No sign of Gunderson.

Not yet, at least.

He stopped a few yards away. Waited. Heard a distant howl of wind.

He couldn't shake the feeling that he was being watched. At any moment, something not quite human would tap him on the shoulder, reach into his chest, and snatch his soul away.

And that would be it. Game lost.

As he stood there, struggling to suppress this fear, a faint but unmistakable sound rose above the howl of the wind. Someone crying.

Someone—

—Jessie?

Oh, Jesus.

It was coming from the passenger car.

Panic rising, he crossed to one of the windows and peered inside, seeing no sign of life. He worked his way along the side of the car, looking in window after window. Nothing.

The crying continued. Deep, terrified sobs.

Moving around to the train car's door, he found it padlocked shut. He searched the ground, snatched up a good-sized rock, and hammered the lock over and over, until it finally broke open.

Throwing the door wide, he was assaulted by a blast of light so intense that he had to shut his eyes—

—and when he opened them again, it wasn't the interior of the passenger car he saw, but the curved cement walls of the Chicago freight tunnels.

He was underground, beneath the city, knee-deep in river water.

And Jessie was still crying.

How long has it been?" Rachel asked, staring down at Donovan's lifeless body. She felt sick to her stomach.

Wong checked his watch. "Little over two minutes, give or take."

"Give or take?"

"Relax," Wong said. "He's just getting started."

There was light down here.

He didn't realize where it was coming from until he discovered he was holding his Mini-Mag.

What the hell?

He supposed he could try to come up with a logical explanation for this, but what was the point? Like a dream, logic was irrelevant here.

The feeling that he was being watched had not abated, and he wondered if this death, this afterlife, was merely a product of some form of communal thought. A kind of metaphysical Internet connecting each of us—both the living *and* the dead—through invisible data lines. While we remain a part of the whole, we also contribute our own little piece of randomness to the equation.

Maybe our thoughts are the programming code. Donovan had needed a flashlight, so he had one. That this had happened without his realizing it only confirmed that he had little or no control here. He was a neophyte, a guest with limited privileges, who hadn't yet mastered this particular domain.

Of course, he could be wrong.

Could be that all of the above was just a bunch of happy horseshit. Hadn't he just told himself to forget logic?

But, he wondered, if it *was* true, was it also possible that someone like Gunderson—who, according to Grandma Luke, had been straddling both worlds and had been raised to believe and have faith in these things—might have a better understanding of how to control the environment? Would he be able to hack into a fellow traveler's thoughts and manipulate him at will? That might explain the feeling that someone was watching him. And the sudden changes in his environment.

It might also explain Jessie's sobs.

Focusing in on them, Donovan raised the flashlight above his shoulder and shone it into the tunnel ahead, seeing little more than darkness. The sound of her tears put a knot in his stomach, but he was convinced now that this was just another of Gunderson's ruses.

After all, hadn't Gunderson used Bobby Nemo to get them to that train yard? Hadn't he left the Suburban parked in plain sight to draw Donovan into those tunnels?

Hadn't he used Jessie's sobs before?

He's playing you, Jack. Don't believe a thing you see. Or hear.

Or feel, for that matter—

(Had something just brushed past him in the water?)

He shone the light toward his legs and saw nothing but murky liquid. A slight ripple on the surface, however, convinced him he wasn't alone.

Feeling the sudden urge to move, he started through the tunnel, letting Jessie's sobs guide him. The deeper into it he got, the higher the water rose. It was up to his waist now.

The fear he'd felt a few moments ago was also on the rise. Something slick and slimy resided in this black water and was stalking him with the practiced stealth of a predator.

Easy, Jack. Get a grip.

It's all in your head, remember?

Staring at the water, he was reminded of the dubious green liquid that Wong had given him to drink. The fleshy bits floating in it that had almost seemed alive. Was he merely transferring that image to this place? Yet another piece of baggage?

Or was Gunderson playing netherworld Wizard of Oz?

Jessie's sobs were closer now.

Following a bend in the tunnel, he continued toward the sound, the water rising to his chest.

Keeping the Mini-Mag raised above his shoulder, he saw a dead end just ahead, a wall of cement that housed a familiar steel door, three-quarters of which stood beneath the surface of the water.

Something brushed past him again. Unmistakable this time. He flinched and wheeled around, shining his light into the blackness, catching just a glimpse of glistening gray flesh as it crested the surface, then disappeared beneath it.

Stifling a wave of revulsion, he whipped back around toward the door. The only way through it was underwater. He'd have to get down to where the thing that was stalking him resided.

The question was, would he be able to get through the door before the thing decided to strike?

The water rippled again, his stalker on the prowl. Unwilling to stand there and find out what its intentions were, he braced himself, sucked in a deep breath, then dove into the murk, heading for the steel door. It was too black down here to see anything, but he swam forward, legs kicking, arms outstretched, hoping to latch onto the wheel that should be mounted at the center.

A moment later, he collided with it. Grabbing hold with both hands, he tried to turn it, but it wouldn't budge.

The thing in the water made another pass. Even closer this time.

Donovan jerked the wheel. Come on, you piece of shit, *move*.

Mustering up every ounce of strength he had, he tried a third time and it gave slightly, turning a fraction of an inch to the left.

He was about to try again when his stalker brushed against him, more aggressively than ever, its slick flesh icy to the touch. Donovan flinched and shot upward, breaking the surface of the water, sucking in precious air.

Sonofabitch.

You're letting him control you, Jack. Don't let him control you. The reality of this world is what *you* make it. No one else. Concentrate and you'll get what you want.

Taking another deep breath, he dove again. A moment later he had the wheel in his hands, and from out of nowhere, the slimy thing bumped hard against him, then circled away.

A low, angry roar rippled through the water. He imagined the thing moving toward him again, its open mouth full of razor-sharp teeth.

Frantic now, Donovan turned hard, but the wheel still wouldn't budge.

Turn, goodammit. *Turn!*

Feeling movement behind him, knowing the thing was surely headed straight for him, he centered his concentration on the wheel, and all at once it gave. Spinning it to the left, he yanked the door open—

—only to be assaulted by another blast of intense white light.

I can't take much more of this."

"Relax," Wong said. "He's well under the limit."

"How long?"

Wong sighed, glancing at his watch again. "A little over three minutes to go."

Rachel shifted her gaze to the ancient defibrillator, then looked at Wong. His face was impassive. Bored. She wondered how many times he'd done this.

Then again, maybe she didn't want to know.

"It's okay," he said, as if reading her thoughts. "My grandfather taught me well. Still gives me pointers sometimes."

"Your grandfather's alive?"

Wong shook his head and grinned. "No. But we keep in touch."

When the light faded, he was standing in an alley between two high-rise apartment buildings. The sky was dark and restless, but the moon was full, giving him plenty of illumination. The smell of rotting garbage filled the air. A row of overflowing trash cans lined a nearby cement wall.

The only sound was a distant wind.

And, of course, Jessie crying.

His beacon.

He headed toward her, moving through the shadows to the mouth of the alley. The hairs bristled on the back of his neck. Was someone behind him?

Looking over his shoulder, he thought he saw movement in the darkness beyond the garbage cans. He picked up his pace and hurried out of the alley onto a familiar city street.

It was empty. Devoid of life.

Not exactly a surprise.

But up ahead, along the curb, ringed by pools of streetlight and spilling onto the sidewalk, was a row of mangled cars. Just off to the left, the news van, Gunderson's getaway car, lay on its side, steam rising from beneath its hood.

This is it, Donovan thought. Where it all started. The wreck that put Sara in a coma and changed all of their lives.

Jessie's sobs echoed from inside the van.

Donovan started toward it, then hesitated. What exactly did he expect to find there? He had to think about it a moment, and when he did, it came to him.

A conclusion. That's all he was hoping for. An end to this saga, one way or the other.

He started forward again, crossing the blacktop toward the van, the sound of Jessie's sobs growing louder as he approached. Glancing at its oil-caked underbelly, he noticed gas leaking from the ruptured tank, the smell of it stinging his nostrils. He quickly hoisted himself onto the bumper and climbed up to the side of the van, where the sliding door hung open in invitation.

It was dark inside, but he could hear Jessie clearly, only inches away. The moment he realized he needed a flashlight, the Mini-Mag once again appeared in his hand. He flicked it on, pointing the beam into well of the van.

A small, naked figure sat huddled on the floor against the back of the driver's seat, head buried in her hands, crying.

Sweet holy Jesus. He hadn't expected this.

"Jessie?"

The girl flinched at the sound of his voice, then slowly raised her head. But as she did, her body began to grow and change shape, morphing like the villain in some low-budget sci-fi flick—

—into Alexander Gunderson.

He smiled and held up a pocket minidisc player, Jessie's sobs emanating from its speaker. It was the same player Donovan had found in the tunnels.

"Fool me once," Gunderson said, flicking it off. "You're awfully easy to manipulate, Jack."

"And you're getting predictable," Donovan said.

"Nice of you to play along." Gunderson gestured to their surroundings. "Not exactly what you bargained for, is it? All those promises of eternal rest and what do we get? Our own little piece of fucked-up reality."

Donovan climbed into the well of the van, facing Gunderson directly. "Where is she, Alex?"

"Ahh. Straight to the million-dollar question."

"Enough is enough. It's over. Just tell me where she is."

"Over?" Gunderson said. "You think I went to all that trouble with Bobby and poor Luther just to get you here for some pointless little con-fab? That took a helluva lot of concentration, my friend. And that kind of work deserves a worthwhile payoff."

"Meaning what?" Donovan said. "Invasion of the Body Snatchers?"

"That's the gist of it, hotshot. When that two-bit witch doctor gives you the touch of life, he and your little girlfriend are in for a nice surprise. Imagine what a guy with a mind like mine could do with a highly re-spected, federally employed body like yours." Gunderson thought about that a moment, then laughed. "What am I saying? You don't have to imag-ine it. You make a helluva copilot, Jack, but this time I'm flying solo."

"Where is she, Alex?"

"You're persistent, I'll give you that. Why don't you hang around awhile? Those air tanks won't last forever."

Donovan felt the urge to lunge, but before he could move, Gunderson dissolved into vapor.

The smell of gas once again filled his nostrils, and with a whooshing sound, the seat in front of him burst into flames. More flames shot up on either side, threatening to box him in.

Surprised, he spun around—

—only to be jolted by the realization that he was no longer inside the van. It had vanished, along with the fire, the streets, and the city sur-rounding it.

Instead, he found himself standing on a rocky precipice, a hot wind whipping past him like a blast of furnace heat. At his feet was a deep chasm in the earth. An endless, dark abyss.

And it could only be described as the gate to hell.

52

"Welcome to the lost and found, Jack."

Donovan turned. Gunderson stood several yards behind him, leaning against an outcropping of rocks. Beyond him was the same stark landscape Donovan had seen on his first visit here.

Gunderson's dark eyes shone in the moonlight.

"I know how you're feeling," he said. "It takes a while to figure this place out. The first question you ask yourself is, how much of it's real? The answer is everything . . . and nothing. Once you wrap your brain around that kernel of absurdity, you're gold."

He pushed away from the outcropping and started toward Donovan.

"I know it's a cliché," he continued, "but people are sheep. They get into that tunnel and hear Grandma and Uncle Bob calling them and forget all about their shitty little lives. They head straight for the light like a teenager homing in on his girlfriend's tit."

He brought out a cigarette, lit it, then took a drag and blew smoke. "Then there's the resisters. The folks who, for whatever reason, aren't quite ready to let go. Accidents, suicides having second thoughts, nature's mistakes, or just stubborn bastards like you and me. We're cosmic anomalies, Jack. We turn away from the light and wind up here, hoping for a way back home. It's the lost and found. Emphasis on *lost*."

Donovan just looked at him. "You're not impressing me, Alex. Where is she?"

Gunderson snorted. "You need to widen your focus, Barney. Pay more attention to the world around you. If you'd done that back home, you could've found her anytime you wanted."

"Meaning?"

Gunderson came to a stop a few feet away. Taking another deep drag off the cigarette, he flicked it past Donovan's ear into the abyss. There was a brief spark of light and something crackled below.

"Helluva view isn't it? No pun intended. Sara used to enjoy a good view. Give her a lakefront window and you'd lose her for half the day."

"No more bullshit, Alex. Just tell me."

"You see what I mean? You're not paying *attention*. When you figure this thing out, my man, you're gonna kick yourself for taking such a huge risk in coming here again." Gunderson shrugged. "But what the hell. No balls, no babies, right?"

As far as Donovan was concerned, the only one taking a risk right now was Gunderson. He was about to rip him a new asshole.

"Let's tackle this in a way you can appreciate," Gunderson said. "One word. Ten letters. Here's the clue—you ready?"

Another goddamn puzzle. Donovan was ready, alright. Ready to castrate the motherfucker.

Gunderson smiled. "Sara's window. All you had to do was look out Sara's window." His eyes hardened. "Too bad you'll never get that chance."

Then he pounced.

It happened so quickly that Donovan wasn't even sure he'd seen him move. One second he was standing there and the next he had his hands wrapped around Donovan's throat, crushing his windpipe with his thumbs.

Donovan tried to breathe, tried to beat him away, but his blows seemed to have no effect. Gunderson increased the pressure, driving him to the ground, and Donovan fell hard, rocks digging into his back. The steady loss of oxygen drained him of strength, narrowed his vision.

"Control, Jack. That's what it's all about. Here . . . in the real world . . . and even down there, where you're headed."

There was a small electric storm brewing inside the abyss, as if waiting in hungry anticipation for Gunderson to finish his task.

As his consciousness faded, Donovan flailed, trying again to beat Gunderson away, but his blows were soft and powerless. A few seconds more and he'd be gone.

Come on, Jack, concentrate. This place is what you make it. Everything and nothing.

Think about Jessie.

Take control, goddammit. *Now.*

In a final, Hail Mary attempt to break free, he brought his knee up hard into Gunderson's groin, centering every bit of his concentration on the impact between bone and testicle.

The connection was solid.

Gunderson howled, grabbing himself, and fell back.

Donovan choked and coughed, sucking air into his lungs. Rolling over, he got up on his hands and knees, then staggered to his feet.

He glanced toward Gunderson, expecting to find him curled up in a fetal position—

—but Gunderson wasn't there.

And before Donovan could pull himself fully upright, a boot connected with his ribs, jolting him with pain, knocking him down again. Looking up at the sky, he found Gunderson silhouetted against it, circling like a predator.

"Not bad, hotshot. You're starting to catch on. Unfortunately, it's too little too late."

He punctuated his words with another kick to the ribs.

"You see, Jack, while you're still trying not to piss all over yourself, I'm already hitting the bowl."

Donovan struggled to get up, but another kick sent him sprawling.

Gunderson continued circling. "You should've seen Sara the day we met. She was a lot like your little pea pod—all ripe and ready to wear. What do you think a mind like hers would be able to do with a sweet fifteen-year-old body?"

Donovan tried to catch his breath. ". . . What are you talking about?"

Gunderson smiled. "I didn't take Jessie just to piss you off, Jack. That'd be a tad shallow, don't you think? I had plans for her from the very beginning."

"What plans?"

"Ever hear of a little thing called controlled metempsychosis?"

Donovan shook his head.

"It's just a bullshit word for a very simple process: the transmigration of souls."

Donovan suddenly remembered the conversation he'd had with Bobby Nemo. About Gunderson's stoned monologues on reincarnation, mind control, the swapping of souls . . .

"Most religions believe in transmigration," Gunderson said. "Even the Christians were into it before they got civilized. But my nasty old aunt, as crazy as she was, always believed it was a lot more than religious psychobabble. She was convinced that there were certain people in the world—people like you and Jessie—who, with the right conditioning, could be used as vessels for migrant souls. Kind of like a car with the driver's door hanging open and the key in the ignition." Another smile. "Guess she wasn't so crazy after all."

Donovan tried to rise again and got another boot to the ribs. Pain blossomed and he clutched his side.

"Unfortunately," Gunderson said, "that fat fuck cop put a stop to the wheels before they really got rolling. And I gotta tell you, I thought the coins had let me down."

"Coins?" Donovan had no idea what Gunderson was talking about.

"The *I Ching*, Jack. *The Book of Changes*. You really need to expand your mind." There was a flicker of disgust in Gunderson's eyes, then he continued, "So after the cop did his deed, I had to improvise, and, surprise, surprise, the coins weren't wrong after all. Turns out the improv is so much better than the original."

The boot came up again, knocking Donovan backward.

"While you were incapacitated last night, I was a busy, busy boy. Stopped by to see Sara. Her nurse tried to bitch me out of there, but I hung around long enough to give her a message."

Donovan could barely breathe. "A message?"

"She may *look* dead to the world, but she's still got a channel or two on receive mode. You just gotta know how to tune her in."

"What did you tell her?"

"Nothing special. Just that we have a prime opportunity here. A chance to start over. And just as I expected, you took the bait. Now, the first order of business in my shiny new, federally franchised body is to pay Sara another visit." He grinned. "And pull the plug."

The sparks from the abyss were reflected in his eyes. "Invasion of the Body Snatchers, Part Two, hotshot. Leave no child behind. It might take us a while to get over the father-daughter thing, but I think we'll manage. Don't you?"

Wong was smoking another cigarette, thinking he might actually be able to make his student-loan payment this month, when the girl said, "He blinked."

Wong jerked his head toward her boyfriend on the table. Motionless.

He looked up at the girl. Damn, she was cute.

"Impossible," he said. "He ain't taking an afternoon nap."

"I swear I saw his eyelids flicker."

She'd been on edge ever since she'd stepped foot in the room. Now she was getting agitated. She was also seeing things.

"Situation like this," he said, "sometimes your imagination gets the better of you."

"No. Something's wrong. Bring him back."

Wong checked his watch. "He's still got a couple—"

"*Bring him back,*" she said, her voice rising.

There was a fierceness in her tone that Wong wasn't about to argue with. Cute, but no pushover. He liked that.

Doffing an imaginary cap, he said, "I aim to please," then stubbed out his cigarette and went to work.

Clutching his battered ribs, Donovan struggled to get to his feet, but the celery sticks were back, as rubbery as ever.

Focus, Jack. You did it once, you can do it again.

Donovan may not have been much of a father, was certainly a failure as a family man, but one thing he'd always excelled at was shutting out the world around him and focusing in on the task at hand. Why should it be any different now?

Willing strength into his legs, he pulled himself upright and stood. He swayed slightly, but the harder he concentrated, the steadier he got.

Gunderson circled toward him. "Like I said, Barney. Too little, too late."

And all at once, he was gone—

—only to appear, a split second later, behind Donovan. But Donovan hadn't missed it this time, had sensed the move before Gunderson made it. He wheeled around and blocked another blow to his ribs, then immediately countered with a backhand to the jaw, once again feeling the solid connection of tissue against bone.

Gunderson reeled, stumbling back, but caught himself, steadied his feet. Wiping the back of his hand across his mouth, he found blood. "You should play tennis, Jack. That's a helluva backhand."

Behind Donovan, the abyss crackled and sparked hungrily.

"Unfortunately for you," Gunderson said, "it's forty–love and I've got the serve."

He brought his hands up, holding his palms outward.

A sound rose in Donovan's ears, like a thousand bees swarming inside his head. What looked like a ripple in the surface of the air emanated from Gunderson's palms, radiating straight toward him.

It hit him with the force of a small tsunami. His feet flew out from under him and he felt himself falling backward—

—straight into the abyss.

Rachel watched Wong work, his hands roaming over Jack's chest and head, finding and massaging pressure points.

For the first time today, Wong looked worried.

Nothing was happening.

"What's wrong?"

"He's not responding. If anything, he seems to have gone deeper."

"What? What does that mean?"

"Shut up and let me concentrate."

He continued to massage Jack's chest, then suddenly balled his fists and pounded on it. "Pump, you piece of shit!"

"The defibrillator," Rachel said. "Use the defibrillator."

Wong glanced at the ancient machine. "You're kidding me, right? Thing hasn't been fired up in decades."

"*What?*"

"It's part of the sales pitch. I tell every client the same goddamn thing. I've just never seen one go this deep before."

"You son of a bitch," Rachel said, crossing to the defibrillator. She found the plug and shoved it into a nearby socket. Grabbing the paddles, she searched the control panel for the power switch and flicked it on.

The thing moaned in protest as if being awakened from a deep sleep, but it was coming alive and that was good. Rachel studied the panel, trying to figure it out. "What now?"

Wong was still working on Donovan. "Third switch on the left, I think."

"You *think*?" Without waiting for a response, she flicked the switch and the machine began to whir, a high, unpleasant whine that quickly rose in intensity.

"Move," she shouted, shoving Wong aside, then raised the paddles over Jack's chest.

As he fell, Donovan flung his arms out, grabbing desperately for the walls of the abyss. Focusing his concentration, he hooked his hands around a grouping of rocks and jerked to a stop, feet dangling.

Hugging the cliff wall, he found purchase on a small, practically non-existent overhang. It crumbled slightly as he stepped on it, sending dirt and rock into the blackness below.

The sparks intensified.

A clap of thunder boomed and a small jolt of electricity shot through Donovan's body—a mild hit to the chest that surprised him, but wasn't strong enough to dislodge him from the wall.

Had it come from Gunderson? Looking up past the lip of the abyss, he saw an already turbulent sky begin to churn, dark clouds gathering, swirling restlessly.

Then Gunderson appeared, crouched near the edge, and glanced up toward the sky. "Isn't that sweet," he said. "They're coming for you, Jack. Too bad you're gonna miss the ride."

There was a second clap of thunder and Donovan felt another jolt. Directly above Gunderson, a vague but unmistakable wormhole began to form in the clouds.

Gunderson watched it a moment, then returned his gaze to Donovan and raised his hands again, palms outward, a fresh new smile on his face.

Rachel was about to go for round three when Wong checked Jack's pulse and said, "Wait, wait! I've got something."

"He's back?"

"No . . . maybe. It's pretty weak."

"For crissakes," Rachel said, then flicked the switch. "Move." There was a whir and a high, sustained whine, and she brought the paddles down on Jack's chest. He jerked in response, his body bucking beneath her.

Wong felt his wrist. "No change."

Rachel wanted to scream. Wanted to grab Jack by the shoulders and shake him awake. Slap him a few times for being such a goddamn fool.

Instead, she flicked the switch again and readied the paddles.

Wong, meanwhile, yanked open a nearby drawer, rifled through it, then pulled out a vial of medicine and a syringe big enough to vaccinate a small elephant.

"What the hell is that?"

"Epinephrine," he said. "Stimulates the heart. If this doesn't do the trick, nothing will."

Rachel stared at the syringe dubiously, then brought the paddles down.

There was another clap of thunder and the wormhole expanded, swirling furiously above Gunderson's head. He felt a jolt in his chest and a twinge of triumph. His time here was about to end. He was only moments away from his new life, his new career.

His new Sara.

Oh, the things they'd do.

He remembered the moment he'd been shot, that sudden feeling of loss, the abrupt end to life as he'd known it. Then the wormhole, the light, the yearning to head toward its promise—but at the same time resisting, not yet ready to go.

And suddenly there he was, stranded in limbo, refusing to accept his fate, using his time here to learn the rules of the place, just like he had in prison.

Then Deputy Fife showed up and he knew that was it. Fate intervening. The *Ching* giving him his second chance.

He'd only had time to hitch a ride, but after a while he thought, why not go for the big prize? Sharing was a blast, but a nice warm body of your own is even better. A nice *new* body, unblemished by a pesky little thing called a criminal record. A body that placed him right smack in the middle of enemy territory.

And the best part? Everyone would think he was one of *them*.

He felt another small jolt and the clouds above him grew more frenzied, the wormhole widening.

Arms outstretched, palms facing Donovan, he gathered up his energy, working up a really good hate, ready to knock Barney even deeper into the pit, where he was sure that Bobby and Luther and God knew who else were waiting for him.

He almost felt sorry for the guy.

Almost.

Donovan stared up at Gunderson's hands and braced himself, knowing what was coming. The minuscule ledge beneath his feet continued to crumble, sending rocks and debris into the abyss below. If he didn't resist this blow, he'd be joining them soon.

Then the bees began to buzz and a ripple in the air rolled toward him. He focused on it, trying to stop it in its tracks, to will it away, but it was no use. This wasn't a fair fight. He didn't have the skills he needed to compete with Gunderson. Not here.

It smacked him head-on like a big rig at high speed. The impact ripped him away from his perch and he was once again falling, arms flailing, the sparks below crackling wildly.

Above, Gunderson turned and flung his arms upward toward the whirling wormhole, waiting for it to snatch him away.

Donovan closed his eyes, knowing this was it, he'd lost, Jessie gone from him forever.

"Forgive me," he whispered as he plummeted deeper and deeper into the pit.

Then a voice in his ear said, "There's nothing to forgive, Jack," and something or someone grabbed his wrist, stopping his fall.

Coming to an abrupt halt, he slammed into the abyss wall. His eyes flew open and there, crouched on the rocks, arm outstretched, hand gripping his wrist—

—was Jessie.

Not his *daughter* Jessie, but Jessie-Anne, his *sister*. And she was smiling at him, her face lit up as he'd never seen it before. A face at peace.

The face of an angel.

"It's not too late," she said. "It's never too late."

Donovan felt a choke of emotion rise up from his chest. Her hand released him and he clutched the wall, wanting instead to throw his arms around her.

"Jessie-Anne . . . ," he said, but couldn't find words to follow it.

"Lead with your heart, Jack. Always remember that. If you lead with your heart, nothing can stop you."

And then, without warning, she began to fade from view, leaving only the trace of a whisper in his ear. "Glass half full," she said.

Then she was gone.

Donovan clung to the rocks, feeling tears well up, her words swirling through his head.

Lead with your heart, Jack.

And with sudden clarity, he understood. Although his physical heart had been stopped, everything that had happened to him here, every change, the baggage he carried, had been based not on intellect—but emotion.

It was Gunderson's hunger for vengeance, a fully formed, unadulterated hate, that had fueled his ability to control and manipulate this world so easily.

The power of the heart, not the mind.

That was the currency here.

And armed with that knowledge, and the desire that accompanied it, Donovan felt a renewed sense of hope.

Just as Gunderson had said in that train yard as he lay in Donovan's arms . . .

This wasn't over yet.

Hands stretched toward the sky, Gunderson stared up at the wormhole, waiting for it to take him. Another loud thunderclap and the now familiar jolt to the chest told him his wish was about to be granted.

"Come on, goddammit!"

The swirling black maw widened in response, wind kicking up around him, and he felt its power take hold. His feet lifted off the ground and he began to rise.

"Yes!" It was finally happening. The moment he'd been waiting for ever since that cop had put a bullet in him. "Take me," he shouted. "Take me!"

But then, from out of nowhere, a voice said, "I don't think so, Alex"—

—and Donovan appeared directly below him, wrapping his arms around his legs.

What the fuck?

Gunderson kicked, trying to shake him off, but the bastard had a lock on him so tight, he could barely move. One look into Donovan's eyes and Gunderson realized that something had changed.

Donovan knew. He understood.

And that, ladies and gentlemen, was not part of the program.

Feeling himself being pulled back toward the ground, Gunderson fought desperately against it, trying to break Donovan's grip. But Donovan was a bulldog, would not let go, and a moment later they hit the earth, a tangle of arms and legs.

Pain shot through Gunderson as rocks dug into his flesh, scraped his bones—a sensation he wasn't accustomed to.

They rolled to the edge of the precipice. Then, all at once, Donovan was straddling him, hands around his neck, an intense, unstoppable fury in his eyes.

"No more puzzles, Alex. Tell me where she is!"

Gunderson brought his arms up, trying to break Donovan's grip, but was powerless against his rage. The earth beneath them began to rumble and crack, steam hissing up from newly formed fissures.

"Tell me, goddammit! Now!"

"Fuck you!" Gunderson croaked, and the ground shifted, another fissure opening up directly beneath him, the earth crumbling away on either side.

Electric tentacles reached up and wrapped around him, pulling at him. Donovan jumped back, narrowly avoiding the widening fissure. There was another loud thunderclap, and above, the swirling wormhole sucked at Donovan, his hair whipping wildly in the wind.

"Where is she, Alex? Tell me!"

But Gunderson ignored the command, watching in horror as the wormhole enveloped Donovan.

"No!" he shouted. "No!"

Then the wormhole swallowed Donovan whole and whisked him away.

And the agony Gunderson felt was so deep that he was almost certain it would last an eternity.

Just when she thought they'd lost the fight, that the epinephrine had been a bust, Jack's body bucked wildly beneath the paddles and his eyes flew open as he gulped a bucketful of air. Feeling a rush of sweet relief, Rachel burst into tears and threw her arms around him.

"Oh, my God," she said. "Oh, my God."

She glanced at Wong, who was now leaning against the wall, his body slack, face full of shock, looking like a man who was seriously considering a career change.

"The hospital," Jack croaked. "Take me to the hospital."

"We've already called," Rachel told him, hugging him close. "The ambulance is on its way."

"No," Jack said. "That isn't what I mean."

"What, then?"

"The convalescent hospital. Saint Margaret's."

"What?" Rachel said. "Why?"

Jack looked at her, a look she knew all too well. A look that meant she wasn't going to like what he was about to say.

"Sara's window," he told her. "I have to find Sara's window."

part four

LIGHT

53

They got there in less than half an hour.

After making it abundantly clear to Donovan that this was against her better judgment, that he needed to go to the hospital—*now*—Rachel brought her car around and used her considerable driving skills to get them there in record time.

No doubt about it. He was gonna have to marry this woman.

Despite the ordeal he'd just been through, Donovan felt surprisingly good, thanks in part to sheer willpower, an abundance of hope, and the adrenaline Wong had pumped into his veins.

There were only a few scattered cars in Saint Margaret's parking lot. They took the elevator to the second floor, and when the doors opened, Donovan was relieved to see that Nurse Baker had not returned. Instead, a lone nineteen-year-old was manning the nurses' station.

"Sara Gunderson," he said. "What room?"

The nurse looked at him as if he were something she'd scraped off the bottom of her shoe. "I'm sorry. Are you family?"

Donovan frowned and flashed his credentials. "Just take us to the god-damn room."

Looking flustered, the nurse came out from behind the counter. "Follow me," she muttered, and headed down a hallway.

A moment later she led them through a doorway into a small, dank room, a single bed against the wall, surrounded by a collection of medical equipment, including a ventilator.

The woman on the bed did not even remotely resemble Sara Gunderson. She looked like ninety pounds of nothing. A sickly old woman on the brink of death.

But it was Sara alright. Eyes closed, chest rising and falling to the wheezy beat of the ventilator.

Donovan looked around, surprised not by what he saw—but what he *didn't* see. His stomach lurched.

"The window," he said. "Where's the window?"

The nurse studied him, clearly confused by the question. "She . . . doesn't have one. This is a converted storeroom."

"How long has she been in here?"

"Sir, if—"

"How *long*?"

The nurse flinched. "Ever since she was admitted. Why?"

Donovan glanced at Rachel, feeling the ground beneath him roll. Overcome by a sudden, intense despair, he found a chair and sat, the nurse eyeing him with mix of distrust and concern.

"Are you okay, sir?"

"Get out," he spat.

"Sir, I'm not sure what you're—"

"Out," he repeated. "Get out."

Looking frightened now, the nurse turned and scurried out the door. Donovan felt Rachel looking at him and held a hand up.

"Don't say it," he told her. "Just let me think."

He lowered his head and stared at the floor, studying the pattern in the linoleum. Everything he'd been through and this was where it ended?

No. There was something here he wasn't seeing. There had to be.

The puzzle. Concentrate on the puzzle.

One word. Ten letters.

All you had to do was look out Sara's window.

Cursing himself for being so bad at these things, he glanced up at Sara, watching her chest rise and fall. "Come on," he said. "Help me with this."

What had Gunderson meant? If there was no window in the room, what other kinds of windows were there? Sara's eyes? The window to her soul?

No. Too literary for Gunderson.

Ten simple letters. What could they . . .

And then it hit him.

Rising, he crossed to the bed and searched the nightstand next to it, but it was littered with medical paraphernalia, nothing else.

"Come on, goddammit."

"Jack," Rachel said. "What's wrong? What are you looking for?"

And then he found it, partially hidden by one of the machines, taped to the wall directly above Sara's head.

Ten letters.

Photograph.

A Polaroid photo he'd seen at least a half dozen times: Alexander Gunderson smiling for the camera, standing in front of the Lake Point Lighthouse.

"What is it?" Rachel asked.

Donovan ripped the photo from the wall. "Sara's window."

54

Hold on, Jessie.
He's coming to get you.
. . . Jessie?

She struggled to open her eyes and peered into the darkness she'd grown so accustomed to.

Was that the angel's voice she'd heard?

Had she finally come back?

The angel had left her a while ago, promising to return, but Jessie didn't hold out much hope. She was too tired, too weak to believe anymore.

She couldn't stay awake for more than a few seconds at a time. The cold and hunger and thirst that had consumed her those first few hours—or was it days?—had been replaced by numbness, and the places on her skin that had been rubbed raw by the duct tape no longer hurt.

The sound of the rain was long gone, leaving nothing to connect her to the real world but the hiss of air filling her nostrils.

Then that, too, had finally gone.

Every so often, that hiss had trickled to a stop, only to kick into gear again, pumping fresh new air.

But this last time, nothing . . .

Only silence.

And as that silence stretched out longer and longer, she began to realize that all that was left to her was the air in this box. Air that was thick with feces and urine and stale body odor.

Air that smelled like death.

Shaking her head from side to side, she had managed to dislodge the mask just enough to allow her to breathe. But each breath she took seemed harder than the one before it, and she knew it was only a matter of time before she'd be unable to fill her lungs.

Like the angel, Jessie Glass-Half-Full had abandoned her. And the funny thing was, she didn't have enough energy to care.

She thought of her father, frantically searching for her. Thought of Mr. Ponytail's wicked smile and Matt Weber's championship rear end and her mother and Roger doing it in their hotel room in the Caymans—and it all seemed so distant to her. So silly.

So many things in her life seemed pointless now that she was about to take her last breath.

Had any of it even mattered?

She wanted to believe it had. Wanted to believe that she'd brought some happiness to the lives of those who had made *her* happy. Wanted to believe that she and her father would finally have patched things up . . .

But what she wanted and what she could have seemed to be two very different things.

And, in the end, maybe what she really wanted was simply to let go.

Her chest felt so tight. No matter how hard she tried, she just couldn't get enough air and she knew that she would soon be leaving this darkness.

Don't resist, she told herself. You have to let go now.

Say goodbye, Jessie.

Your time has come.

55

They converged on the place like a small army, a cluster of federal and CPD vehicles, Rachel's Celica in the lead. Not far behind was an ambulance, its siren cutting mournfully through the afternoon air.

A popular tourist attraction, the Lake Point Lighthouse had recently been closed for renovation, a project that had been stalled by a dispute with the contractor. Except for the ambulance and the converging cars, the place was deserted.

Donovan was out of the Celica and running before it came to a complete stop.

He raced across a wide lawn to the entrance of a small building shaded by trees, the lighthouse towering above it. There was a padlock on the door.

"I need some cutters here!"

A moment later Sidney Waxman appeared carrying a bulldog bolt cutter. He sliced through the lock and Donovan flung the door open, stepping inside.

The building was rectangular, holding a small gift shop, the lighthouse museum, and the keeper's quarters. At the back of the room, a short passageway led to the tower, sunlight streaming in from above, filtering across a wrought-iron staircase that spiraled upward toward the lantern room.

As Sidney, Cleveland, and several of the others filed in behind him and

fanned out to search the place, Donovan headed toward that pool of sunlight, remembering what Gunderson had said about Sara:

Give her a lakefront view and you'd lose her for half the day.

What better view, Donovan thought, than the one upstairs?

Moving to the staircase, he took the steps two at a time, winding his
way upward. Still plagued by an overextended body, he was out of breath
by the time he reached the lantern room.

The view was magnificent, large windows looking out over the water
and at the wide green expanse of the lighthouse grounds.

Donovan scanned the landscape, looking for disruptions in the surface, but to his frustration, the lawn was pristine and perfectly maintained. No signs of a premature burial.

But Jessie was out there somewhere. He was sure of it. She had to be.

His eyes swept over the grounds again, taking it slower this time as he
mentally walked a grid, covering it centimeter by centimeter.

Then he saw it, a good distance away, near a stretch of grass that sloped
downward toward the lake, half-hidden by a tight grouping of trees:

A large aluminum storage shed.

And leaning against its door were two twenty-pound bags of all-
purpose fertilizer.

Donovan flung the door open with such ferocity, he nearly ripped it off
its hinges. The shed was the size of a small garage and shrouded in darkness, the light from the doorway doing little to illuminate it inside.

Finding a pull cord near the entrance, he yanked it, and a string of
bare bulbs came to life. Gardening tools of various shapes and sizes lined
the walls, a rusted lawn tractor parked at the rear. There was no floor in
the structure, only dirt, and a mound of fertilizer was piled near the center, its acrid smell assaulting Donovan's nostrils.

This is it, he thought, his heart pounding furiously.

Grabbing a nearby shovel, he attacked the mound and dug in deep,
tossing aside heaps of fertilizer. Soon, his entire crew had joined him, Sidney and Al grabbing shovels as Darcy, Franky, and Rachel got to their
knees, scraping dirt and fertilizer away with their bare hands.

No one said a word, the only sound the hollow scrape of the shovels.

Time seemed to have temporarily been suspended as they all concentrated on their task.

Within minutes, the mound was gone, leaving only the soft dirt floor. Donovan, Sidney, and Al sank their shovels into it, digging deeper and deeper until, finally, Donovan's shovel hit something solid.

"This is it!" he shouted, voice choked with emotion. "It's her!"

And then he was digging harder and more furiously than ever before, scraping dirt away from the crude wooden lid of the coffin.

As it came into view, he flung his shovel aside and scrambled into the hole, grabbing the lip of the lid and yanking at it, trying desperately to pry it open. Several of the others joined in, uttering a collective grunt as they pulled at it.

The goddamned thing wouldn't budge.

"It's nailed shut," Cleveland said, grabbing his shovel and ramming it into the crevice between the lid and the body of the coffin. Jamming his heel against the blade, he shoved it in deeper, then levered the handle, forcing the blade upward.

The lid splintered, breaking into several pieces, and through the cracks, Donovan could see a pair of hands inside—Jessie's hands—bound together with duct tape.

"Come on!" he shouted. "Get it open! Get it open!"

Cleveland's shovel slammed into the wood again, widening the cracks as Sidney and the others pulled away chucks of it and finally managed to pry what was left of the lid open.

Donovan stared down at Jessie, her eyes closed, skin bone white. She wasn't moving. Wasn't breathing.

Oh, Jesus God. No. No . . .

Ripping her oxygen mask away, he grabbed her by the shoulders and lifted her out of the box. She was cold and limp in his hands. Climbing out of the hole, he laid her down on the floor of the shed, felt for a pulse with shaky fingers.

Nothing. Not even a hint of heartbeat.

Strangling a cry of anguish, he slammed his fists on her chest, then yanked her mouth open and covered it with his, blowing air into her lungs.

She didn't respond.

"Come on, goddammit, breathe!"

He pounded her chest again, administered mouth-to-mouth, but it did no good.

She was gone.

Suddenly a paramedic squatted next him, a portable defibrillator in hand. Shoving Donovan aside, he jabbed a needle into Jessie's arm, as a second paramedic appeared out of nowhere and strapped a fresh new oxygen mask over her face.

The first paramedic flicked a switch on the defibrillator, shouted, "Clear!" and pressed the paddles against Jessie's chest.

Her body bucked beneath them, flopping lifelessly, as Donovan watched, his heart in his throat.

"Please," he whispered. "Please wake up."

But Jessie remained motionless, no sign of life.

The paramedic shouted, "Clear!" a second time and brought the paddles down, her body again bucking beneath them.

A single moment seemed to stretch into eternity, then suddenly her eyelids fluttered and she stiffened, abruptly coming awake, staring up into Donovan's eyes as she sucked in precious life.

Everyone around them began cheering and clapping, and in that moment, Donovan felt what seemed like a lifetime of pain leak away.

He'd found her and she was alive.

"Thank you, God," he said. "Thank you . . ."

And as tears began to gather in her eyes, he pulled her into his arms and hugged her close, feeling as if he'd never let her go.

56

The fallout from the hunt for Jessica Lynne Donovan wasn't pretty.

After forensic tests revealed that the blood on the carpet in Luther's room at the Wayfarer Inn was indeed Bobby Nemo's, the Fredrickville sheriff launched a search for an unknown assailant.

When a woman named Carla Devito came forward with some illuminating information, Agent Jack Donovan became the prime suspect.

Sheriff's investigators concluded that a distraught Donovan had followed Nemo to the motel and, after a particularly brutal interrogation into the whereabouts of his missing daughter, had executed all three men. The removal of Nemo's body was, they explained, a pathetic attempt to stage the event as a murder-suicide.

Unfortunately, they had a couple of things going against them: no murder weapon and a fairly unimpeachable alibi.

Jack Donovan's registered firearm, a Glock 19, was, according to all accounts, lying somewhere at the bottom of the Chicago River. No mention was ever made—by Al Cleveland or anyone else—that Donovan had been given a replacement, and a search of his apartment and locker proved to be a complete waste of time and manpower.

The alibi came from Sidney Waxman, who claimed to have been with Donovan for the major part of his surveillance, leaving him only in the wee hours of the morning, shortly after they'd lost Nemo in the rain.

Donovan hadn't asked Sidney to lie for him, and Sidney never explained why he did.

He was, Donovan realized, a better friend than he deserved.

When it turned out that the motel's owner/manager, one Charles Arthur Kruger, was a registered sex offender known for his fondness for nine-year-old girls, the investigation quickly fell apart due to lack of interest in the law enforcement community.

No prosecutor, particularly one from a nearly bankrupt municipality, was willing to test the reputation of a topflight ATF agent against that of a stripper and three known, now deceased, felons. Especially when the Feds had made it perfectly clear that they'd rather the whole thing just go away.

Thankfully, the news played up the happier aspects of the case. Father and daughter blissfully reunited as the world watched. Mother and stepfather rushing home from the Caymans to be with their little girl.

As for Donovan, Waxman, and Franky Garcia, their stunt with Bobby Nemo did not sit well with the Treasury Department brass. All three were suspended from duty pending departmental hearings into the matter.

Garcia quit and moved to Hollywood. Waxman suggested to Donovan that they take Garcia's cue and start their own security consultant firm, a business that would surely be more lucrative than a government job.

But while Donovan didn't dismiss the idea, he didn't jump at it either. Right now, all he wanted was time. Time alone with Jessie. And Rachel.

Over the next few weeks, as both Jessie and Donovan struggled to regain their strength, they spent many a night watching *The Simpsons* together. Jessie was, Donovan discovered, an incredibly brave young woman—certainly scarred by the experience, but not overwhelmed by it. And with her and Rachel's help, he managed to overcome the guilt he'd carried with him for so long.

Guilt about Jessie. The divorce.

And about his sister's suicide.

Lead with your heart, Jack.

Glass half full.

57

I'm going to bed," Jessie said.

It was nearly two months since the rescue and Jessie was staying for the weekend. She and Rachel had just finished a game of gin rummy, Rachel the victor. Jessie rose from the sofa, stretching her arms and yawning.

Donovan, who sat in his favorite armchair working a crossword puzzle—one he fully intended to finish—looked up at her.

Her therapist had told him she was making good progress, but, to Donovan, she still looked frail. Vulnerable.

"It's kinda early," he said. "You feeling okay?"

Jessie heaved an exasperated sigh. "I'm fine, Dad. Rachel, will you please tell soon-to-be-ex-agent Donovan here to stop worrying about me all the time?"

"A lot of good it'll do," Rachel said, gathering up the cards. "You go on to bed. I'll keep him occupied." She reached across and stroked Donovan's knee.

"Gross," Jessie said, then leaned down and gave Donovan a hug. "Love you, Dad."

The words were like a song. He smiled. "Me, too, kiddo."

Watching her head toward her room, he thought about what they'd been through and how deeply he loved her.

She *was* fine. She'd be okay. There was nothing to worry about.

A year from now, that prom photo he'd wondered about as he stood inside Grandma Luke's apartment would adorn his mantel. And many more would follow.

The nightmare was over.

Finally over.

58

Jessie lay in bed, unable to sleep, wondering if she should tell her father about the headaches. They'd become more frequent lately, and stronger. And after all that had happened, all that she'd survived, she wondered if fate was playing the irony card, giving her a big fat tumor.

She could see the headline now: RESCUED GIRL SUCCUMBS TO BRAIN CANCER.

Get a grip, Jess. You're overreacting.

The headaches were merely the result of tension and anxiety. Nothing more.

But she hadn't told her therapist about them either.

Despite her brave front, Jessie wasn't nearly as strong as she pretended to be. Or as happy, for that matter. When she *could* sleep, she often dreamed of her time on the other side, of the few moments she'd spent there before the paramedics had brought her back. Most of it was lost in a haze, but she couldn't help wondering if the headaches were somehow related.

Massaging her skull, she tried wishing the pain away, but it did no good. It was bound to get worse before it got better.

Realizing this was going to be another long night, that she'd never get to sleep, she climbed out of bed and went to the dresser. Pulling open the top drawer, she dug past a few layers of panties and pulled out her secret stash: a can of air freshener and a pack of Marlboros.

Maybe she'd go for lung cancer instead.

Shaking one out, she lit up the cigarette and inhaled deeply, instantly feeling her headache subside.

Ahh. Just what she'd needed.

Exhaling, she spritzed the air with freshener and studied her reflection in the dresser mirror, noting with mild surprise how dark and lifeless her eyes looked.

It was almost as if they belonged to someone else.

Taking another deep drag, she exhaled, spritzed the air again, then slowly smiled at herself and said:

"Give us a kiss."

acknowledgments

This book would not exist if it hadn't been for the encouragement and unwavering support of my friend and fellow author Kathy Mackel. She suggested I take the plunge and knew this day was coming long before I did. Thank you, Kathy.

Thanks also go to:

Peggy White and Rob and Beth Flumignan, who helped my geography-challenged mind, and Nick Davison, for advice on oxygen tanks, leakage, and rate of intake. Any mistakes are definitely my own;

Marion Rosenberg, my longtime screen rep, who believed in me well after I had any right to ask her to and knew exactly whom to call;

Scott Miller of Trident Media Group, agent extraordinaire, whose excellent story sense helped me get the manuscript into shape for the marketplace;

and, finally, Ben Sevier and Stefanie Bierwerth, my wonderful editors, whose keen minds and ability to focus on minute story and character details have taken this book to a new level.

Every author should be so blessed.